MAKING ANGEL

MARIANI CRIME FAMILY SERIES BOOK ONE

By

AMANDA WASHINGTON

Thank you for your support,

[signature]

MAKING ANGEL is a work of fiction. Names, characters, places, and incidents are the products of the author's imagination and are used fictitiously. Any resemblance to actual events, locales, or persons, living or dead, is entirely coincidental.

ISBN: 978-1517771621

2015 Amanda Washington

Published in the United States

ACKNOWLEDGMENTS

This book would have never become a reality without the help and support of so many people. Special thanks to my husband, Meltarrus, our boys, and all my friends and family for letting me off the hook when I daydreamed storyline and dialog during our conversations.

Huge thanks to my invaluable editors, Ellen Tarver, Kim Gates, Karen Flanery, and Krista Darrach.

I'm greatly indebted to the talented creative team who developed my cover. Cover design: Jackson and Tracey Jackson. Cover models: Alexander Taylor and Tirzah Kauffman.

Sincere thanks to the many people who believed in me enough to back the "Making Angel" Kickstarter for $50 or more: Trevor Campbell, Jared Curtiss, George Hill, Ed Hummel, Fonda Oliver, Mike Olson, Freddie Omm, Randy & Kathy Rodriguez, Pete & Deena Scholl, and Ronald Webb. The generous contributions of you and the other Kickstarter backers made the production of this book possible.

For Aunt Cindy,
The most courageous humanitarian
adrenaline-junkie I've ever known.
I miss you every day.

♠ ♥ ♣ ♦

PROLOGUE
Angel

T HE MORNING OF my twelfth birthday I arose with feelings of anxiety and anticipation. I'd finally reached it: the day that would begin my right of passage into adulthood. I'd be honored as a man of the family, allowed to sit at the adult table, and trusted with family conversations. As I threw back the covers and climbed out of bed, I caught a glimpse of myself in the mirror and paused.

Who am I? Where do I fit in?

Today, I'd have my answers. I grinned and flexed at my reflection before padding downstairs to find my father sitting at the breakfast nook, eyeing his electronic tablet. He lowered the tablet and flashed me a smile.

"There he is. The birthday boy's become a man now. Cappuccino?"

It was the first time he'd ever offered me coffee, and I eagerly accepted it.

Father started up the machine, filling the kitchen with whirring sounds and heady scents. Moments later he handed me a mug so big I couldn't even get my fingers around it. I gripped the cup and followed him across the tile kitchen floor out onto the cobblestone patio. We sat on custom-built furniture and sipped our drinks. The cappuccino scalded my tongue and I winced, but when the old man eyed me I ignored the pain and took another sip.

"Careful, Angel. It burns. It's bitter at first, but you get used to it. Soon, you'll grow to enjoy the taste. That's the way most things

1

in life are." He set his cup on the table, looked me square in the eyes and asked, "Speaking of life, have you given any thought to what you want to be when you grow up?"

I was supposed to be the one asking the questions, but he'd beaten me to the punch. Unprepared and feeling the weight of his inquiry, I squinted into the rising summer sun. Last week I had built my first website and imported a couple of how-to videos on customizing tablets. A commenter told me about a new, local tech school accepting middle school students, and I'd been hoping for an opening to discuss it with the old man. But before I could seize the opportunity, Father cleared his throat.

"As the first-born son, you're expected to take on the family business, you know?" he asked, watching me with such expectancy and pride that I swallowed back my plans and studied him. Olive skin, dark hair and features, and broad shoulders, he towered over everyone I knew. People said I looked like a younger version of him—a younger, scrawnier version—but I lacked his presence. When the old man entered a room, everyone stopped what they were doing to acknowledge him, whereas I had a gift for blending into the background. I idolized him, but sometimes I felt like I didn't know him at all.

"What's the matter, Angel?"

"I don't know what your job is." Heat crept up my cheeks at the admission.

"It's okay," he assured me. "My profession is complicated. I do a lot of things."

I looked away, discouraged by his vague answer. If he wouldn't even trust me with the details of his job, none of my other questions had a chance of getting answered.

The old man leaned across the table and laid a finger on my chin, directing my gaze back to him. "Look at me when I talk to you, Son."

"Yes sir," I replied, this time holding eye contact.

"There." His dark, all-seeing pupils seemed to drink me in. He smiled in fond approval, deepening the lines around his mouth and eyes. Pride lingered in his gaze, and I sat straighter, trying to be worthy of it. "What do you think I do?"

I started to look down, but stopped myself. Vicious rumors floated around my school, but I didn't believe them. There was no way my father deserved the names they called him, the reasons they gave for not coming to my parties. "I don't know."

He frowned. "But you've heard whispers, haven't you? What have you heard, Angel?"

I'd never lied to my father, and I wasn't about to start. "They say you... you do things."

"What sort of things do they say I do?"

The intensity of his gaze dried my throat. I took another sip of coffee.

"Angel?"

The accusations were too heinous to voice. I honed in on the one term I didn't understand. Hoping for an explanation, I replied, "They say you do wet work."

"Wet work, huh?" Father cocked his head to the side while color flooded his neck, creeping up his cheeks. Anger radiated from him, threatening to drown me in its wake. "Like I'm some sort of hired thug? I don't follow anyone's orders, you hear me?"

"Yes sir."

Tense, silent moments passed. Finally, he let out a deep sigh. "Petty, small people will always speak out of jealousy, Angel. They talk and talk, but the world has never been changed by talkers. You really want to know what I do?"

I nodded, increasingly uncertain.

"I build empires. I write legislature and elect officials to enforce it. I keep the economy from collapsing, and the people from rioting. I enforce justice and keep Vegas from falling to gang wars and chaos. The people I work with... we are the government, the economic stimulus, and the peacekeepers."

I breathed his words in, letting them clear my mind. The old man sounded like a superhero. He was brave and strong, shining with god-like power. Caught up in the moment, I abandoned my dreams and blurted, "I want to do what you do!"

"You make my heart proud." He patted me on the head and stood.

As he walked back into the house, I replayed his speech in my mind knowing I'd missed something important. He was great and powerful and the anticipation of being just like him made my chest swell. No more blending into the background. Only I still didn't know what he did.

Uncertainty drained the joy from my birthday as I thought about the other rumors. Kids shunned me, insisting that my father was a murderer and bully. And I still had no clue what wet work was or why the term had upset him so much. I stared at the cappuccino I no longer wanted, now dreading the changes it represented. I wasn't ready to know the truth, wasn't ready to become a man. But when Father returned carrying two pistols, I knew I was past the point of no return.

CHAPTER ONE

Angel

Eleven years later

THE DAY BEFORE Halloween I sat blissfully alone, researching ways to widen the radius of an electromagnetic pulse blast without increasing the pocket-sized dimensions. I palmed the device, estimating the weight, before being interrupted by an annoying tap on my shoulder.

"Angel, we're gonna be late," Bones nagged.

My best friend, bodyguard, and schedule keeper stood just under six feet tall, inches shorter than me, but his build dissuaded muggers and his scowl made hardened criminals drop their gaze and cross to the other side of the street. His suit screamed funeral director, or some other occupation paid to put people six feet under. His real name was Franco Leone, but I'd nicknamed him Bones in fourth grade when he shattered the wrist of an aspiring bully who shoved me against my locker. The nickname stuck, and so did our friendship.

"I know. I know. One more minute."

"The big man's gonna kill us if we're late. You know how important this drop is."

"The drop's at three, right?"

He nodded.

I glanced at my watch. "Then don't worry about it. We got plenty of time." It was too early for rush hour, and little things like traffic weren't exactly a big deal for my family. Our technical guru had the city wired and could control the lights from the comfort of his hidden office.

"Plenty of time? Aren't you forgetting something?" Bones gestured toward my body.

I followed his gaze and swore. T-shirt, jeans, sneakers; I needed to change and had forgotten to bring a suit. We'd have to stop by the condo, which would add another twenty minutes to our commute.

I swore again and ran for the exit.

"Angel." Bones's tone held laughter, causing me to stop and look at him. He grinned and held out a garment bag. "Who's got your back?"

I patted his shoulder as I took the suit. "Aw, you picked up the cleaning? What a good butler you make."

He flipped me off.

Laughing, I headed for the locker room to change. Bones followed me, grumbling like some fed up old woman. I dressed and we took the elevator up to the ground floor, emerging into the busy plastics manufacturing plant that served as a front for my father's technical development business. Nobody even glanced our way as we hurried toward the garage.

"Keys?" I asked.

He tossed them to me. "She's all gassed up."

I climbed behind the wheel of my black and silver Hummer H5 with tinted bullet-resistant glass and tires designed to resist deflation when punctured, glancing over my shoulder into the backseat. Blankets hid the inventory, and I did not check under them. The less I knew, the better.

"Thanks for making the pickup. I'm really close to figuring out a way to keep the—"

"You're really close to making us late." Bones tapped the clock on the dashboard. "Twenty-three minutes. I'm calling Tech."

I nodded and put the Hummer into reverse. As we pulled away from the building, Bones spoke a code and the dashboard screen came to life. The screen blinked, requiring another password. Bones rattled off a series of numbers and then placed his thumb in the center of the box.

The face of a man I'd known for years, but had never met in person, appeared. "We are secure, Bones, how can I help you?" Tech asked. Nobody but my father knew the real name of the head of the technical department. To the rest of us, Tech was the autonomous human version of a digital personal assistant and knowledge navigator.

"We're in a hurry and need a clear route from Plant A to Drop…" Bones pulled a piece of paper out of his pocket and scanned it before adding, "Charlie-four-niner-alfa."

Everyone who worked for my father spoke in code. Codes changed frequently, and were issued on an as-needed basis. Bones—for all his strengths—had one weakness. He couldn't memorize the damn codes. But he was one of the few people Father allowed to write them down. Bones guarded his codes like they were a matter of life and death, and essentially, they were.

"Got it," Tech replied. "I'm sending the navigation now. Everything is covered."

Confident that Tech had control of the lights and eyes on the cops, I stomped on the gas and maneuvered through traffic. Lights turned green before we reached them and once we cleared the downtown congestion, the Hummer ate up the distance between us and the little blinking light on the screen. We were less than a mile from our destination when Tech's face reappeared on the screen.

"You have incoming. Blue. Next light," he said, before disappearing.

"What the hell?" I took my foot off the gas and hit the brakes. A siren blared to life. I'd only slowed to eighty in the sixty-mile-per-hour zone.

Bones swore. "What's going on, Tech? You said we were clear."

The screen stayed blank, but Tech's voice came over the speakers. "You're supposed to be. He's off route. I'm calling it in."

"What do I do?" I wondered out loud. It had been years since I'd been stopped by a cop. The family spent millions to make sure such encounters didn't happen.

"Just keep going," Bones said.

"And go where? If I don't stop now, more will come. The last thing we need is to create a scene." I glanced behind me. If this ended in some high-speed chase, the pigs would search my car and we'd rot in the can. Father could only cover up so much, and there wasn't a rug big enough to hide the evidence in the back of the Hummer. "I gotta pull over. Maybe I can reason with him."

"What? No! That's a horrible idea," Bones objected.

"I'm working with my contacts at the station, but a team has been routed to your location just in case. Be careful, Angel," Tech said.

I slowed the vehicle and veered to the outside lane, rolling to a stop just beyond an on-ramp. Bones reached for the gun in his jacket pocket. I also had a gun in my jacket and another under my seat, but didn't reach for either since I had no intention of using them.

"This is a cop. He's just doing his job," I said, eyeing Bones's pocket.

Bones stiffened. "And I'm doing mine. At least trade me spots?"

"No. I can handle this, and I can do it without violence."

I looked into my rearview mirror, watching as the cop sat in his cruiser, radio in hand.

"He's calling it in," Bones said.

Tech's face materialized on the screen again. "You may have a problem, Angel. The officer has been ordered to return to the station, but refuses."

Damn. "Tech, I need information. Who am I dealing with here?"

"I'm pulling his file now. Roger Hill, typical beat cop, no marks in his file, married, two kids, a third on the way. His family just moved here from the Denver area. That's all I've got, but I'm still searching."

It would have to be enough. The door of the police cruiser swung open and Roger Hill climbed out. He marched toward us, wearing a stern glower with the same efficiency that he wore the signature tan uniform of the Metropolitan Police Force. Clipped to the top of his shirt was a lapel mic with a wire that led past his name badge to the radio at his hip. Clipboard in hand, he tapped on my window. I pasted on my friendliest smile and rolled down the window. Hot, dry Nevada air gushed in.

Officer Hill leaned forward and looked us both over. I could almost see the wheels turning in his head as he took in our nice suits and the tricked-out Hummer, weighing it all against the orders from his department to leave us alone. He had to be wondering who we were.

"You boys in a hurry?" he asked.

I nodded. "We're businessmen, Officer, always in a hurry. But

I apologize, I didn't mean to speed."

His eyes hardened, telling me I'd get no mercy. "I clocked you at seventy-nine, and your brake lights were on. License and registration."

I glanced at Bones, and we both eyed the glove box. Even if registration paperwork existed, there was no way it was in my name. My father had taught me to officially own nothing, that way the IRS couldn't officially take it away. I hesitated, wondering if I should pretend to search the glove box or just go straight for the fake ID in my wallet.

A burst of static came over the officer's radio, followed by a female voice with a hysterical edge. "Officer Hill, you are not on radar. Please report."

He frowned. "Excuse me for a moment," he said to us, before stepping back and answering.

"Tech, what's going on?" I asked.

"I'm working on it, sir. Don't worry. The team is almost to you. Sit tight."

I knew what teams did, and therefore needed to come up with a plan to diffuse the situation before they showed up.

Officer Hill reappeared in my window. "License and registration." His request had morphed into a demand.

Desperate, I lied. "We have this important meeting we're late to and my car broke down. I had to borrow my father's car, and I can't find his registration. Can you just write me a ticket and we'll be on our way?"

"Officer Hill, we need you to check out a possible ten-seventy on Wedgewood Drive. What's your status?"

Keeping an eye on me and Bones, he pressed the button on his radio and said, "I'm still at the four-thirty-eight."

Static. Then, "Officer Hill, you are not authorized to proceed with that four-thirty-eight. You have been ordered back to the station by the chief."

He tilted his head to the side, his eyes hardening. "Your father could be the devil himself, I don't care. Nobody's above the law."

I shrugged, wondering what the dispatcher had told him. Wondering why the hell he wouldn't follow orders. "I told you, we're just a couple of businessmen trying to get to a meeting."

"Oh yeah? What type of business are you in?"

"Officer Hill, report. What's your status?"

He didn't even blink.

"You should probably get that." I nodded toward his radio.

"Don't tell me how to do my job." His hand slid to his holstered gun. Sweat glistened across his forehead. "Now, hand me your goddamn license."

I took a resigned breath and slid the ID from my wallet. Righteous anger radiated from the cop and I understood his frustration. He was from Colorado, a good cop who didn't understand how we played the game here.

He studied my fake license and chuckled. "John Frank, huh? They're not going to let me run this, are they?"

I didn't reply. Even if they did, he wouldn't find anything.

"You part of one of the families?" he asked.

He knew about us. Hell, he was probably some wannabe savior who thought he could bring us down. Thought the good guys would win. In a last ditch effort I switched tactics and tried honesty. "I'm just a man trying to save another man from making a big mistake. Christmas is coming and you have two kids and one in the oven. Am I right, Roger?"

That surprised him. His eyes widened for a second before hardening again. Maybe he'd come around after all.

"You're in a lot of danger right now, officer, but not from me."

He pulled his gun. "Don't threaten me, and don't talk about my family."

I tried to pretend the Glock didn't affect me and opened my wallet again, this time reaching for the bills in the back. My fingers wouldn't stop shaking, making it difficult. "You're a good cop, going above and beyond, so why don't you accept this token of our appreciation for your service and get back in your cruiser while you can still drive away."

"Officer Hill, do you read me? You are not authorized to proceed with that four-thirty-eight," the dispatcher said again. "We need you to return to the station. Now."

I slowly withdrew seven hundred dollars, and then added another three. "Last chance. Think of your kids, Roger. Don't you want to see their Halloween costumes? To spend Thanksgiving with them? And Christmas? They need their father. Your wife needs her husband. Nobody has to get hurt. Just take the money and walk away."

His jaw clenched. He didn't even glance at the cash, and I

knew he was screwed. "I'm an officer of the law and not interested in your chances. Now, hand over your real license and registration before I arrest you both and impound your car."

I sighed. "You have no backup. Nobody's going to impound my car, and there's no way you're taking me in. In a few minutes a car full of men will come and they will… overreact to you pulling a gun on me."

Officer Hill's hand began to tremble.

The screen on my dashboard lost its connection. I didn't have to look at my phone to know I had no bars. All electronics in the area were blocked. I was out of time.

"Incoming," Bones whispered.

My rearview mirror showed a black SUV pulling up behind the cop car. Doors opened. Officer Hill turned toward the sound. Six shots rang out and Mrs. Hill became a widow.

Bile rose in my throat. My vision swam. I lowered my head and closed my eyes, trying to block out the image of Roger Hill's head exploding.

"Angel?" Bones asked, patting my shoulder.

I took a couple short breaths and opened my eyes. A dead father lay on the other side of my door, and I had to pretend it didn't faze me. My stomach clenched and I swallowed back the bile, knowing I couldn't show weakness in front of the men swarming the scene. Keys were tossed, and then the police cruiser started up and drove away. Suits blocked the body from view of freeway drivers and bagged up the officer. Someone handed me back my fake ID.

He should have taken the money. He should have walked away.

My dashboard screen lit up and Tech's face appeared. "Get out of there, Angel," he said.

"There was nothing more you could have done for him," Bones said. "You tried. The fool should have listened."

A couple of the men were watching me. I felt them measuring my reaction, judging whether or not I was ruthless and apathetic enough to lead their merry band of murderers. Shaking my head at my father's sick bastards, I slid the Hummer into gear and merged back onto the freeway. In my rearview mirror, I watched them load the body bag into the SUV. He was a good guy—a good cop—and now he was dead. In Vegas, nice guys didn't just finish last. They didn't finish at all.

♠ ♥ ♣ ♦

CHAPTER TWO
Angel

AFTER BONES AND I made the drop, I wanted to go home and wallow in a guilt-driven mental breakdown, but there was no time. My baby sister was in a ballet recital, and the family would never forgive me if I missed it. We entered the theater and were met by a thin usher, who bowed low before motioning for us to follow him.

"We've been here a time or two," I objected. "We can find our own way."

"It's no trouble. I insist, sir."

His smile was almost as greasy as his hair, and his gaze darted between me and Bones as if he expected us to barge past him with guns blazing. The idiot didn't understand the way things worked. If violence ever erupted at a child's event, Father would probably purge the population and start over.

We followed the usher toward the box seats and Bones pressed in beside me, swiveling his head to watch behind us while keeping an eye on the usher. "Want me to set him straight?"

Having had more than enough action for one day, I shook my head.

"Right this way, please," the usher said, stepping aside and gesturing for us to continue. "Your father is in the center box."

"We know, since that's where he always is. Owns the box," Bones said, watching the usher as I stepped past them both and continued down the hall. Within seconds Bones was back at my side.

"Who does that guy think he is?" he asked. "Where's the regular guy?"

"Paul?" I asked. Paul was a graying man with a slight limp, who usually greeted us.

"Yeah, Paul. I like that old guy. He knows his place. You'd never catch ol' Paul watching us like we're criminals and insisting on walking us in."

I resisted the urge to remind Bones that we were both packing. "He's just doing his job."

"All I'm sayin' is that he should show a little more respect. We're grown-ass men. We don't need to be monitored like a couple of kids."

We stopped in front of a door with guards on both sides of it. All of Father's guards wore their dark hair short and came equipped with stocky builds, strong Italian names, and a plethora of weapons stashed in their tailored suits. For the most part, they were related by blood or marriage. My father recruited for our *borgata*—our cozy little crime family— like a model paranoid mastermind. He distrusted anyone he couldn't trace clear back to Adam, required a minimum of five references, and had a finger on the pulse of the most prized possession of each employee. If the competitive pay and generous benefits packet failed to inspire loyalty, Father made sure he knew what would.

One of the guards announced my arrival into his radio. He pulled a key out of his pocket and unlocked the door, swinging it open and stepping aside.

I followed Bones inside. He walked to the right and put his back against the wall, standing alongside two more of Father's men. Spicy sausage, garlic, and freshly baked breads scented the air, and classical piano music competed with the chatter and laughter of my family. My heart started to lighten, followed immediately by heavy guilt. It was impossible to celebrate with my family after seeing Officer Hill be ripped away from his.

Georgio, my seven-year-old half-brother, called my name and hurled himself at me. I opened my arms just in time to catch him, and then we staggered backward as I ruffled his dark curls.

He wiggled free, swatting my hands away. "You're gonna get me in trouble," he complained.

"Oh really? Why's that, Georgie?" I asked.

"Georgio Augostino," Georgio's mother—my stepmother,

Rachele—said with a huff. "What have you gone and done with yourself? Just look at you! Jumping around like you're some sort of monkey."

She bent down and straightened his tie, adjusted his vest and coat collar, and then started in on his hair.

"Sorry, Rachele. My fault," I admitted.

My stepmother wore a tight, low-cut black dress that walked the tightrope between classy and trashy. Strung around each wrist she wore diamond tennis bracelets worth more than the average American made in a year. Her dyed red hair was styled up so she could display the giant diamond teardrops hanging from her ears, matching the one around her neck. Her collagen-plumped lips drew into a tight line before she seemed to remember we were in a room full of family and gave me a patronizing smile. She had access to all my father's money, and still couldn't buy a heart.

She sighed over Georgio's appearance and stepped forward to greet me. "Hello, Angel. Good to see you."

Yeah, right.

The family was watching, though, so I moved in to dutifully kiss her cheek. "Hello, Rachele. I hope you're well."

Georgio tugged at my slacks. "Do you like my new suit?"

"You look like a stud, Georgie. You know, you're the reason I never bring girls home. One look at you, and I'd be chopped liver."

Georgio blushed. "Yeah right."

"For real, bro."

"Mom said I have to watch all of Luci's boring dance."

Luciana was Georgio's twin sister, and when the two weren't terrorizing the world with all the mischief twins could muster, they were driving each other crazy.

"Well, save me a seat and I'll join you after I talk to Father. I won't let you suffer alone. Promise."

Georgio nodded. "Thanks, Angel. You're the best."

He scurried off and Rachele went back to her conversation with Uncle Mario and Aunt Adona, who were long-time business partners of my father's and not actually related. The trio hovered near the hors d'oeuvres, not far from Father and his brother, Uncle Carlo, who spoke in hushed voices beside the wine. Cousins Naldo and Remo sat with my sisters, Sonia and Sofia, playing on their cell phones and seemingly oblivious to the world around them. My brother, Dante, wasn't among them. Father's cousin, Alberto, reclined in his seat with his eyes all but closed while Aunt Mona and *Nonna* (my grandmother) fussed over his four-month-old baby, Nina.

Nonna looked up, and frowned at me. "What's wrong, Angel?" she asked.

She handed Nina off to Aunt Mona and hurried to my side. Barely above five feet tall, Nonna was heavy-set, dark-featured, and made *cannoli* so crispy and sweet it could mend broken bones as well as hearts. And she was the closest thing to a mother I'd ever known.

"I'm fine. *Buonasera*, Nonna," I said, kissing her cheek.

"Good evening, Grandson," she replied, returning the gesture. "And don't lie to me."

Knowing she wouldn't relent until I told her something, I said, "Rough day at work. I will be fine, though."

She glanced in Father's direction, but didn't press the issue. Instead, she slipped something into my pocket. "I saved you some macaroons, and it's a good thing. These vultures dove in and attacked the platter the minute I put them out."

I opened the baggie and popped one of the treats into my mouth, smiling as sugary perfection exploded on my taste buds. "Thanks, Nonna."

Father called out my name and waved me over. After he greeted me, he gestured for me to check the room. I'd created a device to scan for wires, taps, or anything with the ability to record or transmit audio or video files. I did a quick scan of the room and the readout told me one of my cousins had brought a handheld game to the recital. Each person in the room—even Georgio—had a cell phone, and Uncle Mario was also packing a tablet. There was a device I didn't recognize in Father's left shoe. When I pointed it out, a wide grin spread across his face. He clapped me on the shoulder and beamed at his brother.

"You see, Carlo, I told you the boy's a genius. This new gadget he has can pick up anything."

I had to stop myself from correcting him as he leaned against the back row of sofas and tugged off his shoe, retrieving the pinky-nail-sized bug hidden inside. Technology evolved constantly, and I didn't want to mislead anyone into trusting the device to catch everything. Regardless, Father was the type of man you didn't correct, especially not in front of others.

Uncle Carlo smiled. "He sure is a genius, Dom."

"Mario, Adona, have I told you about this thing?" Father asked, pointing to the scanner. "I bet it gets more bids than that phone distorter we put out last year."

The distorter bounced calls around cell towers and providers, taking family communications to a whole different level. It was my first big invention, and the profits from taking it to market had changed the way the family viewed me. I was still the black sheep, but at least I'd found a way to make money off my pastime.

"We always knew you were a bright young man," Aunt Adona added, her patronizing tone grating on my nerves.

"Yes, we're all proud of him," Rachele replied, fake smile once again plastered across her face.

"Excuse us for a moment," Father said to the group, giving my shoulder a gentle squeeze. He led me to the corner and draped an arm over my shoulder. "You were late making the drop today."

A man's life had ended, and my father was concerned about my tardiness. There was something so messed up about that, I couldn't even wrap my brain around it. "There were complications beyond my control," I replied.

"You're a Mariani, Angel. Nothing is beyond your control."

Every time I closed my eyes I saw Officer Hill's body crumple to the ground. Everything was beyond my control. "Tech said we were covered."

"If you had left on time, you wouldn't have needed Tech's assistance. You get so wrapped up in these stupid toys that you neglect your position."

And there it was… what the old man really thought of my life's work. He expected me to follow in his footsteps, building the family empire, and although he tolerated my work, he'd never respect it.

"Now, why the hell are you moping around here, making your nonna ask after you?"

"Father, that cop—"

"—was unreasonable. He had to be dealt with."

"He was clean."

The old man nodded. "Yes, he was. That's the problem. This city doesn't need clean cops, it needs reasonable men and women, interested in keeping the city thriving and families fed. You're sheltered, Angel. You don't see what it's really like out there. Why don't you use that giant brain of yours to research what's going on in the rest of the country. Check out Santa Fe, Cheyenne, Bismarck, most of Montana and Utah... cities with over fifty percent unemployment, where families starve to death on their morals. Hell, you think that cop's family cares that he was clean? Will that keep his wife warm at night or teach his son how to throw a baseball? Will it put food on their table and clothes on their back? This recession has been a bastard, and the minute we turn soft, our business will dry up. Nobody gives more to the people of Las Vegas than our family, and the city will fall if we fail."

Father frowned and looked away. When he looked back at me, his eyes had softened. "We can't worry about stubborn idiots who refuse to see the bigger picture. We have to make difficult decisions so those who judge us will have a full stomach when they sleep at night."

My heart screamed that there had to be a better way to serve the community—a way that didn't leave widows and fatherless children behind—but in my head, I knew he was right. Life wasn't some fairy tale where heroes won the prize. Life was a battle for the ferocious who weren't afraid to claw, kick, and bite their way to the top, and I needed to sharpen my nails and strengthen my resolve if I had any chance of surviving.

I pulled an envelope of cash from my inside pocket and handed it to my father. "From the delivery."

"Thank you. I didn't want to pull you in on this, but I needed someone I can trust. The Pelinos are gearing up, preparing to make a move." He rubbed a hand down his face, looking tired and worn.

The Pelinos were our rivals. Less than a year ago they made a play for power and failed. A big deal went south and they shot the wrong people, disrupted the balance, and brought the feds down on the city. Their mistake inconvenienced the local families, resulting in several Pelino deaths.

I frowned, wondering why the idiots would try again. "The Pelinos are greedy and incompetent. The families won't support them."

Father studied me, scratching his chin. "Who knows what the families will do? But if I know one thing, Adamo—that crazy bastard—will hang himself. We just need to supply the rope. In the meantime, we stay the course, guard against outsiders, and keep as much business as we can within the family. You get what I'm saying?"

He wanted me more involved. I tried to mask my disappointment, and nodded. "Yes sir."

"Good, good." He patted me on the back. "Now, I need you to pick up a couple of associates from the airport tomorrow afternoon. I'll forward you the details. And don't forget you promised the twins you'd take them out for Halloween. Then family dinner Sunday."

"Of course, Father."

He nodded. "You're a good son, Angel. A good family man."

Considering my family, I wasn't sure if that was a compliment or not.

An announcer stepped onto the stage and prepared the crowd for the start of my little sister's ballet recital. I turned to head to my seat, but Father grabbed my arm.

"Angel, I want you and Bones to spend some time on the shooting range. This thing with the Pelinos is heating up, and we may have to make a move. I want you two ready in case I need to send you in."

My stomach sank as I stepped forward to take my seat. Everyone said my baby sister danced her legs off that night, but I was too busy wondering what the old man was planning to even pay attention.

CHAPTER THREE
Markie

WITH MY SUITCASE packed and set beside the door, I paced the small, dank room I had shared with eight orphans for the past eleven months. Empty, lumpy mattresses sat atop four sets of bunk beds, the absence of their occupants filling my stomach with lead.

The door opened and I stopped in my tracks, hopeful.

Tad stepped into the room, wringing his hands as he scanned the space. "They're still not back," he said, leaning against a bunk.

Somewhere north of forty with skin darker than a starless night and heart larger than Texas, Tad had devoted his life and finances to running this orphanage in the impoverished, AIDS-ridden village of Mwembeshi, Zambia. He had patience for days, but I'd managed to wear it thin on more than one occasion. Today was no exception.

He glanced at his watch. "If we don't leave in the next ten minutes, you'll miss your flight, Ms. Markie."

"I know. I just—" Having no idea how to finish the statement, I closed my mouth. Almost four hours ago the children—six girls and two boys ranging from ages three to ten—had set off to deliver fresh water to a family in the bush north of the village. We'd made the trek together dozens of times, but this time I stayed behind to pack and say my good-byes to the villagers. The delivery should take two hours, round trip, and knowing I was on a schedule, the children had promised to hurry back. And with every minute they were late, my stomach tied in another knot.

"I'm sure they'll be all right, Ms. Markie," Tad said. "They know the land. They will not get lost."

My worries had more to do with Zambia's recent Boko Haram infestation than with the children getting lost. If those psychos got their hands on the children... there'd be nothing I could do. We'd be lucky to ever see them again. Guilt gnawed at my insides, making me wish I'd just gone with them. A little voice in the back of my mind reminded me I was abandoning the children to head back to the states and they'd have to make the delivery without me from now on. Doubting my decision to leave for the millionth time, I checked my cheap, international cell phone again, hoping for a text from my sister. Nothing. It had been weeks since I'd heard from Ariana.

The voices of children calling my name drew my attention from my phone. I looked up just in time to see all eight children rush through the door and stop short, breathing heavily as sweat dripped down their faces.

"What is it? What's wrong?" I asked, wondering if they'd been chased.

"We didn't want to miss you," the oldest boy, Kael, breathed.

I didn't care how sweaty they were, I wrapped each in a hug and kissed their moist cheeks. "Where have you guys been? I was so worried!"

"Ms. Tanishia was having her baby, and Hadiya had to help," the five-year-old girl, Aboyomi, said.

"I had to learn," Hadiya, the eldest girl, defended. "I knew you'd understand, Ms. Markie."

I did understand, but Tad took that moment to remind me we were out of time. The children carried my bags to the jeep, we said hurried good-byes, and then Tad and I were off to the airport. Tad drove as fast as his broken-down jeep could, and we arrived only moments before I needed to board. I barely had time to thank him before being whisked onto the plane and strapped in. As Africa shrank beneath my feet, the reality of my departure hit me. I didn't cry—never been big on shedding tears, especially not in public— but I felt like I'd been sucker-punched in the gut. I lowered my head and tried to pull myself together.

"You okay?" someone asked.

Startled, I looked up to see the elderly woman in the next seat watching me. She flashed me the trust-gaining smile of a politician or a preacher, and, based on the leathery condition of her sun-saturated skin, I figured she was the latter. Probably a missionary, in fact. My first instinct was to lie and assure her I was fine, but as an external processor, I couldn't. We had a long flight ahead of us, and if I didn't talk to someone now, I'd be ranting to myself like a lunatic in no time.

"Honestly, no." I replied. "I've been volunteering at an orphanage, and now that I'm heading back to the states I'm worried about the children. There are so many dangers, and if I'm not there to protect them..." My incomplete thought lingered between us as I fought to form my concerns into words.

The woman nodded, patting my shoulder. "You're worried about their ability to survive without you."

As her words sank in, I realized how arrogant they made me sound. Did I truly believe a group of tough-as-nails children couldn't survive without the help of a five-foot-seven, one hundred-and-thirty-five-pound, twenty-two-year-old white girl? What could I really do for them that Tad couldn't?

"I remember my first mission here," the woman added, clearly oblivious to my inner battle. "I felt the exact same way. Cried the whole trip home. Then some wise old lady reminded me that the children were all right before I came and would be fine after I left. So now I'm going to be that wise old lady and tell you the same thing. Those children have their own path to follow, and you wouldn't be able to control it even if you stayed. Who are you to protect them from life?"

Feeling robbed of whatever empathy I'd been expecting, I bristled. But in the end, I knew she was right. The past couple of years had taught me that control was an illusion easily shattered by circumstances or details. "You *are* wise."

"Of course I am. I'm old and have earned my knowledge the hard way." She smiled and squeezed my hand. "You can always come back and check on the children, you know?"

Even in all her wisdom she was wrong, but I didn't have the heart to correct her. We chatted for a while. When we were done, I put earbuds in and came to terms with my decision, knowing it was far too late to turn back now.

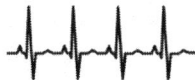

⊣┝⊣┝⊣┝

After what seemed like a lifetime of flights and layovers, Las Vegas appeared in the small window. Swimming pools in practically every yard, replicas of world-famous buildings, flashing lights. I couldn't help but get swept up in the possibilities of the city I'd never seen in person. By the time my flight landed, I felt much better about being in the states and was mentally prioritizing an after-I-smack-Ariana-around list of things to do.

After a brief stop at baggage claim, the welcome aroma of pizza smacked me across the face, reminding my growling stomach that it took more than a handful of airline pretzels to make a meal. Temporarily tabling my search for my sister, I followed my nose to Don's Pizzeria. The place was packed. I sighed and gave my name to the hostess before wheeling my luggage over to sit in the waiting area. I didn't have to wait long before a man stood before me, smiling. Barely older than me, he worked the sexy Italian look like a movie star. His tailored suit might as well have had moneybags taped to it, and as I glanced down at my rumpled sundress and sandals, I hoped he wasn't the manager, appearing to escort me from the premises.

"There's only one in your party?" he asked.

I nodded. "Yes."

"You shouldn't have to wait. My friend and I have an extra seat at our table if you'd like to join us," he offered.

Startled, I gaped at him like an idiot. I understood what he said, but it didn't make sense. Why would someone like him offer someone like me a seat? I thought of the childhood warnings my mother had given, hesitant to trust a well-dressed stranger in what everyone referred to as the city of sin.

His smile melted away and his posture stiffened. "If you don't want to, that's okay. Just thought I'd offer, since we have an extra seat."

My brain kicked into gear enough to realize my hesitancy could be seen as offensive. I jumped up, ashamed. He was offering me a seat at a public restaurant, not luring me into the back of his van with candy.

"Sorry, you caught me off-guard. Thank you, yes. I'd love to join you."

I followed him to his table where he introduced himself, Angel, and his companion, Bones, without offering last names.

"Angel and Bones, huh?" I asked, looking them over. They

seemed like men who worked out. Bones had muscles on top of muscles and very little neck. I could feel several sets of eyes watching us, and wondered who they were. Clearly, they were important. And why withhold their last names? "Nice suits, code names... you're not secret government agents, are you?"

Bones had just taken a sip from his water, and he almost spit it all over the table, coughing and choking. Angel pounded Bones's back until he stopped.

Once Bones started breathing again, I said, "I'll take it that's a no, not government agents."

Angel chuckled. "Definitely not, and they're just nicknames, not code names."

"Good to know. I'm just Markie, no full name, no nickname. My parents wanted a boy, but got two girls." Realizing they probably didn't care about my life story, I pointed at their wine glasses and changed the topic. "What are you drinking?"

"Merlot. Would you like a glass?" Angel asked. Before I could answer he slid one of the two glasses in front of me. "They poured him a glass, but Bones doesn't drink. At least not wine."

"What? Why would they bring you something you didn't order?" I asked.

Bones shrugged. "They're human. They make mistakes. Are you even old enough to drink?"

Since there was still a possibility the two mystery men could be cops, I pulled out my ID and handed it to Bones. "I'm twenty-two."

Bones glanced at the ID before handing it to Angel. "Knock yourself out," he said, gesturing toward the glass.

"Thank you." Unsure whether or not I'd like it, I took a sip. Blackberries and currents danced over my taste buds, reminding me of other reasons it was good to be back in the states. "Mmm. This is delicious! You'll have to excuse me. I barely turned twenty-one before I went away, and I've never had anything that tasted like this."

"Went away? You get locked up or something?" Bones asked.

"Locked up?" I snorted. "As in jail?"

I knew I looked rough, but jail?

"Okay, wait a minute. I realize I look frumpy. I've been traveling for days, and I'm sure I could use a shower and a change of clothes. But do you really think I'm some convict? Is that why you guys brought me over here?"

They gaped at me for a moment, and then the two shared a look I couldn't read.

I scowled directly at Bones. "Is it?"

Before Bones could answer, an Asian man appeared carrying a pizza almost as big as the table and piled with more toppings than I'd ever seen. He set it atop the riser, and then a server handed Angel and Bones each a plate.

"Is everything all right, Mr... Angel?" the man asked, eyeing me.

"Yes. Ling, meet my friend Markie. She was... unexpected, but welcome. Markie, Ling owns this restaurant."

Wondering if Angel expected me to be impressed he knew the owner, I held out a hand to Ling. "Nice to meet you."

Ling's fingertips barely brushed my hand while he insisted that any friend of Angel's was a friend of his before rushing off to grab a third plate. Angel slid a slice of pizza onto his plate and set it down in front of me. The pie looked incredible, and the smell made my mouth water, but the entire exchange was creeping me out. I'd never been confrontational, but I wasn't going to let these guys roll over me either.

I wasn't finished with my tirade, though. I slid Angel's plate back in front of him and added, "Thanks, but I am perfectly capable of ordering my own lunch."

Angel turned back to me and cocked his head. He still wasn't speaking, but he did loosen up his tie. Bones looked from Angel to me, chuckled, and then shook his head.

"What?" I asked, getting the feeling that nobody ever refused them.

"I think you look lovely," Angel said, finally. His gaze drifted down, and then came back up to my face. "That dress brings out the blue in your eyes."

I most certainly did not blush. I bit the inside of my cheek to make sure of it.

"And we didn't mean to offend. Sometimes Bones thinks he's funnier than he actually is."

"I'm hilarious," Bones deadpanned.

"See what I mean?" Angel asked with a smirk. "You know, this pizza is gigantic. Ling really outdid himself, and there's no way we'll be able to finish it. You are welcome to it if you'd like.

If not, we can get you a menu. We didn't want to be rude and eat in front of you. Especially if you've been traveling for days. This is one of the few good airport restaurant choices, so I'm sure you're starving."

And it smelled so amazing. I was moments from gnawing off my arm. Angel's calm and polite response made me feel like a complete hag for freaking out. "I'm sorry I snapped. I'm pretty exhausted."

"Don't even worry about it." Angel offered me the plate again.

There was no way I could refuse it. I thanked him and dove in as Ling returned with the third plate. The pizza tasted even better than it smelled. "Oh man, I've missed pizza. This alone makes it worth coming back to the states."

"Where have you been?" Angel asked.

"Zambia."

"Oh, wow. What were you doing in Africa?" Angel asked.

"Running drugs," Bones said, gesturing at me. "Obviously. I mean look at her."

"You see what I'm dealing with here?" Angel asked.

I giggled. "He's a little funny."

Bones grinned.

"But no, I wasn't running drugs. At least not this time. I orig-inally went to help build wells, but there was this orphanage with the most amazing kids. They needed help, so I stayed and helped out."

"Changed your plans just like that, huh?" Angel asked, shaking his head.

I nodded.

"How long were you there?"

"About a year."

"Wow."

Angel seemed like he wanted to say more, but Bones's pocket buzzed, interrupting the conversation.

"Everything all right?" Angel asked.

Bones studied his phone. "Yeah, but we gotta bounce. They must have made up some time, because their flight just landed."

I couldn't help but wonder who "they" were, but resisted the urge to ask. Bones waved Ling over and offered to pay the bill, but Ling refused his card.

"Sorry we have to rush off." Angel stood and offered me his

hand. "It was great meeting you."

I stood as well. A handshake seemed kind of formal since they'd shared a meal with me, so I hugged him instead. "Thank you for your kindness."

Bones tensed and stepped forward. I laughed. "Still not a convict, Bones." Then I hugged him too. That seemed to really throw the big guy off. He patted my back awkwardly and stepped away from me.

I forced back more laughter. "Thank you both. This was nice."

They muttered in agreement before heading toward the door. Realizing they weren't taking the pizza, I asked if I could. We'd barely touched the pie, and I was certain I could find someone who'd appreciate it.

Angel looked at me like I'd sprouted a giant zit or third eye. It was too late to retract the statement though, so I waited until he nodded.

"Knock yourself out," Bones replied.

Having thoroughly embarrassed myself, I was happy to watch the mystery men leave, confident I'd probably never see them again.

Boy, was I wrong.

CHAPTER FOUR
Angel

BONES HALF-DRAGGED ME out of the restaurant while my brain was still trying to process what had happened.

"What the hell was that?" Bones asked, pulling me into a gift shop. "You leave to use the restroom and you come back with this broad?"

I shrugged. "She needed a place to sit. We had an extra chair."

"And?"

"Did you see her? She was fine, Bones."

He chuckled, shaking his head. "*You* picked up a girl at a restaurant? *You?*"

Offended, I flashed him my best scowl. I could pick up girls, I just usually didn't want to. There was something different about Markie, though. Her dimples. Her perfect lips. The innocence in her bright blue eyes. "She was really fine."

"If she was all that, why didn't you get her number?"

So many reasons. She seemed sweet and untainted and I had no desire to drag her into my wreck of a life. "Turns out she wasn't my type."

Bones eyed me. "Right. Well, fix your shirt. And your tie. What the hell, man? Are you taking these guys to a meeting or to a strip club?"

"Huh?" I followed his gaze, and sure enough, my tie was loose and my collar button undone.

When did that happen?

With no time to worry about it, I fixed my appearance and we hurried out of the restroom. Markie stood outside the restaurant with an open pizza box in her arms. An elderly couple stopped in front of her, and she held the box toward them, saying something. They each reached in and took a slice. Markie closed the box and headed toward the exit, stopping to offer pizza to a mother and two small children along the way. Her long blonde curls cascaded down her back and, as she slipped a rogue lock behind her ear, I suddenly wanted to run my fingers through it.

What the hell's wrong with me?

Bones nudged me. "Never met anyone like her before."

Still transfixed by the natural girl-next-door beauty before me, I stole one more eyeful of her soft curves. "Nope. And we probably never will again." A little pang of regret pierced my chest.

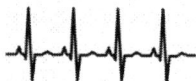

Bones and I made it to the waiting area only minutes before my father's associates. Two Italians and one orange-haired Irishman sported typical wiseguy attire: tailored suits, Italian loafers, luxury watches, and hard-ass attitudes. The family limo took us on a tour of the strip before stopping in front of a five-story glass building, one of several locations where Father conducted his business. The driver let us out and then sped off before the trio could even ask about their luggage in the trunk. That soured their expressions and made for an uncomfortable elevator ride.

Bones led us to Conference Room B where six black high-backed ergonomic chairs surrounded a rectangular stone table that ended in a fifty-two-inch flat-screen television. The opposite wall held a built-in glass-door refrigerator stocked with bottled water and soda. Large tinted one-way windows looked out over the strip and gave us a scenic view of the hills beyond. I offered up refreshments as Bones stood guard by the door.

Small talk was never one of my strengths. I could only discuss the city's history, shows, and restaurants for so long before the tension in the room suffocated us all. Father let me sweat it out until the wait hovered around offensive before making his grand, guarded entry. He greeted his guests without apologizing for their wait, and gestured for me to scan the room.

The room was clean, so I nodded at him and took a seat.

"Did you bring the plans?" Father asked, getting right down to business.

"Yes, of course," the Irishman replied. He pulled papers from his briefcase and offered them to the old man.

Father gestured for me to take them. Curious about what he was springing on me, I grabbed the pages and studied the design of a bomb. The ginger pointed out the sensors and so-called safety features, and then engaged my father in a conversation about keeping production costs low.

A generic, low-cost killing machine. Terrific.

"Angel, what do you think?" Father asked.

He'd brought two guards, knowing Bones would accompany me. Between his visible security, the amount of time he'd left them waiting, and the fact their luggage was still tucked safely away in the trunk of the limo, I knew I wouldn't be bursting any budding friendship with my honesty. "It is economical and the design is simple; production would take no time at all."

"Exactly," the ginger said.

Father looked at the paper in my hand. "Would we use it?"

It was a bogus question. Only he knew what we would and wouldn't use, but he wanted my eyes on it again. Reading past his words, I studied the design once more, committing it to memory. Then I handed the papers back to the ginger.

"No. Our family is precise and our hits are clean."

"This is clean," one of the ginger's babysitters replied. "Nobody can survive this explosion. They open the door and boom, it's over."

He didn't blink, didn't wince, didn't waste a moment considering bodies splattered all over the pavement. I wondered—not for the first time—how many lives a person could take before they grew numb. A room full of people, and there wasn't a single heartstring to tug on. I sighed and tried for a more practical approach.

"That's what I'm worried about. What if a wife or a child is the first to the car? Then what? Your hit is still out there roaming free and you've killed an innocent and broken the code. Now you've got the cops and the families hunting your ass down. That's a lot of trouble to save a few bucks. Hardly worth it."

The second babysitter leaned forward. "Even with a slug to the head, you run the risk of collateral damage. Somebody could duck, or a child could get in the way. There's no guarantee in anything."

"Good point," Father replied, standing to let us know the conversation had come to an end. "Thank you for your time, gentlemen. Now that Angel has seen the specs, we'll discuss this and have an answer to you within the week. I have another meeting I must get to, and my security is calling the limo. They'll be waiting downstairs to take you wherever you need to go. Angel will walk you out."

And with that, Father shook hands and vacated the room with his guards in tow. The trio had flown across the country and waited almost an hour for a five minute chat with the head of the Las Vegas families, and they were clearly expecting more. After a moment of stunned silence the ginger packed up his paperwork and he and his goons followed me and Bones down the hall. They were drowning in outrage, and I refused to so much as throw the callous bastards a kind word. Bones and I saw them to the limo and then waited for a valet to bring the Hummer around.

"Well, that was awkward," Bones said.

I chuckled, shaking my head. "I don't even know what that was."

My phone rang. Knowing the old man would be calling to debrief, I clicked on my bluetooth and answered.

"Angel, thank you for your assistance today."

Father rarely thanked me. I didn't know what to say. "Yeah, no problem. You're not going to buy from them, are you?"

"Of course not. I wanted your eyes on the design so you'll recognize the product when it surfaces," he replied.

The certainty in the old man's voice sent a chill down my spine. If one of the families purchased and used those bombs, all hell would break loose. "Got it. One lousy design for a killing machine etched into my brain."

He sighed and disconnected without so much as a goodbye.

"Everything okay?" Bones asked.

I shrugged. "He thanked me, but then I spoke and he remembered how disappointing I am."

Bones nodded. "It's a screwed-up world."

"Yes, yes it is."

I tried to pretend it didn't bother me, but deep down every son wants his father's approval, and I was no exception. If I could just keep my mouth shut, we'd get along better. Making backhanded comments about the old man's livelihood definitely wasn't winning any son-of-the-year competitions. Frustrated with it all, I changed lanes and hung a left, heading in the opposite direction of my workplace.

"Where are we going?" Bones asked.

"It's too late to go back to the office. Let's hit the gym."

Bones took working out very seriously. The minute we stepped out of the locker room he morphed into some sort of fitness Nazi hell-bent on pushing me until I bled or coughed up a lung. But between the cop shooting and my father's shady associates, I desperately needed to purge my brain, even at the expense of my body. Bones helped me do just that. About an hour-and-a-half into our workout, I collapsed into the Jacuzzi, sore muscles sizzling as they hit the water, and sank down to my neck. Bones—looking no worse for the wear—strutted toward the pool and dove in. I waved him off, giving him my blessing to do laps like some possessed Olympic hopeful while I recuperated. I wanted to rush home, crawl into bed, and sleep for a week, but the twins would never forgive me if I didn't show up to take them trick-or-treating. And somehow Bones had talked me into club hopping afterward.

Cold water splattered on my face, and then the level of the Jacuzzi raised over my chin. "You almost ready?" Bones asked, sitting across from me.

"Ready for what?" I asked, eyes still closed.

"Costume shopping."

"Bones, today's Halloween. I doubt there's going to be anything left."

Bones got out of the Jacuzzi and I heard him walking away as he replied, "I call bullshit. You're just trying to get out of it. I have a friend who runs a costume shop and she's been sending me pictures of their remaining inventory." There was the sound of Bones rustling through his bag, followed by his wet steps on the cement floor as he walked back over. "Think I'll go as Sexy Zorro this year. What do you think?"

I opened one eye. Bones's phone was in my face, flooding my vision with the image of a man dressed all in black, shirt unlaced down to his navel, spandex pants that left nothing to the imagination, wielding a sword. His hat and mask covered more than his outfit did. I closed my eyes and winced, wishing I could unsee the image. "Ugh, Bones. That's like man-porn. Keep that shit out of my face. You do realize we're taking the twins trick-or-treating first, right? I don't know that they're old enough for Sexy Zorro. Hell, I'm not old enough."

"Yeah, yeah, I'll keep it G-rated for the kids, but after we drop them back home all bets are off."

"I don't even know what that means, but I'm terrified."

"What are you going to go as?" he asked.

"I don't know. A dutiful man taking his younger siblings out and then babysitting his best friend all night?"

"That look is so tired; you wear it all the time," Bones whined. "Live a little."

"What did I go as last year?" I asked.

Bones tensed. The sour look on his face reminded me I had stepped into territory best left untouched. Memories of last Halloween came flooding back. My ex-girlfriend, Leilana, had me dress like a pirate so she could be my slutty wench, which really should have clued me in on her extracurricular activities. Later that night, I found out she'd been sleeping with a guy from work. Leilana was gone now, but anger, shame, and guilt still managed to ravage me every time I thought of her. I stood and let the memories slide off me with the water. "Right. Let's go for something with a little less drama this year."

Bones chuckled and tossed me a towel. "Got it. Hmm." Then he cocked his head and a wide grin spread across his face.

"Uh oh. That doesn't look good," I said.

Bones threw back his head and laughed. "You're right, it's not good. It's great. I have the most incredible idea. We are going to look so badass this year!"

Since badass was much better than sexy, I swallowed back a grimace and followed Bones to the locker room, wondering what the hell he was up to.

♠ ♥ ♣ ♦

CHAPTER FIVE
Angel

WITH BONES AT my side, I rang the doorbell of my childhood home and turned my back on the security camera aimed at me. I had a key and would normally let myself in, but today I wanted to make an entrance. Bones and I wore matching black outfits: pants tucked into combat boots, jackets with official police crests on the arm under Kevlar vests that said "Police" on the front and "SWAT" on the back. Even our baseball caps were black with white letters announcing us as "SWAT." Black squirt guns were holstered at our hips, ready to drench anyone who didn't take us seriously. In case the squirt guns weren't enough, we each carried a billy club, handcuffs, rubber gloves, and enough containers of silly string to cover the entire city of Las Vegas, stashed in the pouches strapped to our legs. I had no clue where Bones had gotten the costumes, but I was fairly certain they were authentic, and I couldn't wait to see my father's reaction.

The old man answered the door with a security guard hot on his heels. His eyes widened for a moment as he looked from me to Bones, and then back to me. Then he threw back his head and laughed harder than I'd ever heard him laugh before. The security guard eyed Bones and me, with one hand on the gun in his pocket. Then he must have recognized me, because he chuckled and shook his head appreciatively.

"Al! Come look at these pigs on my doorstep!" Father shouted, sliding aside and waving for Cousin Alberto.

Cousin Alberto hobbled over to the door, took one look at us, and practically spit out his dentures.

"That's the best thing I've ever seen," he said, when he could finally breathe again. "You've gotta get a picture of this, Dom."

Still chuckling, Father disappeared for a few moments and then reappeared with a camera around his neck.

"Those are *some* costumes," he said. "Looks just like the real thing. Where'd you get them?"

I held my hands up. "Don't look at me. This was all Bones's idea."

"I know a guy," Bones said with a shrug.

"Those guns real?" Cousin Alberto asked, pointing at my holster.

I drew my plastic weapon, aimed it for dramatic effect, and then proceeded to water the potted plant next to the door. This only made them laugh harder.

Cousin Alberto shook his head. "The guys aren't gonna believe this. Dom, you gotta get a picture of me with these two."

There were pictures of us arresting Cousin Alberto and Father, pictures of us about to beat the men with our billy clubs, and pictures of them stealing our guns and squirting us. The two laughed hard enough to make me feel like I'd partially redeemed myself. So what if I sucked as a wiseguy? At least I could be comic relief. Too bad the costumes hadn't even been my idea. Father was still chuckling when Luciana came around the corner wear-\ing a long, frilly purple dress.

"Wow! Look at you!" He gasped. "I've never seen such a beautiful lady in my life."

"You're stunning, Luci," I added.

She blushed, pausing to flick a long dark curl out of her face. "I'm a princess."

Father scooped her up in his arms, kissing her forehead. "Of course you are. You're my little princess. The most beautiful princess ever."

"Look at my glass slippers, Angel," she said, showing me her feet.

"Better not lose them. If some guy shows up on the doorstep with your shoe, he's gonna be eating it. You know that, right?" I warned.

Father narrowed his eyes at me. "Where's Georgie?" he asked

Luciana.

"Here, Daddy!" Georgio said. He strutted down the stairs, dressed in a breastplate over a tunic with chain mail sleeves and waving a long plastic sword. His black pants were tucked into fur-lined boots, and on his head he wore a helmet with what looked like a spear point coming out of the top and some sort of winged emblem on the front.

"Angel!" He shouted, running to greet me. "Can you guess who I am?"

I lacked imagination for guessing games and never could figure out what the hell they were drawing or who they were imper-sonating. I always tried, though.

"Of course. You, Georgie, are a mighty Samurai."

He tilted his head to the side and dropped his shoulders, obviously exasperated with me. "Not what, who?"

History was never one of my strong subjects, but as a young history buff, Georgio had a small library on ancient battles and the rulers who initiated them. He couldn't read half the words, but didn't let that minor detail keep him from his passion. I'd spent many hours reading those boring books to him, but still had no clue who he was supposed to be. I looked to Bones for help, but he shrugged. Father tried to mouth the answer to me, but I couldn't make out what he said.

"One of the guys from Mulan?" I asked, taking a stab in the dark.

Georgio groaned. "Genghis Kahn. You know, famous warrior and leader? Didn't they teach you anything in school?"

I tried to hide my smile at Georgio's dramatics. Smacking my palm to my forehead, I groaned along with him. "Genghis Kahn. Of course! How did you not get that, Bones?" I asked, passing the buck.

Bones waved his hands as if he could dispel the accusation. "Hey, you're the genius, Angel. I'm just the muscle."

Father interrupted our verbal sparring to pose us for more pictures.

"Where's everyone else?" I asked. Last year Sonia and Sofia had dressed as storm troopers, and I couldn't wait to see what costumes they'd chosen this year.

"Dante is out with friends, and Sonia and Sofia are eleven and thirteen now. Earlier this week they informed me and Rachele that they're too old for trick-or-treating and asked to attend a dance their school is putting on."

"Too old? Since when?" I asked. Then the rest of his words sunk in. "Wait, you let them go to a dance?"

He chuckled. "They are well chaperoned. Even their mother is there. Now get out of here so I can get some work done. Remember, I don't want them going just anywhere."

"I know, I know." Like I would take them just anywhere. Sometimes my father forgot that he wasn't the only one who turned into an over-protective papa bear whenever the twins were around. "We'll hit their school carnival and then a couple of churches so they can load up on candy."

"Great. Their dentist will thank you." Father chuckled and shook his head. Then he hugged me and added, "You're a good man, Angel."

His words managed to warm my heart, even as they sliced through it. In our world, good men were suckered, taken advantage of, and discarded when they were of no more use. Father didn't need good men. He needed men who were willing to put the family business above all, and I wasn't that man. Feeling disgraced, I scooped Luciana up and grabbed Georgio's hand. "I'll have the twins back by eight."

Father closed the door behind us, and we climbed into the Hummer and headed to the school. The twins introduced us to their friends while dragging us along as they tossed bean bags, hula hooped, jump-roped, raced, and fished for prizes. Our costumes earned us several strange looks, but for the most part, people left us alone. We were watching Georgio and Luciana compete in the cake walk when Bones nudged my arm and nodded at the pint-sized Batman and Spiderman who were whispering and watching us from the wall.

"Couple of wannabes?" Bones asked.

"Man, I hope not."

Occasionally people heard stories about my family. Sometimes the stories glorified our life and made people want to experience it for themselves. It really sucked when these people were disillusioned kids who lacked parental guidance. Batman saw us watching him and nodded like he knew us. Then, with Spidey in tow, Batman strutted over in his hundred-dollar sneakers. The duo stopped right in front of us and waited. I pretended not to notice them, returning my attention back to my siblings on the cakewalk.

I could feel Batman watching me for a while before he finally grew the balls to say hello. I wasn't about to encourage whatever visions of mob life grandeur the kid had, so I didn't respond.

"Hey," he said again, taking another step toward me. "Cool costume."

Bones cleared his throat and stepped forward, crossing his arms and standing with his feet apart.

I glanced down at the kid. He looked at Bones and swallowed, but didn't back down. He focused back on me and asked, "You Luci and Georgie's brother?"

"Yeah. Do I know you, kid?"

He nodded. "I'm Tanner. Tanner Michaels. My dad helps your dad out sometimes."

Spiderman snickered.

I frowned. Some idiot associated with my father had been stupid enough to discuss business in front of his child. And like most children, Tanner clearly had a big mouth. Michaels. I couldn't place the name, but would have to mention it to the old man. Could be the kid was lying altogether, but I'd have to make sure. Focusing back on the problem at hand, I shrugged and asked, "So?"

That seemed to burst Tanner's bubble a little. He took a step back and glanced around. "Just thought I'd say hi," he replied.

The last thing I needed was some punk kid following me around trying to be a wiseguy. I crossed my arms and looked down at him. "Yeah? Well, you said it." Then I dismissed him and turned away.

Tanner didn't know what to do. I watched out of the corner of my eye as he and Spiderman stood stunned for almost a full minute before scurrying off like they suddenly had someplace to be.

"You know who his dad is?" I asked Bones.

Bones pulled out his phone and tapped the screen to life. "Nope. But I'm about to find out."

"Good." I wasn't a violent person, but I'd gladly make an exception for a father who knowingly put his kid in danger just to look cool.

Not long after our encounter with Batman and Spiderman, the twins got their fill of the carnival. It was a little after seven, so we stopped by enough churches to fill their sacks with enough candy to keep them jacked up on sugar until next Halloween before carrying the exhausted duo to the door.

"You're the best brother ever," Luciana told me, kissing my cheek. Then she leaned over to hug Bones around his neck and kissed his cheek. "You too, Bones. Thank you guys."

Bones put Georgio down and gave him a manly fist bump, like he hadn't just given him a piggy-back ride to the door.

"Who wouldn't want to take Princess Luci and the great Genghis Kahn Georgie around for a night?" Bones asked. He bowed and added, "It was an honor, your Highness."

We released them into Father's care and bowed again, several times, making them laugh as we walked away.

♠ ♥ ♣ ♦

CHAPTER SIX
Angel

FOR MY HIGH school graduation, Father gave me the key to a two-bedroom condo located in a high rise just off the strip. He owned the building and controlled the security, but having my own space at least gave the illusion of freedom. While my high school friends escaped their families and headed to college, Father granted me independence he could control, and surrounded me with people he could trust.

The condo was a beautiful prison, complete with earthy tones of bamboo flooring, granite countertops, stainless steel appliances, custom leather furniture, and bold crimson curtains framing floor-to-ceiling windows with a view facing the lights of the strip. Every inch of the space was designed and furnished to remind me of my position as heir, in line to reign over the city through blood and luxury.

As I entered the condo, I dropped my keys in a dish on the console table and turned to face Bones, still engaged in our argument. "Listen, you thrill-seeking maniac, I think the cops will be able to tell these aren't fake." I tugged at my Kevlar vest. "I see 'impersonating an officer' charges all over this one."

"It's Halloween, the one night you can get away with impersonating anyone," Bones replied.

"But what if they start asking pesky little questions like where did we get them? What are we doing with them?"

Bones shrugged. "They fell off a truck."

"Right." I couldn't help but chuckle. Ask a wiseguy a question and get a wise-ass answer.

"Angel, you play responsible big brother to half the city. For one night, I'd like to see you relax and let loose. Do something crazy and enjoy yourself."

I inwardly groaned, wanting to stay as far from crazy as humanly possible. But Bones was my friend, and sometimes friendship required stupidity. "Fine, but if I go clubbing with you in a SWAT uniform, my crazy-card is filled for the next five years."

"Five years?" Bones snorted. "For dressing up on Halloween? This buys you maybe one month. Just wait until you see what I have planned for Christmas. You'll want in. You'll reconsider."

That sounded ominous. I had to find a way to get past Christmas. "One year."

Bones cocked his head. "I can't believe you're negotiating away your fun." Then because he could never resist a good gamble, he added, "Two months. Come on, Angel. The chicks are gonna dig this."

I was more concerned about a real SWAT team taking offense to us terrorizing the nightclubs with cans of silly string and squirt guns. And Father would kill me if I ended up in jail tonight or on Christmas. "Six months. I go clubbing with you tonight and I don't have to do anything else stupid until at least April."

He gave me a hard stare, and then split the difference. "Four months, and that's my final offer. You'll miss Christmas, but we'll have Valentine's Day, and I got a real plan for getting the honeys this year."

Resigned to possible jail time over a stupid Halloween costume and fearing whatever the hell Bones had in store for February, I scooped up my keys and followed my friend out into the cool, autumn night. Bones picked the club, and I drove. As we approached, he pointed to a line of costume-clad club jumpers that stretched halfway down the block.

"Looks packed," I said. "We should probably call it a night and head home."

"Don't worry about it. I got this." Bones pulled out his cell phone and started dialing. "Just park."

I reluctantly handed over the Hummer to the valet and followed Bones to a side door. He sent a text, and moments later the door swung open, pouring loud, thumping music into the street.

A thin, short woman wearing skin-tight black fabric that barely covered her bust and butt struggled under the weight of the door. Black velvet ears clung to her head and whiskers streaked across her cheeks. Her eyes rounded at our costumes for a beat before her face lit up with recognition and she squealed in delight. "Bones! You crazy bastard, you scared the shit out of me!"

Then she looked me over and added, "Why, hello there. You must be Angel. I've heard so much about you. I'm Trixie."

Any chance of blessed moments of anonymity went up in a poof. I glared at Bones, wondering just what he'd blabbed to the girl.

Bones shrugged. "What? Did you wanna wait in that line all night?" he asked.

"Don't worry, handsome, your secret is safe with me," Trixie said. She led us to a booth and we both ordered water.

"That's it?" Trixie asked, clearly disappointed.

"For now," Bones replied with a wink. "We usually don't turn up until after midnight. We just woke up a couple hours ago."

"Oh, I see," she smiled, seemingly satisfied with his answer. "Night people."

When she walked away I kicked Bones under the table. "What the hell are we, vampires? And since when do we 'turn up'?"

"Hey, gotta live up to the image. People expect certain behaviors from you."

I couldn't even live up to my father's expectations. If I had to start jumping through hoops for the rest of the world, I was screwed. "Think she'll be disappointed when we don't get smashed and thrash the place like rock stars?" I asked.

Bones chuckled. "She'll get over it. What's up with them?"

I followed Bones's gaze to find three suits sitting at the bar, two with their heads together and the third watching the bar crowd. The three stuck out in a room full of costumed crazies. "One of the families. Who knows what they're up to?"

"The bartender doesn't look too happy with them," Bones said, ever observant.

I found the bartender in question just in time to watch him set drinks in front of the suits. They didn't offer payment, and he didn't quite hide his scowl before he turned away. One of the suits said something, but the bartender put up his hands and softened his expression. Wasn't my business though, so I shrugged and scanned the rest of the club. Drinks in hand, costumed professionals, tourists, college students, and entertainers bounced, grinded, and swayed, on and off the dance floor. A handful of working girls wove through the crowd, seeking out the lonely and trying to make a buck. A fight between a skeleton and a hippie broke out by the side door, but bouncers swooped in and carried off the offenders before it got out of hand.

Trixie returned with our waters, asking if we needed anything else. Bones ordered me a glass of wine.

"You need to relax," he said as Trixie walked away.

I leveled a stare at him. "If I was any more chill, I'd freeze our drinks."

He chuckled. "So that's where the frost is coming from, huh?"

I couldn't help but crack a smile.

Bones grinned. "There. That's better. Now check out those girls on the dance floor. The ones wearing the belly dancer costumes. You should go up and say hi."

"Sure. I'm just gonna walk up and strike a conversation with a girl wearing gauze. Maybe I'll tell her how pretty her brain looks."

"And that's your problem. I'm not telling you to meet her parents. I'm telling you to have a good time and enjoy the night. Nothing more."

"Right." I took a sip of water. "Bones, if I need to get laid, I'll call Terrance and have him send a girl over."

"I never understood that. Why would D'Angelo Ma... why would *you* pay for sex?"

I shrugged, ignoring his near slip. "Simpler that way. No chance of someone screwing around and catching a feeling."

"No chance that someone has to meet the fam," Bones replied.

I tilted my head to the side. "See? Simpler *and* safer."

Trixie reappeared long enough to pour me a glass of wine. I swirled it around and took a sip, and for some reason the strange girl from the pizzeria slipped into my mind. *Markie.* I tried to imagine her on my arm, meeting my family, but couldn't even fathom it. They'd rip her apart and hang the pieces by her sundress.

"That was almost a year ago. You need to put it behind you," Bones said.

Wondering what the hell he was talking about, I replayed our conversation in my head. *Leilani. Right.* My old on and off again girlfriend would forever direct my future relationships. Leilani was exotic: dark, sleek hair, flawless caramel skin, legs that went on for miles, blue eyes that contrasted with the rest of her appearance. She saw me coming from a mile away and sank her perfectly manicured nails into me, refusing to let go. I knew she was like the others, and understood what she was after, but I was tired of being alone. She danced, and often got a little too friendly with her clientele. I begged her to quit, and in return, she tried to negotiate a ring out of me.

Our Christmas gift exchange was awkward, to say the least. In hindsight, giving her a small jewelry box in a nice restaurant was probably misleading. But since I'd never even invited her to meet my family, I didn't think she'd read so much into it. When she opened that box and saw earrings she threw a public tantrum, aided by the rum and diet soda she'd been guzzling throughout dinner. She started swearing, and I turned to walk away. She attacked me, and I blocked. Bones grabbed her and tried to get her under control. Leilani kicked and screamed about how I used her and tried to control her. People crowded around, watching the spectacle of our crumbling relationship. Hotel security detained Leilani and helped us slip away, but word got back to my father. He, Uncle Carlo, and Cousin Alberto were waiting in my apartment when Bones and I got home that night. Father made a quick call, and then we all sat down and played poker. We didn't talk about Leilani, or the incident, but we didn't have to. The old man would never stand for such an open show of disrespect to our family, no matter who it came from. I knew his presence there meant he was my alibi, and I was his.

A few days later Leilani's roommate reported her missing. Cops questioned me, but I told them the truth. I didn't know what had happened to Leilani. The police had to know my family was in on it, but my building's doorman and surveillance videos kept us above reproach. Leilani never surfaced, and I learned my lesson and stayed the hell away from the dating scene. Just thinking about it now made me cringe.

"I'm good for now. Maybe I'll talk to the belly dancers later."

Thankfully, Bones didn't press the issue.

A tall dark-skinned man paused beside our table and bid us a good evening. He wore a tight smile, a tailored suit, and what was left of the hair on his head had the appearance of running away from his face. "I'm Greg Pines, the manager here, and I wanted to stop by and personally welcome you."

"Thank you, Mr. Pines," I replied, keeping the conversation polite but professional and wondering what the hell he wanted from me. "The service has been prompt. Your people are very attentive."

"Happy to hear it. Thank you." He pulled a six-by-two-inch gray box out of his inside pocket and offered it to me. "Please accept this gift as a token of our appreciation of the family, and all you do for the city."

Bones took the box and angled it away from me as he opened it. Then, he placed it on the table so I could see the contents. A beautiful hand-carved pocket knife was tucked into a dark velvet liner. According to the knife's label, the blade was forged of Damascus steel and the dragon-carved handle was fashioned from twenty-four-karat gold and platinum. It was more than a gift. It was a business offering.

"My father will be pleased," I said, snapping the box closed.

Mr. Pines smiled and tilted his head. "If you need anything at all, please let me know. My card with my personal cell number is under the knife."

"Noted," I replied, careful not to commit to anything.

Mr. Pines thanked me for my time and left. I kicked Bones under the table and glared at him.

"What?" Bones asked, rubbing his knee. "I can't help it if people love you."

"Yeah, that's it. They love me. Now *my* brain is beautiful." I shook my head, disgusted and ready to go.

All of a sudden Bones stood up, knocking his chair back. "That lying asshole!" he said, glaring at the dance floor.

I tried to see who he was looking at, but the place was packed. "Which one?" I asked.

"Matt Deter. That guy right there. The one wearing the giant condom wrapper. That bastard owes me three g's. I called him yesterday and he was whining that his mom was in the hospital and he needed to go take care of her. Looks like I need to send *him* to the hospital."

Bones jumped over the railing "Matt! Hey, Matt!" he shouted.

Matt turned toward us, and his eyes bulged when he spotted Bones. His lips formed a couple of obscenities, and then he turned away and wove through the crowd. I grabbed Mr. Pines's gift for my father and ran around the railing in time to follow Bones toward the side door. It opened and Matt slipped out. We followed him out the door and searched the street. Matt was gone.

Bones swore. "I was lenient and he took advantage of me. I can't wait to catch up with him and rectify the situation."

To be honest, I was glad Matt had gotten away. Bones was my best friend and my constant protector, but when he fought, it scared the hell out of me. He went into some sort of crazed rage that usually ended in me trying to pull him off some unconscious victim before he killed the guy. Not exactly what I wanted to do with my evening.

"Well, looks like he got away." I shrugged. "What do you want to do now?"

"I know where he lives," Bones said.

Shit!

Hoping Matt wasn't stupid enough to go home, I retrieved the Hummer and followed Bones's directions to a run-down apartment building off West Bonanza Road. We parked the car and crept up to apartment one-fourteen.

"Are you sure this is a good idea?" I asked after Bones knocked.

In answer, he knocked again, harder this time.

The door swung open.

Nothing could have prepared me for the person who answered.

CHAPTER SEVEN
Markie

AFTER LUNCH WITH the nice guys at the pizzeria, I took a cab to my sister's last known address. Ariana had sent me pictures of the place, but the photos didn't do it justice. In person it looked more like a high-end resort than an apartment complex. As I walked past the landscaped common area and swimming pool toward the manager's office, I wondered how much the rent was. No doubt way more than I could pay.

It took a while to convince the apartment manager I wasn't a stalker or a bounty hunter, and was legitimately worried about my sister, but he finally gave me her forwarding address. This time the cabbie deposited me in front of a dilapidated building without landscaping or swimming pools. The manager had never heard of Ariana Davis, and since I wasn't interested in renting an apartment, she promptly showed me to the door and went back to her soap opera. Disheartened and unsure of what to do, I wheeled my luggage to the curb and sat down beside the apartment mailbox.

I pulled out my phone and scrolled through our correspondence, searching for clues of where she could be. She'd mentioned a waitressing job, but didn't specify the name of the restaurant. I googled Las Vegas restaurants and the number of them was somewhere north of infinity. But with nothing better to do, I started making calls. The sun set and costumed adults and children emerged from apartments, trick-or-treat bags in hand.

Halloween. Great.

As if it wasn't going to be difficult enough to find Ariana without masks and wigs. Feeling frustrated and a little overwhelmed but unwilling to give up, I dialed restaurant number twenty-three on the list.

Then, my sister almost walked over me. Life is sometimes funny that way. The people you're looking for sometimes pop up and mow you over.

"What the hell?" Ariana said. It took an impressive acrobatic act to keep both her phone and her body from hitting the ground. "Why would someone sit right in front of the mailbox?"

Her attention was still on her phone.

"Probably the same reason someone would try to text and walk at the same time," I replied.

She froze midstep. We locked gazes, and her heavily-lined eyes grew round.

I stood abruptly, knocking my suitcase over. "Ari."

She blinked.

Shock and awe wasn't quite the reception I'd been going for. But that didn't matter. My little sister was alive and well. Relief washed over me, stripping away weeks of worry and stress. Frustration and anger crept in as I stared at her phone. If she wasn't dead, why the heck hadn't she returned my calls or texts? She knew I was worried out of my mind. I'd texted her that exact statement at least six times. Why wouldn't she put my mind at ease? Why wouldn't she save me the plane ticket? Before I could decide whether to hug her or yell at her, she awoke from her stupor and wrapped her skinny arms around me.

"Markie!" she cried, squeezing.

Tears stung my eyes. Ariana wasn't dead. Anything else we could work through.

"What are you doing here?" she asked, releasing me. "I mean… I thought you were still in Africa."

"You stopped communicating and I freaked out. What happened to you?" I looked her over. Her long curls had been chopped to just below her jawline and straightened into a cute do. She wore short shorts, revealing knees knobbier and legs thinner than I remembered. The dark circles around her bloodshot eyes were natural, not from eyeliner like I'd originally thought. She looked older. Much older. Like five years had passed since I'd last seen her. "Are you okay? Why didn't you answer any of my calls or texts?"

Her eyes cut to the side and she shrugged. "Yeah, about that... I forgot to pay the bill and my phone got shut off."

Your phone got shut off?

My gaze cut to the phone in her hand. As an aspiring actress, Ariana lived and breathed by the phone, waiting for "the call" that would give her her big break and launch her career into super stardom. No way would she forget to pay her bill and leave it off for weeks. If my baby sister needed money, she'd be selling plasma or a kidney before she let that phone go. Yet the state of this apartment building compared to her last one led me to believe there were definitely cash flow issues.

"The phone doesn't have service. It's on the building's Wi-Fi."

Which meant she had plenty of options for reaching me, and had chosen not to. "Ari, if you need money, all you have to do is ask."

"Thanks, but I don't need your money." She walked past me to get to the mailbox.

I stared after her, wondering what was going on. Sure, she'd been mad at me when I left for Africa with no plans to return, but we'd worked that out over several lengthy international calls. I had the phone bills to prove it.

I ducked my head and tried again. "I'm sorry. That came out wrong. I know you can take care of yourself."

When Ariana turned back around, she wore an apologetic smile. She grabbed my hands. "I know. I'm sorry. It's just such a shock to see you. I didn't know if I'd ever see... I can't believe you're here. How long are you staying?"

Her hands trembled in mine. No, not trembled; shook. She shook.

"I don't know yet. Ari, are you okay?"

"Yeah, of course." She pulled away and reached for my carry-on bag.

Goose bumps sprouted up my arms, giving me very bad vibes. I grabbed the handle of my suitcase.

She shrugged my carry-on over her shoulder. "Come on, let's get inside." Then she gave me a pleading look and added, "Promise me you'll be cool."

Be cool with what?

"Okay."

"Say the words, Markie."

The last time Ariana had told me to 'be cool' she'd gotten nail polish all over my favorite sweater, which the brat did not have permission to wear. Since I'd given her any clothes I hadn't taken to Africa, I had no idea what to think. I followed her into a small apartment with mismatched furniture, dim lighting, and a haze of smoke, not of the cigarette variety. Someone had been smoking pot in my baby sister's apartment. I really wanted to freak out about it, but before I got the chance, a man asked, "Babe, was the check there?"

Ariana frowned. "Nope. Still not there."

"Damn. I was counting on that money. Well, hurry and get ready. We gotta bounce!"

Babe?

Ariana gave me another apologetic smile. "Matt—my boy-friend—kind of... lives here. You promised you'd be cool."

I was actually thankful for the smoke, because it hid the steam coming from my ears. I was planning to grab my sister and bolt when Matt came around the corner dressed in a giant condom wrapper and holding a beer. My breath caught, and not in a good way. In a bad way. A very bad way. An ohmigosh-my-baby-sister-who-isn't-old-enough-to-drink-is-living-with-a-guy-wearing-a-giant-condom-wrapper-and-drinking-and-smoking sort of way.

Ariana's smile turned to a grimace. "Matt, this is my sister, Markie."

He nodded at me. "Hey, babe." He wrapped his arm around Ariana's waist and pulled her into his lips, and then proceeded to stick his tongue down her throat. At least that's what it looked like from my perspective. She squirmed against his grasp, casting sideways glances at me, but he didn't let up until she pushed him off her.

"Whoa, what was that for?" Matt asked, his words slurring together.

Matt could make me reconsider my stance on violence.

"My sister is right there." She gestured wildly at me.

"Yeah." He shrugged and smacked her on the butt. "Now go get your costume on."

"Actually, I was thinking maybe we can stay home? Markie just got here and I don't feel good."

She didn't sound well, either. She sounded tired. In fact, now

49

that we were in the light, I got a good look at her, and she looked like crap. She shivered while sweat beaded across her forehead.

"Are you kidding me right now?" Matt asked. "After—" His eyes cut to me. "After what I just gave you, you're going to stay in? Tonight?"

What he just gave her?

While I chewed on that little tidbit, Ariana frowned. "No. I'm sorry. You're right. I'll go get dressed." Then she turned toward me and asked, "Do you have a costume?"

Her eyelids drooped, and she looked like she would pass out right there. I moved closer, just in case she did.

"No, I forgot it was Halloween. And you…" I put my hand to her forehead. She didn't have a fever, but her skin felt clammy and cold. "You're sick. You can barely stand. What's going on?"

Matt, the condom wrapper, glared at me. Then he drained his beer and tossed it on the counter. It didn't break, but the clatter made me wince.

"Matt, wait." Ariana reached for him.

He dodged her advance. "You're sick? Really convenient, Ari. You know how important this night is to me, and you don't give a shit." He threw up his hands. "Selfish, Ari. I'm out."

Then he stormed out.

I stared after him, wondering what in the heck had just happened.

Ariana ran out the door, but she was slow. Weak. She barely made it out of the house before she tripped over her own two feet and slammed her shoulder into a pole. She slid down and sat on the ground. Still stunned, I forced my feet into action and hurried to her.

"You okay?" I asked.

A little blue Honda burned rubber out of the parking lot. Matt rolled down the driver's window, shouted, and held out his middle finger at us.

That Matt's a classy guy.

"Why did you do that?" Ariana asked, regaining my attention. Giant tears rolled down her cheeks.

I stared at her, at a complete loss for words. She couldn't possibly believe Matt's blowup was my fault. Regardless, I helped her up and back into the smoke cloud that still occupied her living room. My head felt weird—contact-high weird—and I groaned, because it seemed like an unfair complication when I really needed to think.

"I think I'm gonna be sick!" Ariana announced.

We mostly made it to the sink, and then I held her hair back while she emptied her stomach. My fuzzy brain struggled to process what was happening. The apartment now smelled like vomit and marijuana, something was clearly wrong with my little sister, and her boyfriend had just gotten pissed and bailed because she was sick?

When Ariana stopped heaving, we navigated the path into her bedroom. Shivers racked her body, so I helped her into bed and piled every blanket I could find on top of her. I put a giant bowl beside the bed before cleaning up the mess in the kitchen. Ariana threw up again, so I dumped her barf bowl and returned it to the side of her bed. With each passing minute she looked worse, and I felt too fuzzy to help her. Frustrated, I sprayed half a can of air freshener into the living room, trying to overpower the pot-cloud and hopefully prevent myself from getting contact high*er*.

I was exhausted and knew if I sat down, I'd pass out and Ariana would be on her own. So I drifted around the apartment, cleaning between trips to check on my sister. I was finishing up the dishes when a knock sounded on the door. Hoping it was Matt, returning to redeem himself and prove he wasn't the biggest loser on the planet, I hurried to answer. Two cops in SWAT uniforms greeted me.

I panicked and closed the door in their faces.

Then I sniffed the air. Flowers and marijuana. Awesome.

I am so going to jail.

Only I couldn't go to jail, because that would mean Ariana was going to jail too, and she was way too sick for that.

Another knock on the door.

My dad was a state trooper. I grew up surrounded by cops. Even wanted to be one, and I had the degree in criminal justice to prove it. I could handle this. I just had to play it cool. I opened the door and smiled up at them.

"Sorry, I had to put on a bra."

Yep, that was playing it cool, all right.

It was all I could think of, but it seemed to work. Their scowls disappeared, revealing two hot men in uniform, both with olive skin and dark features. Kind of like the nice guys in the pizzeria.

Wait. The more I looked at them the more I was certain of it.

"Markie?" the shorter body-builder-type cop asked.

"Bones?" I asked.

"Yeah." He stared at me. They both did. No doubt they smelled the smoke, and were preparing to cuff me and read me my rights.

I looked up at the taller, much hotter cop. "And... I'm sorry. I can't remember you name."

He blinked.

Bones chuckled.

And I felt like an idiot.

"Angel," the hotter cop replied.

"Right, Angel. You're SWAT?" I shook my head at my own stupidity and went with a not-so-obvious question. "Of course you are. What are you doing here?"

"We're looking for a suspect. A man, about five-eight, brown hair, medium build, goes by the name of Matthew Deter."

"Matt? You're looking for Matt?"

"Yes. Is he here?" Bones asked.

Of course they were looking for Matt. The guy didn't exactly scream upstanding citizen, as evidenced by the smoke affecting my brain. "No. He took off a while ago. He's a suspect? To what?"

"That's confidential," Bones replied.

"How do you know Ma— the suspect?" Angel asked. "You said you were in town to see family. Are you a relative?"

"He's my sister's boyfriend. Or at least he was. He was pretty pissed when he took off, so I'm not really sure about the status of their relationship right now."

I had no idea why I told them this, but I couldn't seem to stop myself.

Retching sounds came from the bedroom. I leaned back and hollered, "Ari? You okay?"

What sounded like dry heaving answered. I waited for her to stop before turning back to the cops. They still hadn't said anything about smelling pot on me, and I didn't want to press my luck. Besides, my sister needed me. "Ariana's sick. I need to get back to her. If you have a card... I promise I'll call if he shows up."

The dry heaving started again.

"What's wrong with her?" Angel asked, surprising me.

"I don't know. I got here right before Matt bailed. She's shaking, cold sweats, throwing up. She can't even stand."

The two exchanged a look.

"All right. Thanks for your help," Bones said.

Then the two of them turned and walked away. I closed the door and realized neither of them had given me their business card. I wasn't about to press my luck and go chasing after them for one. Instead, I hurried in to check on Ariana.

♠ ♥ ♣ ♦

CHAPTER EIGHT
Angel

SHAKING, COLD SWEATS, throwing up. She can't even stand.

The words assaulted me during the walk back to the Hummer. I made it to the door, even got my hand on the handle, but couldn't open it. I had a bad feeling about Markie's sister, and I needed to know if I was right.

"Angel, get in the car," Bones said, opening the passenger's door. It wasn't a demand—Bones would never cross that line—more like a strong suggestion, softened when he added, "We'll talk inside."

I nodded and climbed in. Bones checked something on his phone.

"Matt's one of your dealers, isn't he?" I asked.

Bones's primary job was to ensure my security, but like all my father's employees, he was also an earner. We never spoke about how he earned, but I knew what was up. I chose to feign ignorance, because being surrounded by my family's secrets had taught me knowledge isn't always power. Sometimes knowledge is responsibility; the kind of responsibility that keeps you up additional nights or adds years onto your prison sentence. Sometimes ignorance is true power.

Bones's jaw tensed. I'd never crossed this line before.

"You really wanna know?" he asked.

I looked back at the door, wondering what was happening inside the apartment. It wasn't any of my business, and the smart thing would be to drive away. Only my brain couldn't seem to settle on the smart decision.

"Yeah."

Bones nodded. "Matt's one of my dealers, but he's slippin'. Been avoiding me, and didn't make the last two drops. His ass is full of excuses and his veins are probably pumped full of my profits. Probably his girl's too."

Shaking, cold sweats, throwing up. She can't even stand.

I was no expert, but that sounded like she was more than just plastered. "And her symptoms?"

Bones shrugged. "Sounds like she got some bad shit."

I eyed him.

He held up his hands. "Don't look at me. Everything I touch is pure."

My attention drifted back to the apartment door and stayed fixed there while I tried to force myself to put the key in the ignition. It wasn't working. My memory kept flashing through images of a dead cop, schematics of a bomb, my father's armory, all the shit I couldn't do anything about. But Markie's sister... I could help her. I needed that, needed to feel like something other than a useless pawn in a war I didn't want.

"We're going in there, aren't we?" Bones asked after a time.

Resigned, I sighed, swung open my door, and got out. Bones followed me back to the apartment door. I knocked with a little more force than necessary, but I was pissed and didn't know if it was because of my decision, the situation, or life in general.

Markie answered. "You're back? Matt's still not here and my sister is—"

"—the reason we're here," I said, cutting her off. "We need to come in, Markie. We need to see her."

"Why?" Markie asked. "Did she do something wrong? She really is sick, I swear. Can't you come back when she feels better?"

I hadn't anticipated her resistance, and it irritated the hell out of me. I was trying to help, after all, and couldn't think of what to say to get her to let us in.

Luckily Bones didn't need an invitation or even approval. He barged right in, somehow squeezing between Markie and the door frame, and marched into the living room.

"Hey!" Markie shouted, jumping aside. "You can't just come

in here! You got a warrant?"

Bones ignored her and kept walking.

Markie looked to me. "What the heck?"

I shrugged and sniffed, confirming what I'd suspected. Recalling her last name from the driver's license she'd showed at the restaurant, I said, "Sorry, Ms. Davis. Smells like marijuana in here and we're looking for a suspect. Reasonable suspicion."

I didn't know if that was a "thing," but it sounded good. Hopefully good enough to keep her from calling the real cops.

Her cheeks reddened. "It was Matt. I swear."

"Angel, get in here!" Bones shouted.

I followed his voice to a small, dark bedroom. Clothes were bursting out of the closet on the left-hand side, and more clothes were folded and stacked on a chest of drawers in the corner. Bones stood beside the bed, tugging back the pile of blankets to reveal a waif of a girl who looked barely out of high school. Sweat glistened over every inch of skin that her shorts and T-shirt revealed.

Markie gasped. "She looks even worse." She hurried to the bed and grabbed her sister's hand. "Ari, honey, what's going on? Talk to me."

Ariana's eyes popped open. She looked up at us and her bloodshot eyes widened. She sat up and reached for the blankets, tugging them with her as she scooted away from Bones.

"What the hell did you do, Markie? Get them out of here. Get out of my house!" Then she winced and grabbed at her lower back. A stream of obscenities shot out of her mouth like a spray gun, drenching us in vulgarity. Midtirade she fell over, passing out cold.

Bones sprang into action. He checked her pulse, her arms, and her eyes. Then he looked around the room. "Do you know what she used?" he asked Markie.

"What she used for what?" Markie asked.

Bones shook his head and ripped open the drawer of Ariana's nightstand, riffling through the contents.

"Hey! I don't think you should be going through her stuff," Markie objected.

Bones pulled out a small plastic bag, halting her protests. He licked the tip of his finger, stuck it in the baggie, and tasted the contents.

"Shit. This is absolute shit." He looked at Markie and added,

"Get her to a hospital. Now."

I expected Markie to argue or freak out or something, but she looked from Bones to the bag to her sister, and her whole demeanor changed. She took charge.

"She doesn't have a car. Can you take us?" She turned her gorgeous blue eyes on me. They were glassy from the smoke and watery from the tears she fought. "Please?"

The smart move would be to have her call an ambulance. But then there'd be cops and probably a search of the apartment. Matt seemed like the type of idiot who stashed enough blow in his home to earn a decent stint in the lockup, and I wasn't about to let Markie take that fall for him.

"Yeah." I leaned forward and sniffed her. "Change into something that doesn't smell like pot. You have some of that fruity-smelling stuff to spray in your hair?"

Bones's jaw dropped.

Eyes wide, Markie nodded at me.

"Good. Do that. Hurry."

Ariana's condition would bring enough drama down on them. I had a feeling Markie was only high from contact and that would clear up as soon as she got out of the apartment.

Markie rushed out of the bedroom.

Bones stared at me. I could tell he wanted to argue, but we didn't have time for that crap, so I stepped up to the bed and bent to get my hands under Ariana.

"Get out of the way," Bones growled. "I got her."

He was pissed, but I'd have to fix that later. Right now, we needed to get Ariana to the hospital. Markie followed us out of the apartment, wearing jeans and a T-shirt, carrying a pair of sandals, and smelling fruity.

I sped the whole way to the hospital, but not fast enough to draw legitimate police attention. When I pulled up in front of the emergency room entrance, Bones jumped out and carried Ariana in with Markie hot on their heels. I parked the Hummer and hurried to join them, arriving in time to see Bones lowering Ariana onto a gurney. Nurses surrounded them.

Markie gave my arm a light squeeze, her gentle touch sending shivers up my spine. She smiled at me, revealing her heart-stopping dimples once again. "Thank you. Thank you both."

Then she took a deep breath and followed the gurney as it was wheeled past the admittance doors.

I watched her go, somehow both grateful and grieved to see her walk away a second time.

"You're doing that thing again," Bones said.

"What thing?" I asked.

"Tugging at your collar. You did it in the pizzeria, then when Markie answered the door, and now you're doing it again."

I looked down, shocked to find that my fingers were—in fact— tugging at the dark T-shirt under my SWAT jacket. "The T-shirt's too tight. Feels like it's strangling me," I said, forcing my hand to let go. We turned and walked back toward the emergency room doors. Real cops would show soon, and we needed to be gone before they did.

"You sure? Looks to me like you have a tell."

"A tell?" I snorted. I lived in the gambling capital of the world and had a lifestyle where predictability led to death. If I had a tell, I would have known about it years ago. "No, I don't."

"As your personal bodyguard, it's my job to tell you that you most definitely do."

I climbed into the Hummer and started it up. "You're being ridiculous. I just met her."

Bones shrugged. "Yeah, and now you need to stay the hell away from her."

I knew he was right, but his words made me bristle. "Oh? Why's that?"

I merged into traffic and toward the strip, feeling his gaze boring into the side of my head.

"Because she's the type of girl who'd be more interested in picking out rings than condoms."

"And you got that from meeting her twice?" I asked.

He chuckled. "You know how good I am at reading people. Tell me I'm wrong, Angel."

I couldn't and he knew it. "Is that really a bad thing? I am getting a little tired of shopping for condoms."

"Dangerous words, my friend. You remember One Nut Brizio, right?" Bones asked.

I groaned. A few years ago, a son of the Porta family named Brizio fell hard for a chick from out of town. As expected, Brizio's father ran a background check on the girl, but she came out clean. Squeaky clean, in fact. The girl didn't even have a speeding ticket.

Since nobody was that clean, Brizio's father pegged her for a cop or worse. He told Brizio to stay away from the girl, but Brizio chose to marry her instead. Turned out the girl was working for one of the other families. She was sent in to get intel, but ended up catching a feeling and blowing off her own family. She disappeared. Then Brizio's father took a hit out on his own son's testicles, declaring that his kid was too stupid to procreate. Losing one of his balls and his new wife sent Brizio over the edge. A couple of days later he put a gun in his mouth and joined her in the great dirt nap.

"Some real Romeo and Juliet shit, there," I said. "Didn't know you were such a romantic, Bones."

He flipped me off. "I knew Brizio. Before that broad appeared and started messing with his head, he was a good guy. A stand-up guy. Don't let this girl mess with *your* head, Angel."

"What the hell, Bones? We've run into each other a couple of times. It's not like I'm stalking her or something."

He eyed me for a second before continuing as if I hadn't spoken. "Look, if you're really interested, let me do some checking into her. I'll dig until I hit bedrock under her dirt, and then we can make sure it's all stuff you can live with. Stuff the family will accept."

A woman had caught my interest, so my best friend wanted to search her closet for skeletons. And they say romance is dead.

"You know, normal people get to know each other organically. They don't start out the relationship knowing whether or not the other person cheated on their senior project or was molested by their uncle."

I couldn't care less about Markie's past. I was interested in her future. More specifically, I wanted to know if I could possibly have a role in it.

"Yeah, we'll you're a Mariani."

I tensed. "Do you think I forgot that?"

When he didn't reply, I added. "No. No background check. I know who the hell I am, Bones. Why do you think I didn't ask for her number? Not planning on running into her again."

Although I'd be lying if I said I wasn't hoping for it.

"Tomorrow I'll forget all about her and go back to my regularly scheduled life of criminal technology, building the toys that'll help my father in his quest for world domination. Hey, look,

I have a slogan now."

Bones looked down. "Angel, I'm sorry, I—"

"You have to do your job. I know, Bones. It's fine. I need some sleep. I'm done for the night, but don't let me keep you from your plans. Drop me off and take the Hummer, okay?" I asked.

Bones had a car; a dark blue jeep which, for the most part, stayed parked in the apartment garage, since he stayed by my side and I drove a bullet-resistant monstrosity with run-flat tires and twenty-four-seven access to Tech. I offered him the use of the Hummer because I knew if he came upstairs to get his keys, he'd probably end up calling it a night. I wanted my friend to go out and enjoy himself, but my motives weren't entirely unselfish. I could really use some time alone.

"I'm just going to go up and pass out," I added.

"You sure?" he asked.

"Yes. Don't make me order you to go out and have a good time."

When I pulled up in front of our condo building, Bones pointed beneath my seat and said, "Take it."

I reached down for the hidden panel and pressed my middle finger in the center of it. It read my fingerprint and popped open, revealing the Desert Eagle .50 caliber pistol inside. Bones handed me a windbreaker from the backseat that I slid over my flack vest. I slipped the pistol into the jacket pocket, put the car in park, and climbed out. Bones circled around and got behind the wheel. I felt him watching me as I entered the building, and greeted the dark-skinned, six-foot security guard who often pulled night duty on the weekends. Despite the security, I kept one hand wrapped around the pistol in my pocket until I checked the apartment. Once I verified I was alone, I stored the pistol in the nightstand beside my bed and hung up the windbreaker.

My mind wouldn't stop spinning, so I opened a bottle of wine and clicked on the television. I watched old comedy show reruns and drank until the knot between my shoulders became a dull ache. I tried to drink until I stopped thinking about Markie, but I finished off the bottle of wine first. Tipsy and exhausted, I crawled into bed.

That night I dreamed of a beautiful, dimpled blonde waving good-bye as she walked away from me, and when I woke up the next morning, I had convinced myself I was happy to see her go.

♠ ♥ ♣ ♦

CHAPTER NINE
Angel

SUNDAYS HAVE ALWAYS been a big deal for my family, full of homemade breakfast, mass, after-church gelato, and then dinner with family, extended family, and friends. The women crowded the kitchen, gossiping while they crafted homemade pasta and simmered sauces and the men watched football in the den or helped father work the grill in the backyard. As a child, I used to follow the old man around with a tray full of seasonings and a pair of heavy metal grilling tongs, beaming with pride at the chance to help him. Looking back, I see that even then, he was grooming me to work with him. Father had groomed Dante in the same way, and now it was Georgio's turn. Bones and I set trays of homemade *bruschetta al pomodoro* down on the table while I watched my baby brother follow Father around, carting tray and tongs, waiting to be of use.

"He's growing up," Bones observed, following my gaze.

I frowned, saddened by the truth of it. "Yeah, he is."

"And what's going on there?" Bones asked, nodding toward my father.

The old man's entourage of ass-kissers swept in around him, led by Renzo, my third cousin who was currently clawing his way to the top of the pecking order. Childhood memories included glimpses of Renzo being a decent human being—laughing, playing catch, and building forts with me and the other cousins—but he was no longer that kid. Now he was just another thug in a suit, trying to make a name and a dollar for himself. Desperate to avoid Renzo and his fellow goons, I headed for the swimming pool while Bones drifted off to go look menacing with the other security guards.

Hidden from view by the gate, I kicked back in a lawn chair and tried to relax. The setting sun had dropped the temperature down to a comfortable level somewhere in the low eighties. Still, I fought the urge to tug off my loafers and socks, roll up my slacks, and dip my toes into the cool water. Instead, I blocked out the conversations from the deck, closed my eyes, and reveled in the peaceful solitude of the moment.

Thoughts of Markie crept into my mind. Curious, I slipped my phone out and googled "Markie Lynn Davis." I got a couple of hits, started clicking them, and then felt someone behind me. I dropped my phone face down on my lap, and turned.

"What are you doing?" Bones asked, eyeing me.

I shrugged, knowing I'd been caught, but still trying to save face. "Just checking a few things out."

Bones sat on the chair beside me, and leaned forward. "Some 'things' or 'someone'?" he asked.

I shrugged again, wishing I could come up with a witty response, but I had nothing.

Bones grumbled a warning about having my nuts removed and stormed off.

Forcing myself to ignore the temptation of my phone, I closed my eyes again. It wasn't too long before I felt the presence of company once again. Through half-lidded eyes, I watched as my baby sister tip-toed toward the shallow end of the swimming pool, watching me as she went. She wore a green satin dress that came to her knees and her long dark curls had been confined in a braid and secured by a ribbon that matched her dress. She kicked off shiny black shoes, hiked up her dress so she wouldn't sit on it, and plopped down on the side of the pool. Then she gently lowered her feet into the water, sighing deeply.

"Better be careful," I said.

Luciana jumped, letting out a little squeak. "Angel! You scared me. I thought you were asleep."

"That was the goal. I was waiting to see if you were going to jump in."

Again, she sighed. "I wish. Stupid Sunday dinners."

"I thought you liked Sunday dinners."

"Yeah, well Mom says I have to help in the kitchen. I tried, but all the women want to do is talk, and whenever I say something, they get all mad and tell me I shouldn't gossip."

I tried to swallow back a chuckle, but Luciana cast me a sideways glare to let me know she'd heard it.

"Why don't you have to help the guys—," she glanced over her shoulder at the men on the patio, "—with whatever?"

I shrugged. "When you move out of the house, you get a little more latitude."

"Yeah? Well, I can't wait to move out. Then I can just swim when I come home." She crossed her arms and stared longingly at the pool.

I didn't have the heart to tell her she wouldn't get that much latitude.

Rachele called for Luciana from the kitchen.

My baby sister laid a finger to her lips to hush me and ducked down, hidden from view by the knee-high cobblestone divider that separated the pool from the lawn. Then she looked over her shoulder at the bushes surrounding the yard. I could almost see the wheels spinning in her head as she calculated whether or not she could make it into hiding before her mother spotted her.

"The bushes would tear your dress," I warned. "Then you'll really be in trouble."

Her shoulders drooped. Head tilted to the side, she asked, "Angel, what's ee's dropping?"

"Eavesdropping?" I asked.

She flung up her hands in a gesture way too dramatic for a seven-year-old. "Whatever."

"Why do you ask?"

"Because Mom and Aunt Mona were talking to Sonia about a boy and I tried to tell Sonia that boys were stupid. Then Mom got all mad and shushed me. She told me not to eeeeevees drop, but I didn't drop anything."

Fighting to keep from laughing, I stood and collected her shoes. Then I walked over and offered her a hand. "Eavesdropping, Luci. It means listening in on a conversation you shouldn't be."

"Well that's stupid," she replied. "Why would they talk right in front of me, if they don't want me to listen?"

From the mouths of babes.

"I don't know. Doesn't make sense to me either. But you better go help your mom before you get in trouble. You don't want to end up spending the evening in your room."

"Maybe I do. It's a lot more fun in my room than it is in the kitchen," she argued.

I kissed her on the forehead. "Yeah, but I barely get to see you anymore. Dinner's gotta be almost ready, and I want to sit by my beautiful little sister."

"Fine." She trudged toward the house like a captured inmate heading back to her prison cell. She was almost to the door when she paused and called over her shoulder, "But it's a good thing I love you, Angel."

Laughing, and feeling lighter after the sweet interaction I'd desperately needed, I straightened my suit and went to see what the men were up to. Cousin Alberto stood in the corner, talking politics with the neighbor. I stayed well away from that conversation and made a beeline for the grill. Father had everything under control, but Uncle Carlo showed up with Nonna and a car full of fresh pastries. Bones and I hurried out to help unload trays of homemade *cannoli, frittole,* and macaroons.

Helping Nonna came with tasty benefits. She kissed my cheek and popped a frittole in my mouth before offering one to Bones. Still warm from the oven, the Italian fried donuts filled with custard and sprinkled with sugar lifted my spirit even more.

Dante opened the door for us, talking on his phone. "Hold on a sec, babe," he said into the phone, then covered the mouthpiece with his hand and flashed me a smile. "Hey, Angel. Bones." Then he put the phone back up to his ear and resumed his conversation, heading out the door we'd just come in.

Bones leaned over and muttered, "Looks like Dante has a more active social life than you do."

I shrugged him off, knowing even seven-year-old Georgio probably had more game than me, and continued on into the kitchen.

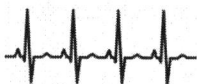

The cool evening was inviting, so we ate alfresco by candlelight. Salads, pastas, breads, wine, and conversation flowed for hours.

Then Nonna pulled out her fabulous desserts and guilted everyone into trying at least one of everything. By the time Uncle Mario started strumming his guitar to provide us with after-dinner music, I was one breath away from a food coma. Bones sat beside me with his head lulling to the side, occasional streams of drool sliding down his chin. At seven fifty-five, Luciana and Georgio bounded onto the chair beside me and begged me to tuck them in. It took a couple tries to stand up, but once I finally did, I grabbed a sibling under each arm and carted them into the house and up the stairs.

"Story, story, story!" they chanted in unison.

Resistance was futile, so I grabbed *Where the Wild Things Are* from their bookshelf and collapsed on Luciana's bed. My two favorite monsters piled on top of me and I read until they passed out and I was in danger of joining them. I carried Georgio to his own bed and headed back downstairs to say my good-byes and collect Bones.

Bones was in the middle of a game of horseshoes with Uncle Carlo and a few of my father's goons, cash piled high on the card table beside the horseshoe pit attesting to the seriousness of the game. I stood back and watched the men pitch horseshoes for a moment, ready to head home but not wanting to interrupt.

Father joined me, keeping one eye on the game. "You wanna put some money on this action?" he asked.

"No sir." Lowering my voice so only my father could hear, I added, "Uncle Carlo is playing them. I wouldn't want to bet on him and tip them off, and I sure as hell won't bet against him."

Father chuckled, clapping me on the back. "Wise man. Never bet against the family."

I nodded. It was the first lesson he'd taught me, and he'd given it while standing over the mutilated body of one of his enforcers. The second lesson was our *Omertà,* or code of silence, a Sicilian proverb that states "He who is deaf, blind, and silent will live a thousand years." That one he'd delivered before sending me off with Cousin Alberto to hunt down a rat.

Every one of his lessons was burned into the back of my brain, and I could tell by his expression that he was about to give me another. Dread crept up my spine.

"So, what's going on with that phone deal you made with your buddy Johnny?" Father asked.

I inwardly groaned, wanting to discuss anything *but* the phone deal. It had been almost two weeks since the family had lifted a hundred and fifty newly-released cell phones. I'd been brought in on the deal because each of the phones came with a built-in tracking device. Removing them without giving away our location had been tricky and included a four-hour ride in the back of a box truck with a chip fryer. Father had asked me to recommend a buyer, and because I wanted to impress him with my contacts, I suggested a loosely-connected fence by the name of Johnny Dominas.

Johnny had jumped at the offer to work with my family, but didn't have the money upfront. Father, feeling unusually gracious that day, gave him one week to sell the phones and come up with the dough. I'd made the drop and arranged a time and location for the payout. Everything was going as planned until Johnny didn't show. Even worse, he'd vacated his apartment and skipped out. Bones had all of his contacts searching for the weasel.

Since admitting I'd lost the fence would disappoint the old man, I said, "We're working on it."

Father's eyes narrowed. "Can you get my money or not?"

Father had four core values: respect, loyalty, money, family, usually in that order. Ripping him off was a blatant show of disrespect, and would put a giant, expensive target on Johnny's forehead. I didn't want my friend to end up dead, so I was hoping to buy him a little more time to wise up.

"Yes," I said with more confidence than I felt. "I'll find him and get your money."

Father frowned. "You never lose sight of someone who owes you. That's bad business, Angel."

His displeasure felt like a knife in my side. Especially since I knew he was right. I'd been suckered by friendship.

Today's lesson... friends suck. Got it.

"Yes, Father, it is."

"I never take my eyes off anyone." He watched me for a moment before reiterating, "Anyone."

"I know you don't."

"Well, Johnny doesn't know anything, apparently. Not only did your boy blow my money at the track, but he also has a good-sized marker there. Now he's hiding out, thinking I don't know where he is and what he's been up to."

My stomach sank. Johnny was the definition of stupid.

"You say you can get my money? Good. You have one

chance."

"What do you want me to do?" I asked.

He shrugged. "Back in the old days, you steal something, they cut off your hand. Johnny stole from me. I want his hand."

I tried not to gape at the old man. Sometimes he had a pretty twisted sense of humor. Hoping he was joking now, I asked, "You want me to bring you a bloody hand? What will you do with it?" My mind summoned up a gruesome scene of Bones and me trying to hack off Johnny's arm as he screamed in pain. Then what? We'd cart it off in a big plastic bag?

Father chuckled, tilting his head to the side. "It would make quite an impression. No, I don't want his hand. I just want my damn money. Lucky for Johnny, he's a coward. You go in there and break a couple of his fingers, he'll find a way to come up with the dough. I guarantee it. Then I'll decide what to do with him."

"I'll get your money. Where is he?"

He patted me on the back. "Patience, my son. I'll give you a call later this week, when I have him where I want this little confrontation to take place."

Some fathers told their children to study or work hard. My father wanted me to break fingers, and nothing I could say or do would change him.

"Yes sir. I'll wait for your call."

♠ ♥ ♣ ♦

CHAPTER TEN
Angel

MY FATHER WAS a complicated man with more layers than any fictional ogre. So many layers, in fact, that Tuesday afternoon he had me and Bones pick up the twins from school to kick off the annual Christmas drive for local orphans and foster kids. Father split a giant typed-out list in two, handing half of it, and Luciana, to me. He and several of his goons took Georgio. Luciana spent the next four hours dragging me, Bones, and a couple of Father's guards up and down the aisles of locally-owned stores, marking clothes, toys, and games off the list as she piled them into our shopping carts.

There was something heartwarming about watching my baby sister shop for kids in need. She didn't ask for a single thing for herself. Not once. I did catch her eyeing a pair of princess pumps, though, and had Bones buy them on the sly. Her gigantic heart had earned every sparkle on those damn shoes. It'd be a miracle if I held off until Christmas to give them to her.

Days like this reminded me of the good my father did for the community and made me proud to be part of the Mariani family. Too bad they couldn't all be like this.

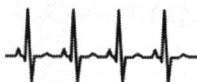

—⌐⌐⌐—

Wednesday morning my team rented out a meeting room at the

Wynn. While there, we hacked into the room's audio, put it on a loop so the guards wouldn't suspect anything, and installed our own hidden cameras and mics. Father had found out about a secret meeting a few of the city officials were holding there later in the day, and he wanted full surveillance.

I was almost finished setting everything up when the old man called.

"Your boy's waiting for you in room ten-twenty-eight of the Strat. All trussed up like a holiday ham."

My boy?

It took me a minute, and then Sunday night's conversation played in my mind.

Johnny.

Next came images of my friend hog-tied with an apple shoved in his mouth. I shook my head clear, disconnected the call, and assigned another technician to finish my work. Bones drove us to the Stratosphere while I hacked into the hotel's security system to get their site code. Since we'd been working, I had my gear. I punched the code into my handheld hotel-card hacking machine and pocketed it.

"You want another piece?" Bones asked, gesturing toward the box under the seat.

I shook my head no, closing up my laptop. "I have my SIG. Besides, Father says Johnny's all tied up."

Bones chuckled. "Can't wait to see what that means."

Since I wasn't so sure I wanted to find out, I didn't reply.

When we reached the hotel, Bones turned the Hummer over to the valet and we headed in. We rode the elevator to the tenth floor and found room ten-twenty-eight. I pulled the small machine out of my pocket, slipped it into the lock, and started up the software. Bones whistled the *Jeopardy* final question music. Before he got halfway through the tune, the lock clicked open.

"Room service," Bones said, drawing his gun as he preceded me into the room.

Rustling noises came from the hotel room. I kept the door propped open with my foot and my hand on the gun inside my jacket pocket, watching the hallway.

"It's clear, Angel," Bones said, his voice heavy with humor.

I stepped in and saw what had Bones chuckling. Johnny was, in fact, all trussed up. Just not like any pig I'd ever seen. He was naked and tied—spread eagle—with fuzzy red ropes to the posts of a queen bed. A brunette with caked-on makeup and wearing a slutty maid's costume stood beside the bed holding a feather duster. She beamed me a sultry smile, dropped the feather duster, sashayed over, and offered me her hand.

"Hi. You must be Angel. I'm Candace." Her eyes seemed to drink me in as she leaned forward, giving me an eyeful of cleavage over the top of her black bustier. She retrieved a business card from between her breasts and handed it to me. "Always a pleasure to help out the family. If there's anything else I can do, don't you hesitate to call me, sugar."

Johnny gasped. "But—"

Candace glanced over her shoulder at him and laughed. "Honey, you really thought I was doing this for you? Sorry, but *you* cannot afford *me*." Then she gave me one more meaningful look before grabbing a dress from the floor. She slid it on over her costume, stepped into a pair of pumps, and headed out the door, swinging her hips as she went.

Dreading the task ahead of me, I used a device finder to scan the room. A small camera was hidden in the smoke detector above the bed, aimed at the scene. Recognizing the design as one of my own, I left it where it was.

The sick bastard wants a show? I'll give him one.

Still, I wouldn't take all of Johnny's dignity. I picked up a discarded blanket from the floor and threw it over his nakedness. Since I wasn't about to sit on the bed, I dragged a chair over and sat, facing the putz.

"Angel, I can explain," Johnny started.

I just stared at him and shook my head. It was far too late for explanations.

"I'm working on a plan. I'll get the money. I promise."

"I told you not to screw with the family."

Sweat beaded on Johnny's forehead. "They said it was a sure thing. An opportunity to double the money and prove I can be an earner. It was gonna get my foot in the door."

"A sure thing, huh?" I asked.

"Yes. I swear to you. I wouldn't have done it otherwise."

"You shouldn't have done it at all. That wasn't your money."

Bones stepped closer to the bed. He rolled his shoulders and cracked his neck, loosening up. Johnny looked from me to Bones, and his eyes widened. He tried to scoot up, but his bonds held tight.

"I-I-I'm gonna make this right, Angel. N-n-no need for Bones. You know I'll get the money. Y-y-you know I'm good for it," Johnny stammered.

I shook my head, frowning at the dumb bastard. "If only it were that simple."

"W-w-we go back a long time, me and you, Angel. I-I-I'll fix this."

I chuckled, wondering if he thought I was stupid enough to buy his promises again. Wondering if he thought I had that kind of power. There was a freaking camera on us. My father wanted broken bones, and by God, he would get them.

"I hope they let you live long enough to do just that. Really, I do. But in the meanwhile, what about me? I have a boss to answer to. I vouched for you, and you left me hanging. How do you think that makes me look?"

Sweat rolled down the side of his face. "I-I-I—"

"It makes me look like a damn fool!" I spat.

A memory flashed in my mind. Freshman homecoming. I didn't have a date for the dance, so Johnny had set me up with his sister, Melody. I was shy and quiet, and she was popular, gorgeous, and a senior. He'd done me the most important favor of my freshman year. I stared at his hand, wondering if I could really break his fingers. Knowing I had to.

"But I never—"

My gaze shifted to his face. The fear in Johnny's eyes made me sick. It made me hate him for being weak, and hate myself for becoming his boogeyman. He needed to know the consequences of his actions though. If Johnny didn't wise up, he wouldn't last the week.

"They'll kill you. They'll kill you, and then they'll come for me. That's what happens when you gamble with the family's money."

Johnny started to reply, but Bones lunged forward, punching the bound idiot square in the jaw. "Enough talking!" Bones shook the sting from his hand.

Johnny's eyes watered. He opened his jaw, as if to gauge the pain, and it made a clicking noise. He winced.

Johnny's beak of a nose started to leak. He tried to wipe it on his shoulder only to wince at the pain of moving his jaw. I forced myself to watch every pathetic, pained move he made, knowing I'd inadvertently put him in this position. I never should have recommended him.

Bones paced a few steps alongside the bed. I hadn't bothered to tell him about my father's orders, mostly because I'd failed the old man, and I felt ashamed. Bones glanced at me, silently promising to rip me a new one later.

Bones stopped and pointed a finger in Johnny's face. "You're lucky to still be alive. And now you got Angel's ass on the line. So help me, if you don't pay—" Bones raised his fist, glaring daggers at Johnny.

Johnny paled even further, if possible. "I'll pay! I'll pay! I swear! Oh God, I swear."

"Now?" Bones asked. "You gonna pay right now?"

"Now? I don't have it right this minute."

Bones flexed, his hand still poised to strike.

"But soon. I'll get it soon. I swear!" He turned toward me. "Please, Angel."

My silence added tension to the room. We marinated in it as I struggled to come to terms with my task. Finally, I leaned back in my chair, lowering my voice to the menacing tone I'd heard my father use when he played the part of the boogeyman.

"I gave you a shot and you disappointed me, Johnny. The boss told me to cut off your hand and bring it to him, like they used to do to thieves in the old days."

Johnny's bottom lip began to quiver.

"I'm not a Neanderthal, though. If it comes down to me hacking off your body parts, I'll just put a gun to your head and end this thing. You feel me?"

He nodded.

"Good. I'm hoping it won't come down to that. It's not lucrative to kill the people who owe you money. Makes it impossible to collect. I can't completely disobey the boss and leave you unscathed, though. Bones, will you please release Johnny's left hand. You're right-handed, right, Johnny?"

Johnny nodded again, his eyes wide with terror as Bones circled the bed and untied his left arm. It fell to the mattress, and then Johnny pulled it close, trying to hide it with his body. "What are you gonna do?" he asked.

Bones chuckled, and the sound made the hair on the back of my neck stand up.

"Give me your hand," Bones said with a smirk.

Sometimes I worried that Bones enjoyed the work a little too much.

Johnny looked from his hand to me. "Two days. I can have the money in two days, max. Maybe sooner. Let me call my mom and she'll get me some—"

"Your hand, you damn *mammone*!" Bones shouted.

Since Bones had spent his childhood providing for his mom, he had no tolerance for money-leeching momma's boys.

Johnny's body began to shake. He slowly eased his hand toward Bones. "What are you going to do?" he asked. Fear hovered over him like a storm cloud.

My stomach clenched. Johnny had been my friend once. In return, I'd been too kind and he'd taken advantage, bringing us to this point. It was his fault. He was the dumbass who gambled away my family's money. So why did I feel so bad? Refusing to show my remorse, I gritted my teeth and steeled my expression.

I knew Bones would do the deed for me; all I had to do was ask. But this was my mess to clean up, and I couldn't afford to show weakness or grace. Father wanted *me* to learn the lesson, and I was sure as hell learning it. I stood and leaned against the bed.

"Hold him," I told Bones.

An objection formed on my friend's lips, but he didn't voice it. He held Johnny's wrist with both hands and waited.

I gripped Johnny's pinky finger. It felt so small and delicate, trembling in my hand.

"Angel, no. Just give me two days. Please." Johnny writhed on the bed, trying to get away. "I'll pay. You know I will."

I couldn't handle his begging anymore. I released his finger and picked up his discarded sock, stuffing it into his mouth. His eyes kept pleading, but they were easier to avoid. I returned my attention to his pinky. Grabbed it and yanked it upward until I heard the bone crack. Johnny screamed behind the sock, and the smell of urine filled the room. Then, I gripped his next finger and did the same thing. Another scream.

Two fingers. Good enough. I couldn't stomach anymore. I stood and told Bones to release Johnny. I was so pissed at him for making me do this, I wanted to break his entire hand.

"We're not friends, Johnny. Not anymore. No friend of mine would put me in the position you did. No friend of mine would steal from my family."

Tears ran down his face. I didn't care. We left him like that, his feet and other hand still tied to that damn bed, lying in his own urine. He'd get free, or the maid would find him. Either way, Johnny would know there'd be no more leniency from my family.

And maybe, just maybe, this knowledge would save his life.

CHAPTER ELEVEN
Angel

I COULDN'T ESCAPE from Johnny's room fast enough. Fear, the smell of urine, and disgust threatened to gag me as I fled through the door, hurrying toward the elevator. The way Bones watched me made me feel like I had horns growing out of my head. The elevator doors closed, locking us inside. I ran a hand through my hair, wishing I could drown out the sounds of Johnny's screams.

Come on, Angel, pull it together.

So I'd broken a couple of fingers. Definitely not the worst thing I'd ever done. Not by a long shot. Johnny would live, after all. Not the case for my first job. I was almost sixteen when Uncle Carlo picked me and Bones up in one of the family's black SUVs.

"Your father put out a contract. He wants you to fill it," my uncle said.

I'd always known the day would come, but still, it took me by surprise. My first hit. My pulse quickened as I climbed into the passenger's seat and fumbled with my seat belt. Bones sat behind me, and I could tell he was as nervous as I was.

Uncle Carlo drove for a while, taking us off the strip and into a run-down residential area off Main Street. He killed the lights and parked beside a chest-high wooden fence.

"Here?" I asked, studying the area. Several blossoming Palo Verde trees blocked my view of whatever lay on the other side of the fence. It would be difficult to see someone, much less shoot them.

"No, there," Uncle Carlo pointed across the street to a blue and white single-wide manufactured home. A waist-high chain-link fence surrounded the property. Green plastic slats were threaded into the fence, but so many were broken or missing I could still see into the yard enough to make out a picnic table. Beyond the picnic table, steps led up to a door.

"Who lives there?" I asked.

"Doesn't matter," Uncle Carlo replied. He leaned his chair back and reached into the seat behind him. When he sat back up, he had a rifle in his hands.

Bones leaned forward, studying the weapon. "That's an m-twenty-ten, isn't it?"

Uncle Carlo nodded. "It's overkill is what it is. But this beauty will definitely get the job done. It's equipped with a Saker silencer. One of the best on the market."

He stroked the barrel of the rifle a few times before handing it to me. I looked from the weapon to the trailer and my heart pounded against my chest so loudly Uncle Carlo and Bones could probably hear it.

"What do I do?" I asked. Stupid question. I shook my head and tried again. "I mean, I know how to shoot. But where is he?"

"He's in the house right now." Uncle Carlo checked his watch. "But in about fifteen minutes, he's going to come out for a cigarette. You'll get one chance when he sits at that picnic table, lights his smoke, and calls his *goomah*."

"His mistress?" I asked, looking over at the single-wide again. "She must be getting all his money."

Uncle Carlo chuckled. "Oh, he's a real piece of work, this guy. Trust me, Angel. You're doing the world a favor. You'll be a damn hero for bumping this one off."

The next few minutes were full of adrenaline and tough-talk, as my uncle prepared me to make my first kill. Then the trailer's porch light flicked on. A door opened, and a figure stepped out onto the porch. He lit a cigarette, put it between his lips, and traipsed down the steps. He sat on top of the picnic table and pulled out his phone.

"This is it," Uncle Carlo whispered. He rolled down my window, leaned over, and helped me position the rifle against the window frame.

"Take a breath," Bones whispered.

I breathed and looked through the scope. It took me a few seconds to adjust the view, but then I studied the man's features. I'd never seen him before. He was a stranger. I took another breath.

I'll be doing the world a favor.

My hands trembled so hard the barrel of the rifle hit the metal of the car. The man stood and looked around. Bones grabbed my shoulders, steadying me as Uncle Carlo coaxed my finger into squeezing the trigger. Once. The rifle kicked against my shoulder. Uncle Carlo gripped my hands and helped me squeeze off a second shot.

Two in the head. Make sure he's dead.

Silencer, my ass. My ears rang, regardless. The man flew backward. Bones took the rifle from me, and Uncle Carlo started the car. Before I took another breath, we were on the way. We made it a full block and a half before I threw up in my lap. Uncle Carlo didn't even blink. He just kept driving. Before long, we pulled up in front of his house. He got me out of the car, and then hosed me off. Then, the three of us got wasted.

The next day, Father took me down to his club and bragged that I'd popped my cherry. But every time the old man looked at me, I knew he saw my failure. He saw Bones holding my arms while my uncle squeezed the trigger. Hell, he could probably smell the vomit on me. I couldn't get the stench to wash off me.

"Angel? You okay?" Bones asked, pulling me back into the present. He nudged me forward.

The elevator doors were open, but I stood there, staring out into the casino like an idiot.

"Couldn't be better," I replied.

Now, I'm no longer killing strangers. I'm hurting friends. That's great, right? Maybe now the old man will be proud.

Bones eyed me, but he left me to my dark thoughts. They called to me like the swimming pool in my father's backyard. I'd dipped my toes in for so long that plunging into the depths seemed like the next natural step. And that realization, above all else, terrified me.

I don't want to be a monster.

I followed Bones out a side door of the hotel and into a crowd huddled around the jump zone and staring up at the sky. Bones stopped short, and I had to do the same to avoid running into him. I followed his gaze to a thin brunette standing on the outside of the crowd. She shielded her eyes from the sun and looked up at the Stratosphere tower. I did a double take, surprised that she was alive, not to mention out walking around.

"That Ariana?" I asked.

Bones nodded and pointed up. "And there's that blonde you got a hard-on for."

"What? Where?" I scanned the tower, suddenly desperate to see her again.

"Getting hooked up," Bones replied.

My gaze fixed on Markie just in time to watch her jump. I'd seen people plummet from the Stratosphere tower before. They screamed and flailed, looking ridiculous. But not Markie. She floated down like some sort of angelic superhero, grinning with her arms stretched out like she was flying. Her long thick hair billowed behind her like a cape, while the sun at her back surrounded her in a golden aura. The sight vanquished my dark thoughts, lightening my spirit.

She reached the ground. The instant her harness was removed, her bright blue eyes swept the crowd until they honed in on Ariana. Still grinning, her wild hair glowing like the sun, Markie floated toward her sister.

"That was amazing, Ari! You've got to try it."

"No thank you," Ariana replied, shaking her head. "At least not while I'm sober."

Markie's smile vanished and she tilted her head to the side. Ariana spun on her heel and walked away from her sister.

"Ari!" Markie called, and then hurried to catch up.

Bones moved, positioning himself in Ariana's path. Then, he crossed his arms and waited. Ariana was two steps from running into him when she froze. She copied his pose, crossing her arms and studying my friend.

Bones cracked a smile.

"Do I know you?" Ariana asked.

"What, Ari, you don't remember me?" Bones asked. "Good to see you again."

Her brow furrowed. "Uh…"

"Angel! Bones!" Markie shouted. She passed her sister and wrapped one arm around each of us, pulling us to her in an awk-

78

ward group hug. It's not that I didn't love Bones as a brother, but hugging in public is not something we did. Ever. Even when being forced together by some beautiful girl. We pushed away and Bones took a big step back.

"Hey, uh...? Sorry, I can't remember your name," I feigned, giving her a taste of her own medicine.

I expected her to get offended, but she only laughed, swatting my arm. "Okay, okay. I already said I was sorry."

Her smile was infectious. I felt it spread, tugging at the corners of my lips. I fought it hard, but in the end I relented.

"I can't thank you enough for what you did on Halloween. I was hoping we'd run into you again." Markie tugged Ariana's arm, forcing the girl closer to us. "Ari, these are the guys who helped me get you to the hospital."

Ariana held back, fighting against her sister's prodding as her cheeks reddened.

"Thank you," she whispered, looking mortified. Then she focused on Bones and added, "And thank you for the flowers."

"No problem at all," Bones replied. "Glad to see you're up and feeling better."

Flowers?

Bones had gotten Ariana flowers? I filed that little tidbit away to question him about it later.

We lingered in awkwardness somewhere between chatting and saying good-bye. Although I knew I should, I couldn't quite make my feet walk away from them. The girls seemed to be having the same problem.

"Can I take you guys to lunch?" Markie asked, surprising me.

No woman had ever offered to buy me a meal. Or anything else, for that matter. I was the one who did all the buying.

"*You* want to take *us* to lunch?" I asked, just to make sure I'd heard her right.

She dimpled and dipped her head in this shy, uncertain move that was sweet enough to give me a toothache. "I know it's not much of a thank-you for saving my sister and keeping me out of jail, but it's the best I can think of right now. And... I'm hungry."

I didn't know the protocol. Was I supposed to counter? Or just accept her offer? I looked to Bones for help, but he just shrugged. This was a new one for him too, apparently.

"We can go wherever you want," Markie added, sweetening

the deal.

"Really?" Bones asked.

She held up her hands, smiling. "As long as it's not a hundred dollars a plate. I am on a budget."

Bones grinned at me. "Cajun."

I groaned.

"What?" Markie asked. "Cajun works for me."

"It's a dive." I complained. "Cheap, everything is fried, and I'm not even certain the fish is real."

"It's heaven. You know I wouldn't eat there if it wasn't," Bones replied. "And you keep promising you'll try it."

"Yeah, but every time you bring home a takeout bag, it smells like heartburn and diabetes."

Ariana's face scrunched up. "I don't really do fried food."

Bones turned toward her. "Angel's a hater. Don't listen to his lies. Not all of their food is fried." He listed off a few of their dishes, licking his lips between each.

"I'm in," Markie said.

"Your opinion doesn't count," Ariana told her. "You spent almost a year in Africa eating God knows what. You'll try anything."

"Guilty." Markie grinned again, showing off her dimples. "And you should live a little and join me. A few more calories in your diet wouldn't kill you."

Bones nodded. "Your sister's right. You weigh practically nothing. You could use a little meat on your bones."

"How do you know what I... oh, right, you carried me. Well, this is awkward." Ariana crossed her arms over her chest. "Fine, I'm in for whatever. But if I get sick, I'm throwing up on you, buddy."

"I'll just pick your ass up and turn you to face the other direction," Bones replied. Then he looked to me. "What do you say, Angel? You up for Cajun deliciousness?"

Resigned to my fate, I shrugged. "Sure. I don't really need my stomach lining anyway. Where the hell is this place?"

As long as I'd known him, Bones had been a big eater. At first, he didn't seem to care about food quality, only quantity. A few days after he'd rescued me from the grade school bully, Bones plopped his tray down next to mine in the cafeteria for the first time. Before he fully sat down, he'd devoured the school's flavorless, dry meatloaf and rubbery mashed potatoes, and was downing his milk.

"You like that?" I asked, eyeing his plate.

He shrugged. "It's food. I'm hungry."

I didn't understand how hungry until that night, when I ran a background check on my new friend and his family. It didn't take me too long to find Bones's parents. Guy and Maria Leone had been married for fourteen years. They had three sons: Antonio (age thirteen), Franco (age eleven), and David (age seven). Guy had worked for a local steel mill until about two months prior to me meeting Bones. About that same time, Maria had filed a missing person's report for her husband. Maria worked as a bartender at a small off-the-strip tavern, and her bank account had been over-drawn twice since the disappearance of her husband, and now held a whopping five dollars and fifty-two cents. Bones and his brothers were all signed up for free lunches and had scholarships for the Boys and Girls Club after-school skills program.

I felt bad for the kid, so I made it my personal goal to make sure Bones ate and ate well. The guy had stuck up for me, after all, and the Mariani family always remembers its friends. I blew the dust off the cover of my mom's old cookbook and went to work, trying to breathe new life into the recipes I thought had died with her. Bones became my official taster, gobbling up whatever I brought to school for him to try.

Then once Bones started earning a living, his tastes expanded. My friend quickly discovered he liked a variety of ethnic foods, from Japanese to Mexican, Thai to Ethiopian. And the more he tried, the more sophisticated his tastes became. In fact, if I wasn't afraid of him punching me for saying so, I'd call Bones a foodie. And although I loved to rib him about his eclectic food tastes, I trusted him with my stomach almost as much as I trusted him with my life.

That trust was rocked to its core when I pulled into the parking lot of Moe's Cajun Eatery.

CHAPTER TWELVE
Markie

ARIANA SULKED DURING the ride to the restaurant. Before we'd gotten into the Hummer, my drug-dealer-dating sister had pulled *me* aside and questioned the wisdom of my decision to get into a vehicle with two strange men. Something inside of me snapped, and I reminded her it wasn't our first drive with them. Also, since neither Angel nor Bones had given her crap-lousy drugs and left her to die, they were both way ahead of Matt in the human race.

I regretted the comment about Matt. Not because it was wrong, but because it was mean. Ariana had made some big mistakes, but she was young and vulnerable, and no matter how much of a slimeball Matt was, she clearly had feelings for him. I needed to be more thoughtful of those feelings. Even if I wanted to throat punch the jerk.

Angel drove the four of us to a dilapidated, red-brick, mixed-use building in a rough-looking neighborhood. He parked his shiny black Hummer next to a rusty Ford truck which had to be older than I was.

"Here?" Angel asked. "Seriously?"

Bones stared at the front door of the restaurant like it was edible. "Oh, hell yeah," he said, unbuckling his seat belt.

Movement in front of the restaurant drew my attention. I looked up in time to see a group of teens descending on an elderly man wearing a backpack. One of the boys reached for the man's pack. The man dodged and his cane wobbled under his weight. Fearing he would fall, I jumped out of the Hummer and hurried to the scene.

While the man shielded his pack from the first teen, a second darted in, reaching into the man's pocket. The old man stumbled back and the boys laughed.

"Markie, wait!" Ariana shouted from behind me.

I ignored her and charged into the fray, positioning myself in front of the old man. "What do you guys think you're doing?"

"Why don't you mind your own damn business, bitch?" one teen asked, sliding a hand into his pocket. He was maybe fifteen. I wanted to smack him and then have a long talk with his parents.

"You better watch your mouth, kid."

"Or what? You'll spank me?" he sneered.

He started to say something else, but before he got the first word out, he was lying on his stomach, faced pressed against the ground with Bones on top of him. His friends all took one giant step away from him.

"Oomph. What the hell?" the kid asked.

"We have rules in this city," Bones said, yanking the kid's arms up until he cried out. "We don't pick on old people and we sure as hell don't swear and threaten to draw on ladies. You feel me?"

"Get off me!" The kid wriggled, but Bones didn't budge. "You're making a big mistake, man. You don't know who I work for."

"Doesn't matter." Bones released the kid's arms, grabbed his head, and angled it at Angel. "Because my boss is a Mariani."

The kid's eyes grew wide. I followed his line of sight to watch Angel. Wearing his suit and climbing out from behind the wheel of what appeared to be a tank, he did pose a striking figure. But the kid looked more than impressed. He looked terrified. His friends all took another step away from him.

"You feel me now?" Bones asked.

"Yeah, man. Sorry. I didn't know." His whole demeanor had changed, instantly.

"Now apologize to the lady," Bones said.

"Sorry, ma'am. No disrespect meant. To any of you. Sorry. Sorry."

"I'm gonna take this, because you don't make good decisions

and you don't deserve it." Bones shifted his weight, but I couldn't see what he took from the kid. "Now, get out of here before you really piss me off." He released the kid and stood.

The entire group of teens pulled a vanishing act that would have landed them a show on any Vegas stage.

I looked from Angel to Bones, trying to figure out how I felt about what had just happened. It would probably be polite to thank Bones, but I wasn't one hundred percent thankful he'd ground some kid's face into the pavement for me.

"Are you okay?" Ariana asked, grabbing my hand.

"Of course I'm okay. I just need a second to—"

"What were you thinking? That kid had a knife or a gun or something, and you just... You could be dead right now!" she shouted.

A knife? Or a gun? I let that sink in for a moment, remembering the kid's hand in his pocket. *Is that what Bones took from him?*

Ariana thanked Bones.

I stepped away from them to check on the old man. He wasn't hurt, but asked me for something to eat. This was something I could help with, so I asked my companions if he could join us for lunch.

The three of them looked at each other, then at the old man, then back at each other.

Desperate to remind them he was a human being, I added, "His name is—" Then realized I didn't know it. I nudged him and waited.

"Max," he replied, leaning against his cane to hold out his hand to Angel. Angel, whose suit probably cost more than first-class airfare back to Zambia, shifted his gaze to Max's outstretched hand. Time froze. I looked into Angel's eyes and saw a battle raging. I'd made a big mistake. Guys like Angel clearly didn't eat with guys like Max. Awkward tension mounted, and I needed to diffuse it. I grabbed Max's shoulders and braced, preparing to angle him in the opposite direction. We'd walk a few steps away, have a little chat, and then I'd go order him some takeout. Then he'd sit on the curb and eat while we lounged in nice, comfy chairs.

Because that's the way the world works. And it sucks.

I shouldn't have expected more, but I wanted Angel to be different. Heck, he'd invited me to pizza when I didn't have a place to sit. He was a nice guy, just not nice enough to draw attention by sitting with a homeless man. Disappointed, I tugged on Max's shoulder. Only I couldn't move him, because his hand was connected to Angel's.

"Nice to meet you, Max." Angel smiled at the man. It wasn't fake or forced, condescending or pitying. It was real and heartwarming. It made my eyes burn and my breath catch. "Please join us for lunch."

They broke apart, and before Angel could reconsider, I swooped in to link arms with Max. Angel held the door open and I helped Max into the restaurant with Ariana and Bones following. A smile tugged at my lips and I couldn't stop it. Max wouldn't have to sit on the hard curb and eat his lunch. And that made my heart soar.

I saw a restroom sign and pointed it out to Max. "Would you like to go wash up?"

He started to nod, but lost his balance. I tightened my grip on his arm, while wondering how he would make the walk on his own.

"Here, I'll take him," Angel said, appearing on the other side of Max. He put a hand on Max's back and another under his arm. Then he leaned in, dirtying the front of his nice suit on Max's filthy shirt.

It was the most beautiful sight I'd ever seen.

Bones headed for the restroom ahead of Angel and Max. Then a waitress showed me and Ariana to a corner booth.

"See? He's a good guy," I whispered, giddy after what I'd just witnessed.

"Did you see the way those kids looked at him?" Ariana fired back. "I'm telling you, Markie, he's dangerous. Gotta be part of the mob or something."

I knew the mob still existed, but I highly doubted big bad mobsters helped elderly homeless men clean up. Still, Angel was clearly in charge, and Bones was muscle. Big, scary muscle.

"Bones said Angel's a Mariani," I blurted out.

Ariana's eyes widened.

"What?" I asked. "What does that mean?" They weren't cops. No legitimate police officer would have directed me to get out of my pot-smelling clothes before we took Ariana to the hospital.

And it was Halloween when they showed up wearing the "SWAT" uniforms.

"Marianis are one of the families." Ariana massaged her temples. "I can't believe we're on a date with a couple of Marianis and you invited a bum."

"A date?" I asked. "I thought you were with Matt?"

"Okay, not me. You."

"I'm not on a date. I'm buying a meal for the men who saved your life."

Ariana snorted. "So you're telling me you have no interest whatsoever in Angel? Right. He's freakin' hot. They both are."

Bones wasn't bad, and pretty freakin' hot didn't even begin to describe Angel, but there were complications to consider. "You know I can't go down that road, Ari."

"Why not? Live a little while you're here. Pull the stick out of your butt and have a fling for once."

"I jumped from the Stratosphere today. I think that counts as living a little. Besides, you just said they were mobsters or something. What are the families?"

She grinned. "Dangerous *and* sexy."

"Stop it right now. We're having lunch with friends. That's all."

She rolled her eyes and mumbled about me ruining all the fun. Truthfully, I was just happy she wasn't still pining over Matt. I'd have to find out more about the Marianis later, preferably from a source who could focus on more than how hot they were.

The guys returned. We ordered lunch and broke into conversation. Max told us he was a Navy veteran, and between bites he entertained us with stories about his time as an engineman, and his worldwide travels afterward. He'd spent his midlife trekking across every continent except Antarctica, which he informed us was too damn cold for his bones. We spent more than two hours in that little dive, and by the time we finished up, Max's stomach was full and his eyelids were heavy.

Angel excused himself to make a call and I settled up the bill. When Angel came back we headed out.

"Well? What did you guys think of the food?" Bones asked when we emerged from the building.

I held two thumbs up. "Super tasty. Good pick."

"Yeah, it was all right," Angel replied.

Bones shoved him.

Even Ariana had no complaints.

A cab pulled into the parking lot and Angel smiled down at Max. "Looks like your ride's here."

I felt my eyebrows creep up my forehead. "His ride? Where's he going?"

Angel opened the back door of the cab. "A bed so he can get some sleep."

"A motel?" I asked.

Angel nodded and helped Max into the cab.

My throat constricted and I couldn't speak. We waved good-bye to Max and then climbed into the Hummer.

"You okay?" Angel asked, adjusting his rearview mirror to see my face.

I smiled and nodded, lying without words.

He shook Max's hand, helped him wash up, and got him a cab and a room. He saved my sister. He helped me.

Ariana was right about one thing, Angel was dangerous. Just not in the way she thought.

No doubt sensing my worry, my sister reached over and squeezed my hand.

Angel was dangerous; the kind of dangerous that made my stomach flutter and my eyes burn.

♠ ♥ ♣ ♦

CHAPTER THIRTEEN
Angel

WE FINISHED LUNCH, and since I wasn't ready to drop off the girls yet, I racked my brain for something we could do. If we took them to a family-run casino, Father would know about Markie before we tossed the first die. Venturing into non family-run casinos had the potential to create serious drama. We could hit a show or the movies, but neither of those options would give us time to talk. And that's what I really wanted; to get to know her.

"Want us to drop you off at your apartment?" Bones asked Ariana.

Before Ariana could answer, I blurted out the first option I could think of. "Have either of you been on the High Roller Wheel yet?"

Bones's jaw dropped. He'd been trying to get me on that death trap for ages, but I kept putting him off. Especially when I found out the damn thing goes five hundred and fifty feet off the ground.

"The giant Ferris wheel thing?" Markie asked, arching an eyebrow.

"Yep, that's the one. We should check it out."

"The High Roller?" Bones asked. "*You* want to go on the High Roller?"

Hell no, I didn't want to go on the High Roller. "Yeah," I nodded. "You in?"

Bones could have called me out. He could have revealed me for the chicken I am, but he saw opportunity knocking and flung open the damn door. "Hell yeah, I'm in. Ladies?"

Having dug my grave, I turned the Hummer toward Caesars Palace and a five-hundred-foot possible plummet to my death.

This was my idea? What the hell was I thinking?

Bones must have been having his own reservations, because he put a hand on my seat and said, "We can't do this now, Angel."

As my security guard, Bones was looking out for me. I made a mental note to make sure he got a raise. Clinging to his out, I said, "Yeah, you're probably right."

"Why not?" Markie asked.

Bones grinned. "I've been trying to get Angel to do this for months and now he decides to go? In the middle of the day? Why? The experience is ten times better at night."

So much for saving me. And so much for his damn raise.

"You've been on it?" I asked him.

He shrugged. "Yeah. Not like I was going to wait around to go with you."

Going in the dark wouldn't be so bad. Maybe the ground wouldn't look so far away. I glanced at Markie and she smiled back at me. "Do you guys have a problem with waiting until dark?"

The sisters decided they could wait, so we found a garage, parked the Hummer, and went for a walk down the strip. My cell phone rang, so I excused myself to take the call. We had just made it to Caesars Palace and were standing beside the replica Trevi fountain. Markie and Ariana continued on to the fountain and sat on the ledge, turning sideways to take in the sights. Bones stayed beside me, but kept an eye on the girls.

"Hello?" I asked into my phone.

It was my cousin, Renzo. Renzo hadn't called me in ages, not since he tripped and his nose fell up my father's ass. Knowing it wouldn't be a social call, I glanced around to make sure nobody was paying too close of attention. "Hey, what can I do for you?" I tried to keep my tone friendly.

"The boss said you might have a use for some merch I can't move."

If Father wanted me on it, it was tech. Wondering what the family had stumbled upon now, I asked, "Okay, what you got?"

"You expect me to just tell you over the phone?" His tone dripped with condescension.

Two could play that game. "Yes. Do I need to remind you how my phones work? Again?"

"I don't have a lot of faith in your gadgets," he replied.

Now I was pissed. I turned away so the girls couldn't see my expression. "Understandable. Most people fear what they can't seem to understand. I hear you have trouble booting up your computer."

There was a pause, and I could almost see Renzo taking deep breaths and trying to regain control. Finally, he replied, "Look, I don't have all day. Do you want these things or not?"

"What the hell are they?"

Another deep breath. "Self-checkout stands."

Of all the bizarre shit…

I slipped behind Bones, just in case there were lip-readers about. Then, to make sure I'd heard him correctly, I asked, "Self-checkout stands? Are you talking about the terminals? Or just the stands they sit on?"

He growled. "So sorry I don't speak geek. The terminals. The things at the grocery store where you can scan your own—"

"I know what they are. I just can't understand why you have them." Of course he wouldn't be able to move checkout stands. They were the most visible equipment in any store. Why someone had lifted them was beyond me.

"Yes or no?" he asked.

"Your team bump off the wrong truck?"

"Yes or no, Angel?" he growled.

"How many do you have?"

"Six."

I wasn't sure which components a terminal held, but I was fairly certain I could salvage something useful. "Sure. I'll send a team over to pick them up. Which warehouse?"

Renzo gave me the location and then I called my team lead and sent him to round up the troops and go after the goods.

With business out of the way and finally a few minutes alone with Bones, I asked, "Flowers, Bones?"

"Hm? You offering? You know you're my boy and all, but I just don't swing that way."

I shook my head at him and clarified. "You bought Ariana flowers?"

"Oh. Yeah." He shrugged. "She's a source. She's connected to

Matt and connected to this broad you seem so crazy about. It's not personal, Angel, it's business. You know how this works."

I did know, but it seemed like there might be more to it than he was letting on.

The rest of our walk went off without a hitch, and once the sky darkened we got into the maze-like line for the High Roller. Markie stood beside me with Bones guarding my back and Ariana standing at his side. Bones was drilling the girl for information about Matt, but doing it in a way that kept her from telling him to get lost. Bones knew how to handle people.

I, on the other hand, did not. Striking up a conversation with Markie proved more difficult than I'd imagined.

"What?" Markie asked, dimpling at me.

If I had a little more game, I'd tell her how beautiful she was, or how happy she'd made me by agreeing to venture onto this death trap with me. Then she'd throw herself at me, and I'd actually be able to catch her. Unfortunately, I wasn't that guy and I didn't have much game. So my opening line went something like, "Tell me something about the enchanting Markie Davis."

The line shuffled forward.

She dimpled again. "Enchanting, huh?"

I nodded. "Absolutely."

Her smile widened. "What do you want to know about me?"

Uh-oh. I needed a line. Something witty and charming. "Like… Hello, my name is Angel, and at midnight I turn into a wraith who eats small animals and haunts local opera houses."

She giggled, so it must not have been too bad. "Good to know. Busy nightlife you've got there."

I shrugged. "Hey, someone's gotta terrorize dachshunds and frighten the fat lady."

"Indeed." She leaned against the metal railing and chewed on her lip, looking down at the floor. One lone curl dangled in front of her face. Before I realized what I was doing, I reached up and tucked the hair behind her ear. Markie looked at me and froze, her eyes wide.

"I'm sorry," I said, dropping my hand to my side.

She blinked, and then blushed. "No, it's okay. You just surprised me." She smiled, but it seemed forced. "Okay, something about me… Well, I don't transform into any mythological characters, and I'm not a big fan of opera. I do like to dance, though."

The line lurched forward again, and we followed it out of the metal line-maze and into another room and another line. A wall-length screen showed ads for local businesses and coming attractions.

"To dance, huh?" I leaned closer, intrigued. "Tell me more. What style of dancing?"

"All of it. Ballroom, ballet, pop, hip-hop." She looked away and her cheeks turned the slightest tint of pink. "Disco."

"Disco?" I asked, forcing down a chuckle.

She shrugged, her blush deepening. "What? I like to get down. I like to boogie."

I laughed. How could I not? She was adorable.

"All right, all right, that's enough mocking me, mister. Your turn. Tell me something about you."

I ducked my head and wiped the grin from my face. "I, too, like to boogie *and* I'm big into oldies, so top that." I had no clue when my ploy to get to know her had morphed into a contest to see which of us was the most awkward, but judging by her smile, it was working. I decided to stick with it.

"I'm not very familiar with oldies. My family listened to a lot of country and I was kind of shielded from the wide world of great music. I didn't discover my love for disco dancing until last night when the casino Ari works at had a disco dance competition."

"You entered the competition?" I asked, impressed.

She nodded, her cheeks turning even redder.

I laughed. "Man, I'm sorry I missed that. How'd you do?"

"Not great. You're probably lucky you missed it."

I doubted that. I couldn't see myself regretting a single moment spent with this girl. She was so sweet and real. For the first time ever, I was involved in a conversation not about people, fashion, makeup, or drama, and I loved every second.

"So now that you're not digging wells or volunteering at orphanages, you're dancing. Or is there something else you do with your time?"

"Actually, I'm still volunteering at orphanages. My application just cleared with one of the rescue missions. I start tomorrow."

"Ah, so will you be staying in Vegas for a while?" I asked, hoping my question didn't sound as desperate as I felt.

She shrugged and looked away. "As long as I can."

Strange answer. I filed it away to reevaluate later and changed my line of questioning. "What do you do at these orphanages?"

"Whatever they need me to do. In Africa I did a lot of administrative stuff like marketing and finding sponsors, but here I'll probably do things like laundry, maybe help out in the kitchen, read to the little ones, shoot hoops with the bigger kids, stuff like that."

Wanting to test her sense of humor, I decided to rib her a bit. "Oh, I see. You're kind of short for basketball, so you play with the kids."

She gasped in mock offense. "For your information, I made the southern Idaho all-star team my junior *and* senior years of high school." She crossed her arms and tried to scowl at me. "I got hops."

"Hops? You think you can jump on those short legs, huh? I'm more of a believe-it-when-I-see-it kind of guy." Then seeing my golden opportunity I added, "So you're gonna have to prove it. Give me your number and we'll settle this on the court."

Turns out I wasn't above goading Markie into a basketball game to get her digits. Truthfully, I could get her number with a few clicks on my computer, but didn't want to go down like a stalker.

"Nope. Sorry, but I don't give out my number to strange men."

You'd think a zing like that would make me back off, but it just made me like her more. This time it was my turn to gasp in mock outrage. "Strange? We shared pizza, I took your sister to the hospital, and we've spent most of the day together. We even risked food poisoning together, eating at that Cajun dive. In a few minutes, we could plummet to our death together. What's a guy gotta do to prove he's not a psycho killer these days?"

We followed the line out of the room and onto a loading platform. Twenty people in front of us were loaded into a big glass and metal pod. The door closed, and the pod rotated up, bringing another to rest in front of us. People were unloaded.

Markie tapped her chin thoughtfully. Then she reached into her purse and pulled out a business card, handing it to me. "Volunteer with me," she replied.

"Huh?" I studied the card and then looked up at her. Of all the things I'd been asked to do in my life, this was a first.

"Volunteer with me," she said again. "They don't let psycho killers volunteer at orphanages. If they okay you, I'll know you're somewhat safe, at least."

I chuckled and pocketed the card. "Why orphanages?"

Markie glanced at her sister then leaned closer to me and lowered her voice. "We lost our father when we were in middle school, and then Mom in high school."

I ducked my head, feeling like an ass. "I'm sorry."

She shrugged. "Me too. Sometimes life just sucks, you know? Family took us in, so we never had to live at an orphanage, but still, I get those kids. I understand how lonely and scary it can be. Besides, I really like hanging out with kids. They're brutally honest and unintentionally funny, and they just want someone to care about them."

Our small group moved forward again. An employee looked up at us and then smiled in recognition. "Mr. Angel!" He offered me his hand.

I shook it. "Fernando. Good to see you."

Fernando's family did lawn maintenance for Father's estate. They were nice people, hard-working, and knew how to keep their mouths shut. If I had to run into someone I knew, I was glad it was Fernando.

"Pleasure is all mine."

"These are my friends Markie and Ariana, and you know Bones, of course."

He shook their hands as I explained he was a family friend.

"You are some lucky ladies to be out on the town with these two. Stand-up gentlemen you got here. Real nice guys."

Markie smiled at him. "Good to know."

Fernando wasn't done, though. He inclined his head to me and said, "Mr. Angel, my parents got the floral arrangement you sent for my *abuela's* funeral. Thank you. It meant much to us."

Fernando's grandmother was almost as precious as Nonna. And although I'd never admit it aloud, she could bake almost as good.

"I was sorry to hear about your loss."

"Yes, she was a wonderful woman." Fernando ushered us toward the pod. I tried to ignore the gaping hole on either side of the ramp and walked in. Once the pod was full, an announcer appeared on overhead screens and welcomed us onto the ride. Then he droned on about the city's history as we began our ascent. Bones and Ariana headed for the bar while Markie and I pressed against the glass. She looked out, while I looked anywhere but down.

"It's all so beautiful," Markie breathed.

I followed her gaze to the lights of the strip and saw something different. Connections, money, ties, some buildings would welcome me, and some would call my presence a sign of disrespect. I knew the managers, the back door operations, and the family who got a cut from each one. My father's world called to me through neon signs and dancing lights, reminding me where I belonged. Looming and confining, there was nothing beautiful about it.

"Look at the stars," Markie whispered.

At that moment, I didn't want to think about the city or the stars. I pressed closer to Markie and breathed in the coconut fragrance of her hair. Something soft and crooning played over the speakers. I touched the soft fabric of her T-shirt, locking the moment into all my senses. Bones and Ariana returned, carrying drinks for all four of us. I handed my phone to a stranger and the four of us posed for a picture against the backdrop of the city lights.

"We're nearing the top," the announcer said over the speakers. "Starting the countdown from twenty, nineteen, eighteen."

"I love this so much," Markie said. She grabbed her sister's hand, and then mine. As our fingers intertwined, little electrical jolts danced up my arm toward my chest.

"Thank you, Angel," She flashed me another dimpled smile.

"Fifteen, fourteen, thirteen…"

My brain screamed at me to pull away from her. Just hours ago I had broken a guy's fingers. What if someone came after Markie for revenge? Her fingers felt so thin and delicate between mine. How long could I keep her safe from my family? Sooner or later she'd figure out who my father was, and she'd hate me for the things he did. The things I sometimes did. But by then she'd know too much, and if she didn't accept us, the old man would get rid of her. I needed to let her go.

Not tonight.

I wanted this. I needed it. Her hand felt like a lifeline to everything clean and good about humanity. I stared into her bright, blue eyes and joined in the countdown.

"Ten, Nine, Eight…"

We were almost at the top of the High Roller, but I'd already fallen.

CHAPTER FOURTEEN
Angel

BY THE TIME Bones and I dropped Markie and Ariana off that night, I knew I was royally screwed. Bones knew it, too. He didn't say as much, but he didn't have to. I could tell by the way he frowned at me when we got back in the car.

"I know, I know, One Nut Brizio. Got it. Just give me a minute, and let my brain clear up so I can actually think."

"If she affects you like that, why don't you just stay away from her? Why play with fire?" he asked.

I stared at the road, trying to put my feelings into words. I couldn't think about anything but how incredible Markie was. But, nobody was perfect, and if I spent more time with her, her imperfections would come out. I needed a way to explain that to Bones.

"I don't know. It's like... remember when you were hooked on those lemon bars from that bakery by Caesars?"

Bones eyed me. "Lemon crack bars. They were the shit."

I chuckled. "Yeah, and you were a fiend for them."

"Angel, you don't understand. Buttery crisp shortbread; subtly sweet curd filling." Bones licked his lips. "Perfection. Damn, I miss those bars."

Freakin' foodie. "Right. How'd you break the addiction?"

He looked thoughtful. "I didn't. They did. They got a new baker who didn't know what the hell she was doing. Made the shortbread soggy and the filling too sweet. Haven't been back since."

"Exactly," I replied.

Bones raised an eyebrow.

"There is no perfection, Bones. I don't know this girl, so she looks damn good right now. But I know she's gotta have a deal. Everyone does. I just need to hang with her long enough to see what that is. Then I can forget about her. You know?"

He rubbed his chin thoughtfully. "Yeah, I think I get it. This broad's your lemon crack bar and you need a new baker."

I chuckled, realizing how stupid that illustration sounded.

Bones joined me, his deep laugh shaking the vehicle. "You know how messed up this is, right? A broad catches your attention and you're hoping she'll morph into a psycho bitch."

He was right. I was losing my godforsaken mind.

Bones laughed himself out, and then he grew serious. "This can be settled quick and easy, you know? Run a check and shine a spotlight on all her crazy."

I stopped for a light. "No. I'm gonna check her out, but I'm going to do it the organic way."

"You're just makin' shit up now, aren't you?" he asked.

I retrieved the business card Markie had given me from my pocket, passing it to Bones.

He studied the card for a second before asking, "What the hell's this?"

"It's where Markie will be volunteering. Do you know anyone who has a contact at this place?"

He cocked his head. "I got people in the casinos, the strip clubs, restaurants, government offices. I even got contacts in old folks homes thanks to Nonna. But I don't have anyone in the orphanage scene."

"I need to get approved to volunteer without them running my information," I said. "Maybe a healthy donation to the cause would help?"

"You want to volunteer here? With kids? Angel, you got some cool little siblings, but orphans aren't like that. They got issues. The kind of issues that land them behind bars serving twenty-to-life. You get what I'm saying?" Bones asked.

I nodded. "Yeah. You're saying you're afraid of kids. Now can you bribe this orphanage so I can prove what an upstanding citizen I am and get Markie's number, or what?"

"This is all about getting the broad's phone number? Seriously man, now I know you've lost your mind. We can have her number in seconds."

"And have her think I'm some stalker? No. She has to give me her number. Can you get me in or not?"

Bones studied the business card for a few more seconds before pocketing it. "Yeah, man. This is nuts, but I'll see what I can do."

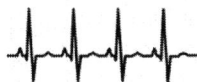

I didn't get much sleep Wednesday night, so Thursday was brutal. One of the self-checkout terminals my team had picked up from Renzo was waiting for me in the center of my office. The seventeen-inch touchscreen monitor was the first thing I salvaged. I started disassembling the body, and activated a beast of a tracking device. Tech jammed the signal while I fried the tracker, bumping my head and slicing my hand open in the process. Once inside, I found a sixteen-gig DDR memory stick and an octa-core CPU. All-in-all, not a bad load. After my team dissected the rest of them, a decent tech fence would be able to fetch Renzo at least two large for the parts. I was bandaging up my hand when Bones reminded me that we had an appointment at the shooting range.

The range was operated by a friend of the family who not only allowed us to bring in our own handguns, but also gave us free rein to fire everything they had. We checked into the VIP room and once we brushed up on our pistols, we tried out the M4, the M249 S.A.W, the Remington 700 sniper, the Beretta M9, and the Tommy gun. Of course we had to try the Tommy gun. How could we not? Bones and I spent the afternoon competing to see which of us could destroy the most targets. By the time we grabbed dinner and headed home, my arms felt like jelly. I was so ready for bed that I even resisted the urge to drive by Markie's apartment to see if I could catch a glimpse of her.

The next day, Bones and I made it to the office early. I went back to the self-checkout terminal in the middle of my floor, while Bones scurried off to do whatever he did when I was in Geekland, as he liked to call it. By the time he brought me lunch he'd scheduled an appointment with the orphanage director for three p.m. We cut out of work early, suited up, and strolled into the joint like we had money to throw around. And when we threw that money around, the director's eyes went wider than silver dollars. He was too busy counting the bills to even ask me to fill out an application.

"You're sure it won't be a problem for us to stop by every now and then? We'd like to make sure our contribution is being put to good use." Bones asked.

"That's a perfectly reasonable request, and the children will benefit from spending time with upstanding male role models like yourselves," the director replied, sliding the cash into a drawer.

I wondered when money had become a sign of good character, but held my tongue. The meeting couldn't have gone better if I'd scripted it, and I didn't want to screw it up now. By the time we left the director's office, I was ready to cash in on my end of the deal and get Markie's phone number. I marched up to the front desk and asked for her.

The lady behind the desk nodded. "Yeah, I know Markie. She's the new volunteer. The kids really like her. She was here earlier, but went home with a migraine."

Feeling completely let down, I thanked her and turned to leave.

A little black kid holding a basketball blocked my path. His shorts and tank top looked about two sizes too big for him, and his sneakers had a hole in the toe. He dribbled the ball a couple of times and then cocked his head to the side and studied me. He snorted, clearly unimpressed. The kid had to be about ten, but packed at least twenty years of attitude.

"You know Markie?" he asked.

The little punk needed to mind his own damn business, but since I wasn't trying to get kicked out of the orphanage, I nodded. "Yeah, she's a friend."

The boy looked from me to Bones and snorted again. "Yeah right."

What the hell? "What's that supposed to mean?" I asked.

"Markie's tough. She's a baller and she don't take no shit. You? You brought your bodyguard into an orphanage. What are you scared of, rich boy?"

I had to hand it to the kid, he had a point.

"I'm smart, not scared. And how do you know I'm not a baller?"

He tossed me the ball and shrugged. "Only one way to find out. Prove it."

I caught the ball, barely. But hey, I hadn't been expecting it. I could shoot hoops. Bones's shoulders shook, and I knew my friend was trying not to laugh. I hesitated, wondering what he knew that I didn't. Besides, I didn't have time to teach the little punk a lesson. If we left now, we could take Markie some flowers and a get-well card.

"That's what I thought," the kid sneered. "Just another stick in a suit."

I'd been in the place less than ten minutes and had paid one guy off and had another challenging me. Turns out that Markie's world wasn't too far from my father's after all. Never one to turn down a challenge, I tilted my head toward Bones and asked, "What do you think? We got time to straighten this kid out?"

Bones removed his jacket, loosened his tie, and rolled up his shirt sleeves. He flexed and cracked his neck. Then he leveled a stare at the kid and said, "There's always time to teach manners." He stepped forward.

The kid's eyes bugged out.

Hiding my laugh, I held out a hand to stop Bones. "Save it for the court, big guy. Where is your court anyway?"

The kid pointed to the north side of the building. "That way."

"Cool. Bathroom?" I asked.

Still keeping an eye on Bones, the kid pointed in the opposite direction. "Down that hall. First door on the right."

I tossed him the ball. "Go find a few of your little friends and meet us in the gym in ten minutes."

"But you're wearing suits."

"Don't worry about it. Not your problem." We had gym clothes in the Hummer, but I wanted him to think they just materialized on us like superheroes.

"Hey kid, you look scared," Bones said. "What's wrong? You just a big-mouthed chicken?"

"I ain't no chicken, and I don't play for free. Let's talk stakes. What's in it for me when we wipe the floor with your tired old asses?"

Tired old asses? Nobody had ever called me old before. Stakes, though? The kid was a gambler, and that was something I knew how to deal with. I crossed my arms and eyed him. "What do you want?"

"If I win, you take me and my friends to play paintball."

"Paintball?" I asked. "You sure you're old enough for that?"

He snickered. "Yeah. I'm good."

"Okay, I'll bite, but what do I get if we win?"

The kid eyed me for a minute longer before answering, "I'll put in a good word for you with Markie."

Bones coughed.

I almost swallowed my tongue. It took me a minute to recover, and then I asked, "What makes you think I need a good word with Markie?"

He blinked. "How dumb do you think I am?"

I didn't want to touch that one, so I shrugged.

"I could call her right now. I got her phone number."

My jaw dropped.

"Ah, you want her number, huh? I can give you that if you can take us on the court."

I seriously considered beating the kid and taking it from him. Since I was sure that sort of behavior would be frowned upon, I refrained. "Markie and I are tight. If I wanted her number, I'd ask *her* for it."

He laughed. "Uh-huh, sure. Markie's been in this city all of ten minutes and she comes here lookin' to help us out. Then you and your bodyguard come strollin' in askin' for her. I bet you lived here your whole life and you never thought about volunteering at no orphanage. You're tryin' to get a piece of that action."

The casual way he sexualized Markie pissed me off. I tensed. "You better watch your mouth and stop talking about her like that. It's disrespectful."

He raised his hands in defense. "Okay man, chill. We got a deal or not?"

I wanted to get the little punk on the court and school him. "Fine, kid, you got a deal." I held my hand out.

He slapped it. "The name's Myles."

Besides being observant, Myles was a phenomenal basketball player, especially for someone barely over four feet tall. We played street ball, first team to twenty-one won. He and his little gang of pocket-sized thugs were all over me and Bones from the instant our sneakers hit the court. The four young boys had at least thirty elbows between them, and each one ended up in my ribs at least twice. By the time we reached the second half, Bones and I were sweating harder than we ever did working out. We barely eked out a win, beating them by two points.

Myles tossed me the ball. "Double or nothing?" he asked.

"How are you going to double giving me Markie's number?" I asked.

He shrugged. "I'll think of something. I'll give you her number *and* might even be able to buy you some alone time with her."

I looked to Bones and he nodded. He wanted another crack at the punk. Myles's team won the second game, but thankfully he couldn't resist the challenge of a third. Bones and I won, and then I met Myles midcourt.

"Markie's number?" I asked.

"Hand me your phone. I'll put it in."

I chuckled. "You must think I was born yesterday. I'm not giving you my phone." I pulled it out of my pocket and started entering a new contact. "Just tell me her number."

Myles rattled off a seven-oh-two number and I entered it, and then confirmed it aloud.

"Yeah, that's it. Just don't rat me out for giving it to you," Myles said.

I had every intention of ratting him out. That was my whole plan for having her number without looking like a stalker.

Heads down, looking defeated, he and his goons cleared the court. Every muscle in my body was on fire but I held my head high as we walked out of the building and toward the Hummer. I thought about stopping by Markie's but I was tired and sweaty, so I headed for home instead. Besides, I had her number. I pulled up the contact and dialed, running my opening line through my head.

"Vegas Paintballers, David speaking."

I pulled the phone away and double checked the contact. Yep, that was the number he gave me. Of course. I dragged my hand down my face, amazed I could be so gullible.

"Sorry. I must have the wrong number." I disconnected and threw the phone on the seat.

Bones started chuckling, and then he broke into a full-on belly laugh. "I can't believe you just got played by that little shit."

I flipped him off.

More laughter.

"Yeah, yeah," I said, still shaking my head.

CHAPTER FIFTEEN
Angel

SATURDAY MORNING I woke up to an absolutely delightful text from my father which read, 'You get my money yet?'

I formed a number of responses in my mind, but since they'd all piss the old man off, I rubbed the sleep from my eyes and replied with some badass line I'd heard Uncle Carlo use, promising money or blood by the end of the day. Contrary to my bravado, I dragged ass to the coffee machine and fired it up. A series of swear words preceded Bones's appearance as he emerged from his room, stretching and groaning.

"I hear ya," I replied. "Damn kids. I'm sore in muscles I didn't know existed."

"My ribs feel like I went five rounds in the ring against Muhammad Ali." Bones stepped into the kitchen and went straight for a mug. "So, what's on the agenda for today?"

I pulled up my father's text and handed it to Bones. He groaned, setting his cup beside mine. We stood there and watched the coffee brew like it was the most fascinating process in the world.

"You still haven't heard from Johnny?"

"Not a peep."

"That dumbass." Bones tapped his fingers on the counter. "You know where to find him?"

"No, but I know someone who does."

I poured us each a cup of joe. As we caffeinated our bodies, my mind served up memory clips of Johnny tied to the bed. Tears streamed down his cheeks while he screamed in pain, begging for mercy. We'd done a number on him, and I'd been so sure he would pay. Now we'd have to go further. How far? What would we have to do?

Bones let me brood in silence and retreated to his room to get ready. Since I didn't feel much like eating, I did the same.

Less than an hour later, we climbed into the Hummer and called up Tech.

His face popped onto the dashboard screen. "Angel, Bones. Good morning. How can I help you?"

Tech had to be the busiest man I knew; too busy to waste time with things like sleep or small talk. "Mornin', Tech. I know you got eyes on Johnny Dominas. Where can I find him?"

Tech looked down. There was the tap-tap-tap of a keyboard and reflections of changing screens in his glasses. Although I'd never seen his set-up, Father had described it as a wall full of monitors, with which Tech watched the city.

"He's staying in a little roach motel off the strip. I'm sending you the address now. Room twelve."

My GPS started up, telling me to head out of the garage and take a left.

"You watching him right now?" I asked. If Johnny was with a broad, I didn't want to bust in and scare the crap out of her.

"No. He checked in late last night and the boss didn't want to waste any resources setting up eyes in the room. We greased the motel clerk and he promised to notify us if Johnny moved. Let me just hack into the motel security cameras."

More keyboard taps.

"His car is still in the lot. I'm sending the property site code to your phone now. Do you want me to dispatch a team?"

My phone buzzed with the incoming information. "No. This is my mistake. I'll handle it. Thanks for your help." I disconnected and rubbed a hand down my face. My stomach felt sick, and I was pissed at Johnny for putting me into this position.

"He said two days," Bones said.

"Yeah, I know. Must have already wiped out his mom."

"Such a *mammone*," Bones spat.

Italian men were notorious for being mamma's boys. But since I'd grown up without a mom and Bones had become the man of the family in middle school, neither of us had any respect for mamma's boys. Especially ones who bled their mamas dry.

"You don't have to take care of this. I can—"

"Can you wipe my ass for me, Bones? You and I both know what has to happen. I can't hand this off to you. It's my mess, and I need to clean it up. Anything less, and the old man will..." I paused, realizing I had no idea what my father would do. Would he kill me for my cowardice and finally rid himself of the disgrace I regularly caused him? Would he strike Bones for interfering? Would he finally realize I didn't have the balls to be his clone? The tension in my back crept into my head, pounding at my right temple. "I have to do this."

I followed my GPS into the parking lot of a gaudy concrete building, painted to resemble gold. A smoke shop and a sex toys retailer were connected to the hotel.

"Classy place," Bones observed, sliding out of the Hummer. He opened the back of the vehicle and returned with the handheld machine I kept in my toolbox.

I powered up the machine and entered the site code Tech had sent me. Bones released the safety on his gun and slid it back into his pocket. Then we walked over to room twelve. I inserted a card attached to the machine and waited. Seconds later, the lock clicked open. Bones drew his gun as he entered the small dark room. I held the door open, peering in so my eyes could adjust while I waited until Bones signaled me in.

The room smelled like shit. Literally, like someone had taken a dump on the floor in front of a fan. I covered my nose and followed Bones to the other side of the bed and a body facing away from us. A packet of white dust was on the nightstand beside a burnt-out candle and a metal spoon, telling us exactly what Johnny had been up to.

Bones crept forward and nudged the body with his foot. Johnny flopped over. His lifeless eyes stared up at the ceiling and a syringe rolled across the carpet. The stink was overwhelming, forcing me to step back. Bones squatted and felt for a pulse.

"Dead. We need to get out of here."

My feet couldn't carry me away from the scene fast enough.

"He killed himself to avoid me." The thought had been tumbling around in my head, and finally vomited out while I drove away from the motel.

"He OD'd. People do it every day."

My hands tried to shake. My stomach soured. My body wanted to react, and I had to fight for control. I breathed deeply, forcing my emotions to settle. "He wasn't a junkie."

"Which makes it easier to OD."

I drove until my body went numb. My mind kept spinning, though. I couldn't stop myself from feeling relieved about Johnny's death, because it kept me from having to deal with him. And that felt cowardly and wrong. I glanced into the rearview mirror, disgusted at the sight of my own reflection. Fear of me had driven my friend to kill himself, and I had the nerve to feel relieved.

"Where are we going?" Bones asked.

That was when I realized I'd unconsciously headed for the orphanage. "I know it's stupid and I'm probably making a huge mistake right now, but I need to see her." In the darkness of my mind, I desperately needed the light of her smile. To hear her laugh. I wanted to flee from my world and escape into hers.

"All right, man, do what you need to do," Bones replied.

We entered the building in time to watch Markie set a stack of papers on the admittance desk. Her back was turned to us, but I knew it was her. She wore a long dark skirt with blue flowers on it, a blue blouse, and dark flats. Her hair was up in a messy bun.

"Here's the food pantry inventory you asked for. Is there anything else I can do to help?" Markie asked the woman sitting behind the desk.

"Thank you, no, this is perfect. You saved me so much time." The woman gave Markie a quick smile before her attention shifted to me and Bones. "Hello. How can I help you?"

Markie smiled at us. "Michelle, this is Angel and Bones."

"Angel and Bones?" Michelle grabbed a post-it off her desk and her smile turned sugary-sweet. "Oh, right, Angel and Bones. Welcome. The director is on a call right now, but I'll let him know you're here." She stood.

I held up a hand. "No need. We're here to volunteer."

"Oh." She eyed our suits. "Okay then."

"We had a business meeting this morning," I explained.

"Yeah, be lucky they didn't come in their SWAT costumes," Markie added.

"That sounds like an interesting story," Michelle said. The

phone rang and pulled her attention from us.

"Are you okay?" Markie asked, searching my face as she grabbed my hand. It felt like she opened a valve, releasing all the pent-up tension and guilt I felt over Johnny. I didn't know how she did it, but I wanted to hug her and thank her for it.

"Stressful day," I replied. "I'd like to forget about it."

She nodded. "Understood. You guys any good at card games?"

I loved that she didn't push or prod. She just accepted my answer and moved on.

Bones snorted. "We did grow up in Vegas."

"Good. I heard you met Myles." She watched my face, but I was careful not to give anything away. I only nodded. "Well, he and his friends are setting up a game in the great room. I'm sure he's in there stashing cards right now. I could use some help bringing that little cheater down."

"Yeah, well cards isn't the only thing that little punk cheats at," Bones said, rubbing his side.

Markie frowned. "He's a work in progress, but then again, we all are. Speaking of which, we should get in there. Last time I left him and his crew alone, they got into the packing tape and stuck a couple of the bigger kids to the wall."

She led us down the hall and turned into a room with several mismatched ratty couches. Myles and his crew sat in folding chairs surrounding an old scratched-up table. He was hunched over, rubbing his calf, but the second he saw me he sat up straight, crossed his arms, and scowled. Bones snickered.

"You sore, Myles?" Bones asked, patting the kid on the shoulder.

Myles pulled away from him and Bones laughed.

Markie joined the boys, sitting at the head of the table.

"Hey guys. You got room for two more?" I asked.

Myles kicked an empty chair toward me. I reached out and stopped it right before it slammed into my leg.

Markie shot him a look. "Be nice," she said.

His scowl only darkened. "Five card draw, fifty dollar buy in," he said.

Markie cocked her head. "I told you, no gambling. It's a friendly game, no buy in."

"It'd be a lot friendlier if you'd let us make some money," one of the kids argued.

Markie stared at him and he ducked his head. "Sorry, Ms. Markie."

Myles was right. She didn't put up with anything from anyone. Bones and I sat while Myles dealt. I caught him cheating twice in the first deal alone.

"How can you tell?" Myles asked, after the second time I called him out.

"Because you're not very good at it. If you're going to deal yourself extra cards, your dealing has to be seamless. These cards are slick. They slide and one of the edges is going to show. If you're going to cheat, it's easier to do it when you exchange your cards."

Markie gaped at me. "Are you really giving him tips on cheating?" she asked.

"Someone has to," Bones replied. "He sucks at it."

Markie dropped her head to her hands. I knew she was going for angry, but her shoulders shook with laughter. She took a moment to compose herself, and then glared us all down. "No gambling and no cheating," she said.

"Of course not," Myles said, holding his hands up.

Bones won the first game and Markie won the second. The third went to one of Myles's little cronies. I sat back, counted cards, and threw the game to the best of my ability, lest she peg me for a cheater. After all, I was going for her phone number, not trying to ignite her temper. In the middle of the fourth game, the boys were called to do their chores. They moaned and groaned before throwing in their cards and taking off. Then it was just the three of us.

Markie pulled out her phone and studied it. Minutes ticked by, thickening the awkward silence that settled over the room. Bones looked at me and his eyebrows rose in question. Then he got up from the table, pulled his phone out of his pocket, and walked down the hall to give us some privacy.

More awkward silence. I had to break it. "Did I do something wrong?" I asked.

She set her phone down and picked up a card. She turned it over in her hands a few times, and then flicked it to me.

"No. Thanks for showing up. It means a lot to them. To me too." She blushed. That's when I realized Markie had even less game than I did. "I'm just surprised to see you, is all. I'm trying to figure out what you want, Angel."

"What I want? I thought I was pretty clear about that. I want your number," I said.

"Yeah, Myles told me you cheated to get it."

"*I* cheated? You *have* met him, right? He's a pint-sized thug."

She laughed. "That's a surprisingly accurate description."

"You know what he gave me? The number to the paintball place he wants me to take him to."

This only earned more laughter. "Do you really think I'd give Myles my number?"

"Nope. I figured he lifted it."

She tilted her head to the side. "Okay, I can see that. The boys are going to be busy for a while. What are you two up to today?" she asked, changing the subject.

"I'm hungry. Can we go get something to eat now?" Bones asked from the doorway.

"He's always hungry. You want to join us for lunch?" I asked.

She nodded. "Sure, I could eat."

We headed to a local diner and engaged in some light conversation before Markie asked what we did for a living.

"Well, we're definitely not secret government agents nor SWAT," I said.

She blushed. "Yeah, I figured as much by the way you kept me from a possible jail cell on Halloween. Thanks for that by the way. But if you're not cops, how do you know Matt?"

I looked to Bones. I didn't want to lie to her, but I couldn't exactly tell her the truth.

"He owes me some money," Bones said. "Since we were in the neighborhood, we stopped by so I could collect."

Markie blew out a breath. "Matt's a slimeball, isn't he?" she asked Bones.

He frowned. "If I had a sister, I sure as hell wouldn't let her date him."

Markie nodded. "Thank you for your honesty." Then she turned back to me. "So, where do you work?"

"In a computer lab, mostly. I also drive around a lot." Both of those answers were true.

"He's a geek," Bones added.

I would have flipped him the bird if Markie wasn't sitting with us. "I manipulate computer programs, write some code, install

110

security devices, stuff like that. I handle some sales, too. That's why the suits are necessary. Gotta look professional."

That seemed to sate her curiosity, and before long we headed back to the orphanage. Bones and I had errands to run, so we couldn't stay. We idled in front of the door to drop Markie off, but I could tell she was struggling with something. She took a post-it out of her pocket and fiddled with it.

"Before I give you this, I need you to know I can't promise you anything other than friendship. I don't know how long I'll be here and what the future looks like."

It had to be her phone number. She was finally going to give it to me. "Understood. I promise not to stalk you."

She laughed and handed me her digits.

"Is this real?" I gaped at the post-it. "I'm not gonna get Chuck E. Cheese or something, am I?"

She laughed. "That Myles... he's a riot, isn't he?"

"Riot. Yeah, that's exactly the word I was thinking of," I deadpanned.

She bit back more laughter. "Yeah, this one's real. Use it."

I stuck the post-it to my dashboard, wondering when she'd written it. A grin tugged at my lips. "Yes ma'am."

She opened her door, and then turned to say good-bye. "I am really glad you guys showed up. Surprised, but glad. Myles needs good men in his life. He's probably the biggest punk on the planet, but I seriously love that kid. Thank you."

Then she climbed out of the Hummer and headed toward the door. As I watched her go, I thought about what she'd said. If Markie could find it in her heart to love a smart-ass little punk like Myles, maybe there was room in her heart for someone like me after all.

♠ ♥ ♣ ♦

CHAPTER SIXTEEN
Angel

SUNDAY WAS THE twins' birthday, so the family rented out Adventure Canyon and spent the day riding water rides and shooting electronic guns at "bad guys." The festivities at the park lasted into the early evening, and then we moved the party to my father's house and sent the kids to bed so the adults could swap stories by the fire pit in the back yard. By the time Bones and I made it home, it was almost eleven and too late to call Markie.

I made use of her phone number throughout the rest of the week, though. Tech had my team out on installs and I managed to text Markie periodically throughout the days, asking what she was up to and whether or not Myles had robbed a bank or conned some little old lady out of her social security yet. Markie always texted back, giving me details about her day and telling me funny stories about the people she encountered. The way she genuinely cared about people was refreshing. I started looking forward to the buzz of my incoming messages, knowing they'd make me smile. I wanted to get back to the orphanage and visit her, and maybe even have another go at Myles on the court, but my busy schedule didn't allow for it.

On Wednesday, Father called me and Bones into his office to discuss a deal he wanted me in on. He needed me to head to San Diego Thursday and make an offer on some "fallen off a truck" swag. This was a first for me, so he detailed the negotiation tactics and gave me a maximum offer amount. The way he spoke about it, dealing with his associates in San Diego would be a lot like haggling with street vendors in Tijuana.

"Give them twenty-four hours to make a decision," Father added. "They'll stall, trying to squeeze us for more. You stay in San Diego until the deal is finalized, then I'll send a driver to pick up the goods."

I nodded while cringing inside. It had been almost a week since I'd seen Markie and now I was going to be stuck in San Diego for the weekend.

"What's your issue?" Bones asked once we were on the road. "We're getting a free weekend in San Diego, a break from the grind. We'll relax on the sand, maybe hit the race track. The Chargers are hosting the Chiefs this weekend. I bet I could score us a couple of tickets."

I shrugged. "Yeah, we'll have more than enough down time for all of that."

"That's what you're worried about? Down time? Shit, Angel, you work too much. Take a weekend and enjoy yourself. My boy Tony works as a bouncer at this club in downtown SD, and he's always bragging about the girls. We can go check it out and…"

Bones droned on, but I was done listening to him. The only girl I wanted to see this weekend would be here in Vegas.

Unless…

Bones was driving the Hummer, so I sent a quick text to Markie, asking if she was available for a phone call.

"What's going on over there? Are you even listening to me?" Bones asked.

I waved off his question. "Yeah, yeah. Race track, football game, girls, sand, I got it. It'll be legit, I'm sure."

"This is about that blonde broad, isn't it?"

I leveled a stare at him. "You know her name is Markie."

He shrugged. "Not like I blame you. Great smile, nice rack, sweet girl, but you sure you want to go down that path?"

It was my turn to shrug. "She still hasn't turned into a psycho bitch."

My phone buzzed with a yes, so I dialed Markie and asked her what she was up to.

"Ariana and I found this adorable little thrift store with board games still new and in the box."

"You like board games, huh?" I asked.

113

She giggled. "I'm buying them for the orphanage."

"Why are you doing that?" I asked. "The bookshelves in the great room held dozens of games."

"Donated games. The games most people donate are missing pieces. Do you have any idea how difficult it is to play *Monopoly* without any get out of jail free cards? I spent half of our last game in the slammer."

"You read the rules, right?" I asked.

"Rules? Angel the game doesn't even have a box anymore. We keep the pieces in a plastic baggie."

I chuckled. "Well, according to the rules you can only spend three turns in jail before you're required to pay $50 and get out. I'm betting Myles knows this."

She growled. "That little punk!"

"Indeed." I thought about her carting a pile of games onto the bus, trying to get them to the orphanage. Then I realized I actually didn't have anything I needed to do for the rest of the day. It was a perfect opportunity to play the hero and to see her. "Hey, do you want a ride to drop off the games?"

"It wouldn't be too much trouble?" she asked.

"Nope. Bones and I are just out driving around right now. Where are you?"

Markie gave me the store name and I put it into the GPS. Moments later, Bones idled the Hummer at the curb while I jumped out and helped Markie and Ariana with board games stacked well above their heads.

"Did you buy the place out?" I asked, filling the back of my vehicle.

She laughed. "Apparently this is what happens when a hobby store goes out of business. I can't wait to see the kids' faces. They're going to be so excited. It'll be good for them to see you and Bones, too. Myles keeps asking about you guys. I think he and his posse are looking for a rematch."

Even the thought of hitting the court with Myles made my legs ache. But strangely enough, it also made my smile widen. I liked the cheating little punk.

Markie and I climbed into the Hummer, but Ariana stayed on the curb.

"Isn't she coming?" Bones asked.

Markie closed the door behind her. "She has to head to work.

She's just gonna hop a bus."

Bones cocked his head to the side and looked at me. I'd seen him break bones, shoot fools, chase down some idiot who tried to rip him off, intimidate the piss out of hardened criminals, but I'd never seen him leave a broad standing on the street. We ended up taking Ariana to work.

Once we were on our way, I turned so I could see all of their faces and asked, "Have you ladies ever been to San Diego?"

Bones cleared his throat, but I ignored the way his eyes bugged out like he knew what I was doing and couldn't believe it. Hell, I couldn't believe it either, but it felt right.

Neither Markie nor Ariana had been to the coast, so I asked if they'd like to join me and Bones on our trip. Bones kept driving and didn't say a word.

"I'd love to, but I have to work this weekend," Ariana replied.

Markie nudged her sister. "Oh, come on. You could call in and take some time off. It would be so fun. We've never seen the ocean. I mean, I flew over it, but I'd kind of like to feel the sand between my toes."

"I can't. Not after that little episode with the hospital. I've got bills to pay, and if I miss more time at work, they'll probably fire me." Ariana sighed. Then she smiled at Markie and added, "But you should go. This could be your only chance."

"I don't want to leave you alone all weekend," Markie said.

"Puh-lease. I am a grown-ass woman. Besides, I could use a little alone time without my big sis all up in my business. Go and have fun. Bring me back a couple of seashells."

"Are you sure you'll be okay?" Markie asked.

Ariana rolled her eyes. "Ohmigod yes. Go, already."

Markie eyed me and Bones. "I don't know how I feel about going out of state with two guys I barely know."

"You didn't know anyone in Africa, and you *lived* with them," Ariana pointed out.

"You'll have your own room," I insisted. "And I promise we'll be perfect gentlemen."

"See?" Ariana asked. "They'll be gentlemen. Sounds boring and right up your alley."

Markie and Ariana argued until we dropped Ariana off. Then Markie caved and promised to come with us. We made plans before we dropped her and the games off at the orphanage. Bones bottled his anger until we were alone again and back on the road. Then he let me have it.

"Do you trust me?" he asked.

I gaped at his ridiculous question. "Bones, you know I do."

"I know that, huh?" he spat. "My job is to protect you. How the hell can I do that if you're off making plans and doing shit you don't even clear with me first?"

"She's a friend. She's never seen the ocean before. What's the harm in bringing her along?"

He tensed. "What's the harm? Seriously? I like the broad, don't get me wrong. Seems like a nice girl, and I see what she does to you and it's good. But we got nuthin' on her, Angel. It's like she just appeared one day. Says she's been in Africa for the past year, but how do we know that for sure? You seen any pictures of her there?"

I shook my head. "We're not quite to the sharing photo albums stage."

He scowled at me. "This isn't funny. You got a screw loose over this girl and you're gonna get us both killed."

"What do you want me to do?" I asked.

"I'm running a background check on her tonight," he replied.

I rested my head in my hands, knowing I wouldn't win this battle. Bones would check into Markie's past no matter what I said. Hell, he probably already had. "Fine, but I don't want to know what you find unless it's something I need to know."

Bones rubbed the stubble on his chin. "You should help me. I can't get everywhere, but you—"

"I'm not helping you invade her privacy."

Bones' face turned a dangerous shade of red. Veins popped out of his neck. He punched the dashboard and swore. Several times. Then he took a few deep breaths and nodded. "Okay. I'll outsource it. It'll take more time, but I've got a guy."

I held up my hands. "Sounds like you got it all figured out."

Bones grumbled and opened his door. "Yay, me, now I get to be the third wheel. Great. Thanks for that, buddy."

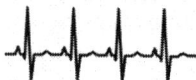

The next morning, Bones met me in the kitchen, extending a travel mug of coffee like an olive branch. "She has a bachelor's in criminal justice."

I wasn't expecting that. It gave me pause for a few beats before I asked, "Has she done anything with it?"

"Not that I can find. She went to Africa right after she got her degree. But why would she spend the money for an education and not do anything with it?"

I chuckled. This was a question I could handle. "Ask the one-third of college grads who never work in their degree field."

"A third? Really?" he asked.

I pulled up the statistic on my phone and showed it to him.

"Well for the record, I still think this is a piss-poor idea," Bones said, grabbing a second travel mug of coffee.

"Didn't find anything else, huh?" I asked.

"Still looking," he replied as we headed out.

Markie answered the door wearing a knee-length gray skirt, purple blouse, sandals, and a shawl draped over her shoulders. Her long blonde hair spilled over the shawl in loose curls and when she walked past me, she smelled like wildflowers and summer. I breathed her in while I bent to grab her bag. Bones climbed into the backseat, so I opened the passenger door for Markie. She slid in and turned on the radio.

"What are you doing?" I asked, merging out of the parking lot into traffic.

"You said you like oldies, and I want to see what that means, exactly." She turned up the volume. Music filled the vehicle and she looked at me. "Who is this?"

"Gladys Knight and the Pips," Bones said, leaning forward. "Angel was born in the wrong era."

Bones didn't trust Markie, but he liked her. And he sure as hell wouldn't be rude to her.

"He's like some crusty old man trapped in the body of a twenty-three-year-old," he added.

Markie giggled. Then her head bobbed to the music for a few beats. "I like it. It's different."

"Wait, you've never heard this song before?" I asked.

Markie waited for a few more bars, and then shook her head. "I don't think so. Ari and I grew up in the sticks. Our music options were pretty limited."

"Turn it up, turn it up," Bones said, tapping Markie's shoulder. "This is my favorite part."

Markie cranked up the volume and Bones broke into the verse, shaking his body with the beat. It was good to see him more relaxed; well worth the background check on Markie. The Hummer bounced a little with his weight and Markie laughed.

Bones nudged me. "Come on, Angel. This is our jam, right here. You know you want to join in."

Another challenge I couldn't resist. I sang with Bones as we tried—and failed miserably—to meet Gladys Knight's pitch and tone. Markie laughed, cheered, and then joined us on the chorus. Then the next song came on, and Bones and I harmonized (kind of) with Aretha Franklin. We sang song after song, amusing Markie throughout the drive. By the time we stopped at a small diner to grab brunch, my cheeks hurt from smiling so much.

"You guys are the best traveling companions ever," Markie crooned as we headed into the restaurant. "I think that's the most fun I've ever had on a car ride. I can't believe it's almost noon. Feels like we just left."

"Yep, we'll be walking on the beach in no time," I replied.

"So what else do you like to do?" Markie asked over our waffles and bacon.

"Angel fancies himself quite the dancer," Bones said for me.

I groaned. "Must you tell all my secrets?"

"And this after you gave me such a hard time about the disco dancing?" Markie asked.

"He took classes and everything," Bones added, as a big grin spread across his face.

I resisted the urge to punch my best friend. Just barely.

"I see how it is." Markie grinned. "What type of dancing are we talking here?"

Glaring at Bones, I replied, "Ballroom mostly. Sometimes my family attends events where it's a necessity. We all had to learn."

"A computer geek who ballroom dances?" she asked, grinning.

Bones cleared his throat, no doubt ready to give Markie all sorts of incriminating information designed to make me look like a sissy. I glared at him and he threw his hands up in mock innocence.

♠ ♥ ♣ ♦

CHAPTER SEVENTEEN
Angel

IT WAS ALMOST two o'clock p.m. when I rolled the Hummer to a stop in front of where we'd be spending the next two nights. Because I was laying low, I avoided my family's usual haunt on Coronado Island and booked a couple of rooms in a small hotel blocks away from Seaport Village. The hotel manager was a friend, not connected to my family, and unlikely to scurry off and tell my father I'd brought a date on my business trip.

As soon as we pulled up, Markie made a beeline for the restroom while I checked us into our rooms. Markie's room was adjacent to the two-room suite I shared with Bones, and we headed there first.

"Omigosh, this is amazing!" Markie squealed, rushing out onto the patio. "The smell! And the sounds! The air feels so different. I have never seen anything so beautiful in my life! Can we go walk on the beach right now?"

Her joy was worth every mile we'd driven, worth risking Father's anger to see. We had time to kill before our meeting, so Bones and I checked our rooms, dropped off our bags, and grabbed jackets. Markie changed and then waited for us in the hall, bouncing on her toes like some kid on her first Disneyland adventure. We had to hurry to keep up as she led us out the doors and onto the beach. Then she removed her sandals and dug her toes into the sand.

"Feels like the sandbox we had in our backyard as kids." She glanced around before adding, "Except there's no cat poop."

Bones chuckled. "You're even more awkward than Angel."

She was, and I loved it.

The temperature was in the low seventies. There weren't many people walking the beach and even fewer braving the water. Markie walked between me and Bones, her eyes round with wonder. "It's so beautiful. Do you guys have your swim trunks on under your shorts?" she asked.

Bones and I shared a look. He chuckled and shook his head.

"What?" Markie asked.

"Uh, no. That water's like sixty-five degrees. I'm not going near it without a wetsuit on," I said.

"Me either," Bones added.

"Really? Sixty-five degrees, huh? Back home we had swimming holes that were colder than that in the middle of summer. I think I can handle it. Will you hold my stuff?"

"Yep. Knock yourself out." I held out my hands expectantly.

"Thanks!" She tugged her blouse over her head and slipped off her skirt. Then she handed everything to me.

I tried not to stare, but Markie was gorgeous. A modest lavender one-piece swimsuit hugged her hourglass figure, perfecting the balance of soft curves and hard lines. She spun around, giving me a view I would never turn away from as her perfectly toned legs sprinted toward the water.

"Damn," Bones whispered.

Markie ran until the waves crested above her knees, and then she dove under. Bones nudged me. Then he gestured toward my hand—the hand tugging the collar of my shirt away from my neck—and chuckled.

I released my collar and rubbed at my hairline. "Damn, indeed," I breathed.

Markie surfaced, gasping for air and visibly shivering from the cold while she pushed her hair out of her face. She splashed her way out of the water and ran back toward us.

"No way that's sixty-five degrees!"

I took off my jacket and held it out to her. She ran straight into it, her lips turning blue.

"Okay, maybe the time in Africa spoiled me, because that water is f-f-freezing."

I rubbed her shoulders, feeling the cold of her body seep

through the fabric of my jacket.

"We tried to tell you," Bones said.

"Yeah, well I'm going to try out that huge jetted tub in my bathroom while you're at your meeting."

I swallowed back the fantasies that visual invoked, took deep breaths, and fought to keep my body from physically reacting. All of which would have been easier if I'd given Markie a trench coat instead of a jacket that barely passed her ass.

Bones and I saw Markie into her room, where she promised to wait until we got back, and then we went to our own room to dress and get ready for our meeting. Before we got into the Hummer, I scanned it for devices, pausing when something unexpected popped up on the screen.

"What is it?" Bones asked, leaning in to study the scanner.

I reached under the back bumper and pulled out a quarter-sized polycarbonate disk, flipped it over in my hand a few times, and handed it to Bones.

"What the hell is this?" Bones asked, examining it.

"It's sending a signal and it's not a bomb, so my guess is some sort of tracking device. I'd have to take it apart to verify that, though."

"Not one of your father's?" Bones asked.

"Not unless he's keeping tech secrets." Father usually brought me in on his new technical toys, but he also liked to test me. I wouldn't put it past the old man to plant foreign tech on my vehicle and see if I caught it.

Bones leaned back, his mind probably spinning in the same circles as mine. "Did you do a scan before we left the apartment?"

I'd been mentally retracing this morning's steps since the anomaly beeped on my device finder, but I couldn't remember. My excitement over picking up Markie and beginning our trip had made me sloppy, and that was dangerous. "I'm not sure."

Bones stared at me and then looked at the device. "If you scanned it this morning, then someone followed us here. Or…" He looked up at the hotel.

Markie. Was she alone with the Hummer? When would she have put it on? It was barely under the bumper, and she could have popped it on when nobody was looking. Maybe when she went to the restroom at the diner.

"No." I forced my mind to stop convicting her. "I must not

have scanned it."

Bones slipped the device under the bumper of a nearby minivan, and we climbed into the Hummer.

"I could have used that," I said.

"For what? If you take it offline they'll know you found it. This way, maybe they'll keep tabs on someone else for a while."

He had a point, so I resisted the urge to steal back the tracking device and make it my next project. "Yeah, but they already know we're here."

He shrugged. "Nothing we can do about that now."

By the time we pulled out of the parking lot and merged onto the street, my stomach was twisting into knots. Anyone tailing us would have seen Markie with us, putting her in danger. I called her cell.

She answered and I realized the flaw in my plan. How could I warn her that she might be in danger without revealing my identity or the fact that I'd found a tracking device under my vehicle?

"Angel? Is everything okay?" she asked.

Anything I said would only confuse her and put her in more danger. I'd been stupid to bring her along on the trip, and even stupider to think I could get away from my life for even one weekend. Now I was on the phone with nothing to say, instead of driving like I had a possible tail to lose. Turning my brain back on, I flipped a u-turn and checked my rearview mirror.

"Markie? Oh, crap. I must have butt dialed you. Sorry about that. We'll see you soon, okay?"

She hesitated before replying, "Okay."

"Enjoy the tub. 'Bye." I hung up.

Bones shook his head. "She's still in the lead, but you're plenty awkward."

I told him what he could do with his opinions.

He turned on the back camera and watched for a tail as I gripped the steering wheel and turned down an alley. I sped through it and merged onto a street, going the opposite direction.

"All right, Bones, help me. What would you do?"

"I'm a bodyguard. I'd call in security."

Security. Of course! Why didn't I think of that?

"You're a genius, my friend." I drove through two connecting parking lots and then made another turn.

He tilted his head to the side. "Yeah, I get that a lot. You want me to call someone to keep an eye on your girl?"

"My friend," I corrected. "She's just a friend. And do you know someone in the area who's trustworthy, but not loyal to my family?"

Bones threw his hands in the air, snorting at my ignorance. "Sometimes it's like you don't even know me."

It was all too easy to forget that my bodyguard doubled as a social butterfly, which, in turn, helped to make him even better at his job. Bones had contacts everywhere, in every industry, probably around the globe. Where my passion ran to gadgets, his ran to relations.

"Sorry, sorry. Please work your magic and get protection for Markie."

Bones multi-tasked, making calls while he studied the rear camera. He hired out Markie-watch and confirmed we didn't have a tail. Then he powered up the navigation and we headed for the agreed-upon meeting place: a warehouse in La Jolla. After we parked, I called Father to let him know about the tracking device. He swore a few times before warning us to be careful and hanging up.

Bones and I climbed out of the Hummer and followed Father's associates into a warehouse where we inspected a load of new computer processors. I made the opening offer and, as the old man had predicted, they hemmed and hawed about it being too low. I shrugged and started walking away. They countered. The cycle repeated a few times before I gave them my final offer. They told me they'd need time to see if they could find a higher bidder. I gave them twenty-four hours.

Once we were back in the Hummer, I checked my phone and saw that I had three missed calls from the hotel.

"Everything okay?" Bones asked.

"No clue." I dialed the hotel, only to find the manager—who was the one trying to reach me—had stepped into a meeting. Worried, I tried Markie's phone. No answer.

Bones dialed his security hire. No answer.

We burned rubber back to the Hotel.

♠ ♥ ♣ ♦

CHAPTER EIGHTEEN
Markie

THE JETTED TUB called to me, but before I could melt into it, I needed to handle business. Eager to do so, I threw a sundress over my wet bathing suit and headed down to the hotel office. I told the front desk lady my room number and handed over my credit card. She punched in a few keys on her computer and blinked.

"Uh, this room has already been paid for."

So Angel had put my room on his card. Well, that wasn't going to work for me. "My friend used his card to hold the room, but this is the card my room needs to be billed to."

She looked at the card. Then she looked at me. It was like I was speaking Hebrew or something.

"I'm sorry, ma'am, but I can't bill your card."

I inched the card closer to her. "Sure you can. Just credit the card on file and put the charges on this one."

We weren't exactly talking about astrophysics, but she still didn't seem to understand me. She called the manager. He wasn't much taller than me, with brown skin, a round face, straight black hair and eyes, and wearing a suit. The manager and the front desk lady put their heads together for several minutes, casting glances my way. Then he held up a finger in the universal gesture of asking someone to wait, and disappeared into his office. When he re-emerged several minutes later, his expression was tight and worried.

"The room is taken care of," the manager said like he was

giving his final answer on some old gameshow rather than discussing my room charges.

I took a deep breath and tried again. "Yes, I know. I was in the restroom, so my friend paid for it. Now I need to get it off his card and put it on mine. Easy-peasy."

The manager cleared his throat. "It's not that easy, ma'am. Angel is a good friend and he gets a discounted price."

So that's what the hold-up was about? "Okay. Well, you can either charge me the full rate or the discounted rate. Either way, it needs to go on my card, not Angel's."

He shook his head. Sweat glistened across his forehead. "No, you're not understanding. Angel and I have an agreement. He doesn't pay for his rooms."

"He doesn't pay *anything* for his rooms?" I asked, certain I'd misunderstood. We had suites, after all. Nice suites, right on the ocean. Why would the manager put Angel up for free? And why would he give me so much grief about paying?

"You should really discuss this with Angel," the manager said.

That did my patience in. "Look, this is none of your business, but since you're hell-bent on arguing and keeping me from jetted-tub bliss, Angel and I are just friends. That's all. He's not going to pay for my room, because that could cause confusion about the status of our relationship. You understand?"

He gave me a barely perceptible nod.

"If you want to give me a discount, hey, I won't complain. But whatever it costs, I will be the one paying for my room. So charge me now, or I swear I'll walk up there, pack my things, and find a different hotel. Understand?"

His eyes widened. "No, please don't do that."

He stepped up to the computer and hit a few keys before charging my card a whopping fifty dollars for two nights. I could have argued for a bigger victory, but I had a tub to get to. Besides, it seemed kind of stupid to ask him to charge me more.

I got a weird vibe on the way back to my room—like someone was watching me—but the hallway was empty. Still, the hair on the back of my neck stood up. I hurried to my room and threw the deadbolt behind me. Then, I sneezed. I sucked in a fragrance and turned, searching for the source as I sneezed again and again. Sure enough, a vase of red roses sat atop the bar. Still sneezing, I picked up the vase—keeping it as far from me as possible—and rushed it out into the hall. I placed it outside my door and returned to the suite to search for some sort of spray to break up the lingering allergens. After dousing the air with Lysol, I headed for the bathroom to find the perfect balance of bubbles and jets.

Roses. Angel had gotten me roses. They were beautiful and it was a sweet gesture, but I was crazy-allergic to the flowers. Making a mental note to text him and tell him of my allergy when I was out of the bath, I sank down and let lavender scented bubble bath take me to my happy place while the jets worked out the tension in my back. I melted into a puddle of goo until my stupid brain kicked into hyper-drive and started cycling through the pesky questions my subconscious had been storing up about Angel.

Free hotel rooms? Why?

That manager... what was up with him? So weird.

Bones said Angel was his boss. Angel works in technology. Did Bones ever tell me what he does?

What do I really know about them?

Angel was a Mariani. Bones called him a Mariani outside of the Cajun dive, and the kid's reaction had been full of fear and a strange sort of reverence. Ariana's reaction had been different.

Why?

I reached for my phone and turned off the jets, pulling up a browser to research the name. There was nothing online about D'Angelo Mariani in Las Vegas. No social media, no contact information, no school achievements, nothing. I did find a few articles on the Mariani family, though. They were apparently among the rich and powerful, sponsoring Christmas toy drives, funding a wing of a local hospital as well as an addition to a Catholic church. Nothing nefarious. But a family that wealthy had to have some clout.

The kind of clout that got free hotel rooms and terrified kids?

Still confused, I called Ariana, hoping she'd be more helpful than she'd been at the diner.

"Tell me everything you know about the Mariani family?" I blurted out the second she answered.

"Hi, I'm good. How are you? How's your trip? Did you get to San Diego okay? Weren't you supposed to call when you arrived?" Ariana asked.

"Sorry. I have a lot on my mind. We made it. The hotel is gorgeous, and I'm lounging in a jetted tub right now. How are you?"

"Dreaming I was lounging in a jetted tub, thank you very much. And like I said, Mariani is one of the Las Vegas family names."

"Like there's a family in Vegas with the last name of Mariani?"

"Not quite."

"What do you mean, not quite?" I asked.

"Look, Markie, I don't know much about the families. It's not like people hand out pamphlets on them or anything. Working at the restaurant, I've heard things. I don't know how much of it's true and how much is gossip."

"Okay." I leaned my head back and closed my eyes, giving the call my full attention. "Tell me what you've heard."

Over the next several minutes, my sister gave me a rundown on what she'd heard about a handful of powerful families who basically ran the city. When she was finished, I let it all sink in before asking, "And the Mariani family is one of *the* families?"

"Yes."

"Are they bad? I mean do they do illegal stuff?"

She hesitated. "I'm not sure. Nobody messes with them, though. Anyone associated with the family is… it's like they're protected. Almost like they're royalty. You think Angel and Bones are with the Mariani family?"

"That's what Bones told that kid outside of the Cajun restaurant. Didn't you hear him?"

"No. I was too busy freaking out about the possibility of my sister getting shot or stabbed. But if Bones said it, it's gotta be true. Nobody would be stupid enough to claim a family unless they were really in."

"You hear a lot, Ari."

"Yeah. I guess having parents who worked for the justice system affected me too. Damn it."

I laughed. "I feel your pain, sis. Why do you think I can't just sit back and enjoy this tub?"

Ariana sighed. "You know, there are a lot of douche bags in Vegas. Trust me on this one. Working at the restaurant, I've met several."

I resisted the urge to remind her that she'd been dating the biggest one of them all.

"But Angel and Bones are different."

"You said they were dangerous," I reminded her.

My phone buzzed with an incoming call from Angel but I sent it to voice mail.

"Yeah, but not to you. Have you seen the way Angel looks at you? Like you're some sort of goddess or something. It makes me want to hurl."

I giggled. "Why, thank you."

"Seriously, though, why can't you enjoy the weekend and let him worship you? Why do you have to over think everything? What does your gut tell you about the guy?"

My gut kept reminding me that Angel had saved Ariana's life, rescued me from possible jail time, put Max up for a night at a motel, and played basketball with Myles and his crew. All of those memories made my eyes sting and my chest swell.

Fighting the feeling, I replied, "He tried to pay for my hotel room."

Ariana gasped. "That asshole!"

I laughed. "Yeah, yeah, I see your point."

"Markie, you aren't afraid of anything. You're afraid of this guy because you like him and it's—"

"And it's complicated."

"Everything's complicated. Stop trying to simplify it and just relax and enjoy yourself for one weekend."

Sometimes my little sister could be very wise. Annoyingly so. I promised to take her advice to relax, hung up, and started making plans. I opened my phone's browser and searched for local restaurants and events. An ad for an authentic Mexican restaurant with a live mariachi band and dance floor caught my attention. They didn't take reservations, but I bookmarked the website and climbed out of the tub to get ready.

I still had my bathrobe on when a loud knock sounded on my door. Angel's face greeted me through the peephole, so I cracked the door and smiled at him. Then I caught a whiff of the roses and pointed at them. "Can you please move those?" Another sneeze. "They're beautiful." Sneeze. "And thank you for them." Sneeze. "But I'm allergic."

He was breathing heavily, like he'd sprinted up the stairs. He looked from me to the flowers and his features tightened. I'd discarded his gift and made him angry.

"Sorry. They really are pretty. I love them, I just can't—" Another sneeze.

"No." Angel shook his head. "It's not that. It's… I didn't send you flowers." He picked up the vase, ran it down the hall and gently set it in the garbage can by the elevator. When he returned, his forehead was creased with lines of worry.

"If they weren't from you, they're probably from the hotel." There was no reason anyone else would be sending me flowers. Another sneeze. He seemed so upset, I tried to reassure him. "It's really nice of them."

He didn't look convinced.

"Okay, well I'm gonna finish getting ready for dinner. Oh, and Angel, don't make any plans. I've got tonight, okay?"

His brows scrunched together. "You've got tonight?"

"Yeah, I've planned out the whole thing. I'm taking you and Bones to dinner, and you're going to love it."

"Where?" He didn't look like he liked the idea even a little bit.

Another sneeze. Desperate to get away from the lingering allergens, I motioned him into the room and grabbed my phone. Then I pulled up the browser and handed it to him.

He frowned at the screen. "A Mexican restaurant?"

"Yes. Well, dinner and dancing." I knew he liked to dance, so I thought he'd be happy. His expression told me otherwise. "What's wrong? If you don't like Mexican food, I can find something else."

"No, no, Mexican's good. Nice picture," he said, handing me back my phone.

I glanced at my screen. African children smiled back at me. "Thanks. I keep it as the background to help me remember my time there."

His shoulders relaxed a little. "You have any more photos from your trip? I'd like to see them sometime."

"I'd like that, too. Unfortunately my camera was stolen somewhere along the flight. It was tucked away in my checked bag, but by the time I unpacked at Ariana's, it was gone."

"You lost all of them? Do you have any more phone pictures?"

"No. I had a great camera. I used it for everything." Now it was my turn to frown. Wondering why it felt like he was pumping me for information, I asked, "Is everything all right?"

Before he could answer, his cell phone rang. He turned away from me and spoke into it.

"Yeah, she's here. Okay. Be right there."

"Angel, what's wrong?" I asked.

He waved me off with a hand. "Just work stuff. Don't worry about it. I need to help Bones out with something. Get dressed. I'll be back in a while and we'll go. Okay?" He walked out the door without waiting for my response.

Sure. Now that I was ready to let loose and have fun, Angel was brooding and weird. Just my luck. Feeling baffled and more than a little irritated by his odd behavior, I sat on the sofa and turned on my phone. Then I clicked open the browser to see if something about the restaurant had set him off. My search on the Mariani family came up. He must have hit the back arrow and saw it. Now he knew I was checking into him.

But why would that irritate him?

No, it had to be more than that. But since I had no answers, I did the only thing I could do and got dressed.

CHAPTER NINETEEN
Angel

BY THE TIME I returned to the suite I shared with Bones, the blond-haired, blue-eyed, two-hundred-and-fifty-pound weight lifter Bones had hired to keep an eye on Markie was coming to. He sat slouched on the sofa, holding an ice pack to his head.

Bones stood against the wall, his arms folded across his chest. "Angel, this is Jamie Matthews."

I extended my hand to the blond. "Thanks for taking this on last minute. Sorry about the head, man. What happened?"

"Bones here sent me a picture of the girl you wanted me to watch. When I got here, I saw her in the lobby having it out with the girl at the front desk."

"Markie?" I asked, certain I'd misunderstood. "What do you mean by 'having it out'?"

"She was trying to get her room charged to her card. The manager showed up and that chick threatened to pack up and leave if they didn't reverse the charges and put them on her card. Never seen someone so insistent on paying for their room."

I shook my head. "Well, that explains the calls from the hotel. What happened after that?"

"I followed her back to her room. She didn't see me, but she did seem spooked so I stayed back. I watched her walk into her room, and that's the last thing I remember. Woke up with Bones shaking me and a hell of a goose egg."

My mind clung to the one hopeful phrase he'd muttered.

"You're one hundred percent sure Markie didn't knock you out?" I asked for clarification.

"Couldn't have been the girl. I saw her walk into her room. Unless she has super speed, she was in her room when I got hit," Jamie insisted.

"Yeah, but it could be someone working with her," Bones said. "It all feels a little too convenient."

I paced the small space between sofa and kitchenette, sifting through the facts. It was too convenient, only it wasn't. I was the one who approached Markie at the restaurant the first time we met. Someone would have had to place her at the restaurant, and then at Matt's, and then outside of the Stratosphere. The locations were random, not exactly places I visited on any particular schedule. Only a handful of people knew about them, and Bones had dragged me to Matt's in a last-minute decision to bust the guy's face in. Nobody could have known we'd see Matt at the club and go there.

And the roses.

I called the hotel front desk, but they assured me that no flowers had been delivered to Markie's room or any other room yet that day. Frustrated, I continued to pace. Why would Markie have roses—which she was clearly allergic to—delivered to her own hotel room? Nothing made sense.

Still, I couldn't pretend Markie looked squeaky clean. She'd been checking into my family on her phone! We had less than fifteen minutes before we were supposed to leave for dinner and I didn't know what to do. If Markie was dirty, and we went to the restaurant she'd selected, it could be a trap. If Markie was dirty and we called off the night and stayed in, she'd know her cover was blown.

And what if she is clean?

Truthfully, it was impossible for me to imagine Markie— homeless-feeding, orphan-serving, dimpled, sweet Markie—as dirty. I didn't even want to entertain the thought. But her story had holes in it.

Someone stole her camera? What's the chance?

Curious, I opened a browser on my phone and checked it out. Several sites warned of luggage theft, strongly suggesting that passengers carry on their valuables.

"What are you thinking, Angel?" Bones asked.

I pulled up the restaurant on my phone and passed it to Jamie.

"What do you know about this place?"

Jamie shrugged. "Not much. It's legit. Family owned. None of the locals have sunk their teeth into it yet."

I handed my phone to Bones. "Markie wants to take us there."

Bones didn't even look at the phone. "No. Absolutely not."

I ignored him. "You have friends in the business, Jamie? Enough to cover this place?"

"Yeah. If I remember right, there's three doors. We could watch it with six men. Two at each."

"Angel," Bones scowled, gesturing toward the closest room.

I excused us and we left Jamie sitting on the sofa so we could talk in private. Bones ranted and raved about what a horrible idea this was, and I stood and listened. Once he finally ran out of steam, I jumped in.

"Do you really think Markie's dirty?" I asked.

His brow furrowed. "She could be."

Bones was hands down the best judge of character I had ever met. Over the years, I'd seen him make hundreds of judgment calls—who to trust, who to watch, who to avoid—and never once had he been wrong. So I pushed him into giving me his opinion.

"Yeah, but do *you* think she's dirty."

"Angel, if I'm wrong—"

"Answer the question."

His scowl told me he knew what I was doing and didn't appreciate it. But I only had to suffer through his glare for a handful of minutes before he finally conceded, shaking his head. "No."

It was all I needed to hear. I set up security for the restaurant with Jamie and sent Bones down to scan the Hummer while I went to collect Markie, feeling much more hopeful about the situation and determined to have a little fun.

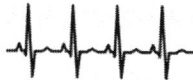

We stepped through the swinging double doors of the restaurant and over the Mexican border, landing somewhere south of Tijuana. Heady spices tickled my nostrils as an authentically dressed door-man, sporting a sombrero and all, greeted us. A lively mariachi band played in the left corner, next to a busy dance floor. To the right, families crowded around brightly-painted wooden tables sharing platters piled high with food.

Despite his foul mood, Bones's stomach growled.

Markie's smile stretched across her face. "This is perfect! Better than I'd imagined." She grabbed Bones and me by our sleeves and towed us toward the hostess stand. We were shown to a booth not far from the band. Markie and I ordered margaritas while Bones asked for water and soda.

Atmosphere lively and energetic, food smells intoxicating, it wasn't long before Bones eased up and helped us pick out dishes to share family-style. Then Markie tugged on my hand and asked me to dance. Bones nodded. His hand stayed wrapped around the gun in his pocket. My friend was neither relaxed nor calm, but at least he wasn't turning green and flexing through his clothes.

Mariachi music wasn't exactly a genre my dance classes had covered, but I followed Markie onto the floor anyway. The two of us stood back and watched dancers for a half song before she dragged me in to try it. There were lots of spins and kicks, a few claps and sidesteps, and we struggled to follow the flow. There was one move—a half-spin step—that Markie couldn't quite master. Every time we tried it, she mis-stepped, tripped, and then threw her head back, laughing. Her whimsical laughter was infectious and before I knew it, the tension in my back was gone. Face glowing, breathing heavily, blonde curls framing her dimples, Markie was hot in more ways than her temperature. It took everything I had to focus on the dance steps. By the time Bones waved us over to eat, both my body and my breathing were responding to her.

"So much fun! You wanna dance after we eat, Bones?" Markie asked, sliding into the booth.

He chuckled, shaking his head. "Thanks anyway, but I'm not much of a dancer. It was fun to watch you two, though. Been a while since I've seen Angel enjoy himself like that."

Bones nodded at me, and I could see all he wasn't saying. Although my friend was apprehensive about Markie, he wanted this for me as much as I did. Regardless, we both knew it wouldn't last. It couldn't. But for now, I'd enjoy the moment and to hell with the consequences.

"After we eat I want another shot at that spin-kick move," I told Markie.

She laughed. "Deal!"

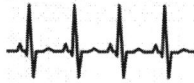

By the time we returned to the hotel, the sun had gone down and a cool breeze had picked up. Bones, Markie, and I grabbed our jackets and flip flops and headed to the beach. Bones followed closely as I strolled beside Markie, thinking about the day's events. Dinner had gone off without a hitch, and Jamie's team saw nothing to alarm them. Still, the tracker on the Hummer and Jamie's attack kept bugging me. I couldn't help but feel like I'd missed something.

Markie stopped, picked something up, brushed it off on her dress, and then offered it to me. "A sand dollar for your thoughts?" she asked.

I accepted the little white disk, turning it over in my hands as we resumed our walk.

"Either you don't know how this works, or you must think your thoughts are worth more than a sand dollar?"

"Hmm?" I asked.

She giggled. "Here's the deal. I give you something and in exchange, you tell me what's on your mind. You're not holding up your end of the bargain."

I inclined my head. "Oh, sorry, I was just relaxing and enjoying the evening."

Even in the dark I couldn't miss her look of disbelief. "Did you just lie to me?" she asked.

"Excuse me?"

"Nothing about you is relaxed, Angel."

"What are you talking about? I'm the poster boy for relaxation."

The musical notes of her laugher floated through the night. I savored each tone like they were my favorite treats.

My phone buzzed with an incoming message. Bones, standing less than five feet away from me, texted me to tell me he was going to sit on the boat dock we'd just passed, where he could keep an eye on us. My friend was giving us privacy. Or getting a better look at the surrounding area. I couldn't decide which.

"You guys are always together, aren't you?" Markie asked when Bones was out of earshot.

Another question I needed to skirt around. "I do a lot of technical design, and these designs would be... inconvenient in the wrong hands. Bones is my bodyguard, and his job is to make sure that doesn't happen."

It wasn't the full truth, but it was close. I'd danced this dance my whole life. The steps were all about containing enough truth within the lie.

Markie looked toward the dock. "Your bodyguard? You seem so close, though."

"We are. We've been friends since grade school."

"Wow. That's really great," Markie replied.

Waves rolled in and out, drowning out the sounds of the city. She turned and walked just to the water line, staring out to sea. We stood in silence as the water tickled her sandaled toes, and the wind whipped her hair around her in a blonde halo. She looked almost ethereal, bathing in the moonlight by the ocean. It took my breath away.

"It's so incredible," Markie whispered.

"Yeah it is," I replied, meaning so much more than the scenery and feeling like a giant loser for thinking it.

She stood for a few moments before plucking a piece of driftwood from a wave. Then she took a few steps away from the water and bent, using the driftwood to write in the sand. The tide was coming in, and as she wrote, the waves rolled closer until they finally erased her work. She took another step inland and wrote again.

When curiosity finally got the better of me, I asked, "What are you writing?"

She finished off the word she was working on and stood. "Mistakes, regrets, anything holding me down."

I don't know what I'd been expecting, but that definitely wasn't it. "Why?"

The gentle rise and fall of her shoulders answered me. "It feels like confession. Like getting rid of all the junk holding me down. Seemed like a good idea to write it all down and let the waves take it away." She offered me the stick. "It's very freeing. Would you like to try it?"

I shook my head, unable to speak. She was such a beautiful person, and so different than anyone I'd ever met.

"No biggie. You should give it a shot someday, though." She tossed the stick into the waves and sucked in another deep breath.

"Better. Want to dance again?"

Actually, I did. One problem, though. "No music."

"It's okay if you don't want to," she hurried to say.

"No, I do." I grabbed her hand and pulled her closer to me. "I really do. I just... are we talking slow dance to the sound of the waves?"

She tilted her head at me.

I chuckled. "Wow, again with the corny line. What about you makes me talk like I'm trapped in some cheesy chick-flick?"

Markie laughed. "I don't know, but I apparently make you forget you're supposed to be some sort of tech-loving geek, too." She pulled her phone out of her jacket pocket. Moonlight glinted off its face as she waved it from side to side.

I did a face palm. "You're really showing me up here."

Markie thumbed her phone on and within a few seconds "Earth Angel" blared through the surprisingly loud speakers. "That's okay. Good songs can solve all problems," she announced.

The fact she'd chosen one of my favorites made me want to hug her and bury my face in her hair. "True," I acknowledged, knowing my biggest problem kept growing.

She slid the phone back into her jacket pocket, muffling the sound as she positioned her hands on my shoulders. I pulled her against me and settled mine on her waist. We swayed slowly to the music as the notes fought to be heard over the sounds of the surf. Halfway through the song, Markie lowered her head to my shoulder. Our bodies moved in sync, melding into one. Every inch of me was alert and aware of how close she was, wanting her even closer.

The song ended and another began, another of my favorite tunes from the drive. A smile tugged at my lips as the thought warmed me from the inside out. I closed my eyes and held her close, afraid the darkening night would somehow extinguish my beautiful ray of sunshine.

My phone buzzed with an incoming text. I glanced at my cell long enough to see the message. "Pelino planted the tracker. Proceed with caution. - Tech."

A chill ran down my spine. Why the hell would the Pelinos be tracking me? Of all my father's men, I was probably the least interesting. They had to have put it on in Vegas. Or maybe they followed us to the diner and put it on there. Either way, my father's enemies were keeping tabs on me, and that didn't exactly give me warm fuzzies.

Bones jumped from the dock and started walking toward us.

"What's wrong?" Markie asked.

I slid the phone back into my pocket. "Bones wants us to move back to the hotel. We're out past bedtime and I'm sure he thinks I'm going to turn into a pumpkin or something."

"A pumpkin, huh?"

Markie was shivering, so I took off my jacket and put it over her own. Bones was almost upon us, and motioning for us to hurry. I grabbed Markie's hand and we picked up the pace. Once we reached the hotel, Bones asked Markie if he could check her room. She seemed startled by the question, but didn't object. She opened the door and waited for him to go in and invade her privacy. She even closed the door behind him, leaving the two of us waiting in the hall.

"What's going on?" she asked.

Now that she knew Bones was my bodyguard, I could use her knowledge to bend the truth a little. I waved off her question. "Bones is paid to be paranoid. He runs a lot of drills, acting like we're in danger or something to keep himself sharp."

"Sounds like he's good at his job," Markie said.

I shrugged. "Yeah. Sometimes a little too good."

Bones opened the door, announcing that the room was free of threats before heading next door to check out ours. I knew I only had a few precious moments before he reappeared and dragged me out of the exposed hallway. Desperate to make those moments count, I stepped closer to Markie.

She leaned against her door, hair wind tousled and face flushed. I leaned in and wiped a streak of smudged makeup from her cheek. Her eyes widened at the contact, and I wondered if she felt even a smidgen of the electricity bouncing between us.

"You had something on your face," I explained.

"Oh, thanks."

Was that disappointment? Did she want me to touch her?

Her cheeks reddened. "So, tomorrow…"

I cut her off with a wave of my hand. "Nope. You planned tonight. I have tomorrow handled."

"You do?" Her eyes lit up. "What's on the agenda?"

"It's a secret, but I think you'll dig it."

"A secret, huh?" Her smile widened, and she pulled away from the door. "Not even going to give me a hint, are you?"

An answering smile tugged at my lips. "Nope. But I will thank you for a lovely evening. Great pick on that Mexican restaurant."

"Major score. And those margaritas: perfection." She kissed the tips of her closed fingers, and then spread them out as she pulled her hand away.

As her hand fell back to her side, my attention lingered on her perfectly shaped lips. I wondered what it would be like to feel them against my own. My gaze drifted down her neck. She noticed me looking and took off my jacket, offering it back to me.

"Thank you for this," she said before turning to leave.

I grabbed the door handle, stopping her. She leaned into my arm, her gaze traveling to my face. Then she licked her lips. It was the only signal I needed. I put my hands on the door, on either side of her face, and leaned in. Our lips touched. My tongue tasted tropical lip gloss and lime. Her hands traveled up my arms and then gripped my biceps, pulling me closer. She opened her lips to me and I explored her mouth. She tasted beautiful. Magical. My senses came to life, touching, tasting, smelling. I breathed her in, and every inch of my body responded. I wanted to hold her, to caress her, but I kept my hands where they were. Markie needed to control the situation.

And, she did. Suddenly her body bucked forward, shoving me away. She pushed open the door and leaped backwards, over the threshold of the room. She stared at me, cheeks pink and lips swollen, a combination of desire, fear, and regret spinning in her bright blue eyes. She took another step back and lowered her head.

"Sorry, Angel, I can't," she whispered, her voice husky.

Can't what? Can't kiss me? Can't be with me? Can't let me in?

"I gotta go. I'll see you in the morning, okay?" she asked.

Before I could answer, she closed the door.

CHAPTER TWENTY
Angel

AFTER LAST NIGHT'S cold-shower-worthy exchange, I was worried about how the day would go. Regardless of my concerns, Markie answered her door wearing a sundress and a smile. She welcomed me in as her gaze drifted over the long-sleeved gray T-shirt, blue jeans, and sneakers I wore, my jacket draped over my arm.

Her attention shifted back up to my face and she said, "All right, buck-o. I know you're being super secretive about today's plans, but I've got to know what to wear."

"Buck-o, huh?"

"Yep. Now spill. Where are we going?"

I gave her my best poker face and leaned against the back of the sofa. "Yeah, I'm not telling you that. I can, however, suggest you change into jeans. Maybe grab a jacket. Also, bring your swimsuit."

"Okay, I'll change, but I'm planning on bringing all of my clothes. I just called down and checked out of the room. We're going back to Vegas tonight, right?"

It wasn't like I expected her to want to stay with me at the coast forever, but did she have to sound so ready to go home?

"Right. Bones and I got a late checkout, so we can stash your stuff in our room until after we're done adventuring." And with any luck, we'd stay another night. After all, Father's associates had until this afternoon to make their decision, and the old man hadn't ordered me home yet.

Markie slipped into the bedroom to change, leaving me alone and too curious for my own damn good. I pulled the device finder from my jacket pocket and scanned Markie's suite. Cell phone, hotel phone, laptop. Nothing nefarious or unexpected. Relieved, I breathed deeply and slid the finder back into my pocket.

When Markie emerged from her room, she wore jeans and a blue and white three-quarter sleeve baseball T-shirt that hugged her curves in all the right places. A small bag hung from her shoulder, and she wheeled her suitcase while carrying her sneakers and socks. "Is this okay?" she asked.

I somehow managed not to throw myself at her feet and instead nodded. "Perfect."

She released the suitcase handle, dropped the bag, and sat on the sofa to pull on her socks and shoes. "Where's Bones?" she asked.

Bones and I scanned the Hummer earlier. It was free of all bugs and tracking devices, but he stayed behind to make sure the vehicle remained that way. "He's waiting in the Hummer. Here, let me grab that."

I wheeled her suitcase into my room. When I headed out the door, she grabbed my hand, stopping me.

"Angel, can we talk for a second?"

My stomach sank. We'd shared something special last night, and I was hoping she wasn't about to reveal feelings of regret or guilt. "Yeah. What's up?"

"I… I need something from you."

Why was she stalling? What did she need? And why the hell was I so nervous about it? I nodded, encouraging her to continue.

"I need coffee. Desperately. Must have caffeine. I lived without it in Africa and I have no intention of going without while I'm in the states. I hope this day you've got planned out allows for that. Please?"

Coffee?

She wasn't going to ask me to back off. Releasing a breath I didn't realize I'd been holding, I chuckled. It sounded nervous and maybe a little manic. "Of course. There's a coffee shop next door, and we can hit that first."

I texted Bones to get his coffee order as we waited in line. Then Markie and I stood in silence as last night's events worried my brain. What had she thought? Was she at all interested in me? What couldn't she do? Did she think I was pressing her for sex?

Finally, I couldn't take it anymore. "About last night—" I started.

"It was fun." She dimpled. "The dancing, the margaritas, the beach, perfect night. I wouldn't change a thing."

She leaned into me, saying so much. Desperate to keep contact with her, I laced my fingers in hers. She didn't pull away, and I was ridiculously happy we were holding hands like a couple of kids.

We joined Bones at the Hummer, ordered breakfast from a drive-thru, and headed out. Bones sipped his coffee from the backseat, positioning himself to watch for a tail. Markie didn't seem to notice, because she was too busy trying to guess where we were going. By the time we turned into the safari parking lot, I thought she was going to burst with excitement.

"You didn't get too much of this in Africa, did you?" I asked.

"Although the kids could sometimes be little beasts, I never actually went on a safari."

The closest Bones and I had gotten was a show at the MGM Grand. Wanting to get the most out of the experience, I'd purchased a customized VIP package. We were ushered inside to a box truck, customized to look like a safari caravan with a gate around the back and a canopy over the top. We climbed in and the driver welcomed us through speakers mounted on the back of the truck's cab as the vehicle lurched forward.

Markie was like a child—eyes full of awe and wonder, perma-grin stretched across her face—as we started along the path. We stopped for crossing rhinos, fed giraffes, chatted with gorillas, lazed around with the lions, held a lemur, petted elephants, and then walked through a butterfly world. Throughout it all, Markie beamed, excited by each experience.

"So it wasn't like this in Africa?" Bones asked Markie as we trekked through the tropical butterfly world.

"I don't think you understand what I did in Africa," she shot back.

Bones spread his hands out. "Enlighten me."

"Well, I went to work. To help. Not to sightsee."

"None? At all?" Bones scoffed.

Markie stopped and turned to face him, crossing her arms.

"Look, I don't know how much you know about African current events, but there's not a lot of safe areas down there right now. Boko Haram has—"

"Boko Haram?" Bones interrupted.

"The militant Islamic group that keeps beheading people down there," I supplied. Then I smiled at Markie and added, "Bones watches the races. I watch the news."

Markie nodded, ever patient. "Yeah, they're scary dudes. Even though the villagers are great and extremely hospitable, they're terrified of Boko Haram. If I wanted to be a horrible person, I could have asked, and any one of the locals would have taken me sightseeing. But they would have been risking their lives. And so would I. I can't even begin to tell you what the Boko Haram would have done to me—a single white woman—if they'd seen me. I saw bodies and heard stories, and they were enough to keep me from leaving that orphanage. You understand?"

Bones nodded. "Wow. I didn't know things were that bad over there."

Markie shrugged. "There was a lot of good, too. Now if you're done with this weird line of questioning, I want to go hold a python."

I'd never seen Bones so thoroughly shut down. I expected him to get angry or ask something else, but he backed off with a shrug and a measure of respect in his gaze.

After the snakes, we watched cheetah races, and then were herded to the high ropes course. Bones took one look at the wooden ladders going up the trees and shook his head.

"Nope. Not for me. I'll wait right here for you two." He leaned against a tree, pulled out his phone, and began scrolling.

"You sure?" Markie asked.

"Oh yeah. No way in hell those flimsy little boards are gonna hold all this sexiness."

Markie giggled, shaking her head. "Well, I'm going. Are you in or out, Angel?" She was staring up at the course, bouncing on her heels, no doubt excited as all hell at another chance to defy death.

"I'm in," I blurted out before I could change my mind. Then I followed Markie over to get harnessed up. I'd never been on a high ropes course, but it didn't look too bad in the video. Turns out, it was much worse. We went up a sketchy wooden ladder and then walked across a bridge that looked like it should have been in an Indiana Jones flick. We climbed another ladder until the ground was a long way down.

"You okay?" Markie asked.

I wiped the sweat from my forehead. "Yeah, no problem. No sweat. Heh."

Yep, that sounded stupid.

Markie gave me a courtesy laugh and then closed the distance between us. "We can go back down if you need to."

Her eyes were sincere and concerned and there was no way in hell I was backing out of this and making myself out to be a coward. Still, I appreciated her concern. "Thanks, but I'm okay. I just need a second."

She dimpled at me. For that smile, I would follow her across a million rickety bridges and probably end up in a wheelchair for my trouble. I swallowed back my fear, pulled my attention from the ground, and followed her over a wide log, holding on to the rope above our heads for dear life. The log lurched forward, and I decided Bones probably had the right idea by staying on the ground. Markie turned and smiled at me, and I'm fairly certain I grimaced back. We reached the platform, and I was rewarded by her sharing it with me as we huddled together to catch our breath.

Her eyes were bright and excited. "That one was intense," she said.

I nodded. Sure, I wore a harness connected to the line above us that would keep me from falling to my death, but I could have slipped and severely racked myself on the log bridge. And racking my nuts would have been much worse than death.

She leaned into me. I think she was preparing to step around, but I grabbed her waist. She froze and our gazes locked. She arched an eyebrow. It felt like a challenge, and I answered it. I bent my head and pressed my lips against hers. The act was insane. We stood on a four-foot-by-two-foot wooden platform, well above ground level. If we lost our balance, we'd fall until our safety line caught us, which I was guessing wouldn't be pleasant. But, to be honest, tumbling from that landing was the least dangerous outcome of us making out. Still, I did it. Once again, sparks ignited. Her hands felt hot on my back. My fingers hooked two of her belt loops, keeping her close to me.

Markie broke off the kiss, but then she leaned her head against my chest, holding me. Thankful she didn't pull away, I wrapped my arms around her and rested my chin on her head. We stood there for a few minutes as air currents tousled her hair. At the top of the trees with nobody around, we connected on a level I couldn't explain, without words, promises, or sex. Yet it was the strongest connection I'd ever felt in my life. Then, Markie moved. She edged around me and continued on the route, leaving me no option but to follow her.

♠ ♥ ♣ ♦

CHAPTER TWENTY-ONE
Markie

I NEVER APPRECIATED my parents until I lost them. It was only after they could no longer hug me, give me advice, or tell me how proud of me they were that I realized the value of the moments we'd shared. But by then, it was too late. Those times could never be reproduced. So, desperate to feel something again, I had started doing whatever made my adrenaline rush. It wasn't the same, but at least I felt something. But that all changed at the top of the high ropes course.

He did this for me.

Understanding slammed into me while we were on top of the world together. I was thrilled, but he was a nervous wreck. Heights were clearly not his thing, yet he selflessly shared the experience with me. No, more than that, he'd organized the experience for me, knowing I'd love it. When he kissed me on the high ropes course, he stirred emotions I never thought I'd have again. And now, this handsome, considerate man was leading me toward a zip-line. My heart swelled at the thought.

"You sure you want to do this?" I asked, squeezing Angel's hand.

"Yeah, why wouldn't I?" he asked.

We stepped onto the platform and I swear I could hear Angel's heart speed up.

"What about you, Bones? Aren't you afraid of heights?" I asked.

Bones bristled, looking very offended. "I'm not afraid of heights. My fear is of flimsy little wooden bridges. But this… this is safe." He sat and got strapped in. Then he bounced up and down to prove how secure it was.

Angel wasn't looking at Bones. Or the ground. Or anything else. His eyes were closed as a safari associate secured him into his seat.

I felt bad for him, but wasn't about to step on his ego and tell him he didn't have to do this. It was his idea. Again, for me, because he knew I'd love it. Instead of worrying about him, I strapped in and prepared to fully enjoy the experience. The safari associate released us, and wind rushed at my face like I was flying. I laughed and slowed my speed, determined to savor every second.

Angel still had his eyes squeezed shut. I called his name and held out my hand. He took it. Then he looked down and turned a little green.

"Don't do that," I said. "Look at me."

He gave me a grateful smile that melted my heart. I squeezed his hand. "See, it's not so bad."

"Right." He chuckled. "Why the hell would anyone *want* to do this?"

My chest tightened. I wasn't ready to share my reasons for wanting to jump from high places and soar through the air with him yet. I could share the outcome though. "Because it makes me feel alive!"

And zip-lining over the safari made me feel like I was part of something so much bigger than myself. Below my feet wildcats roared, zebras raced, and hippos bathed while we flew over them, hand-in-hand. It was a unique and strangely romantic experience, and I didn't want it to end. All too soon the park was in our rear-view mirror though.

"You are planning to feed us, right?" Bones asked when Angel started up the car.

Angel chuckled. "It's barely past noon. Don't act like I'm starving you."

Despite their banter, our next stop was at a nice seafood restaurant right on the beach where Bones drilled me for more information on Africa while we waited for our lunch.

"Tell me about the kids. What was the orphanage like?" he asked.

I fidgeted with my silverware, struggling to find the words to describe the people I missed the most. "The kids were incredible. They were just so... so..."

"Underprivileged?" Bones asked.

I shook my head. He didn't get it.

"Needy?" Angel asked.

He didn't get it either. And the words they'd chosen couldn't have been further from the truth. "No. They weren't like that at all. More like the complete opposite. The kids had virtually nothing, but they were content with their lives and the things they did have. They were... different than the kids here. They were more compassionate and giving. I mean, these kids were ridiculous. They shared everything. Gladly."

My eyes burned. I squeezed them shut and remembered each of the eight kids. Names, personalities, the sound of their laughter, the way they looked when I said good-bye. I blinked back tears and tried again. "They weren't materialistic. It was like they didn't know, or even care, about all the crap they didn't have. They didn't cling to stuff the way we do. The missionaries would give them gifts, but then they'd turn and share those gifts with their friends. They didn't hoard things to themselves, like you'd think people in need would. They saw value in each other, not in objects, and it gave them so much joy to make someone else happy."

"The kids in the picture looked happy," Angel said.

"What picture?" Bones asked.

I turned on my phone and handed it to him so he could see the background photo. It wasn't my picture, but it was all I had.

"Looks like a big age span," Bones observed.

I nodded. "Yeah, infant to early teens. The older kids took care of the younger ones, and they were protective and nurturing. Especially the boys. They wouldn't eat until the younger ones ate, and they wouldn't accept gifts until the younger ones got theirs. It was frustrating for me at first, but then I saw what they were doing and it... it wrecked me to see such selfless behavior. The whole experience blew my mind. The oldest boy in the orphanage was thirteen, but his instincts and his sacrificial love for the others... it was a beautiful thing."

I could feel Angel watching me. "Why did you leave?" he asked.

I'd wanted to stay. Those kids knew nothing of my life and the crap I was going through. When they looked at me, I'd felt beautiful and immortal. I wanted that. I missed it so much. And yet, I'd found it here. Angel looked at me the same way. It made butterflies dance in my stomach and it made me feel a little guilty. Even though I hadn't wanted this, I was strangely glad to be here.

"I had to. As much as I needed those kids, they didn't need me. I know it sounds weird, but they had everything they needed. But Ari... I knew Ari needed me."

"You knew what she was messed up in? With Matt?" Bones asked. He passed me back my phone.

"No. She didn't tell me anything. In fact, that's what did it. She stopped e-mailing and video chatting with me, so I knew something was up."

By the time our food came, I was beyond tired of talking about myself. Besides, the smell of *cioppino* made my mouth water. I tore off a hunk of fresh, warm bread and used it to sop up some of the stew. "Your turn. Tell me about yourselves. I want to know all about your families."

The two shared a look, and then Bones went first. "Just my mom and two brothers. Not much to tell," he said.

There had to be at least a little to tell, but I didn't press. Instead, I looked to Angel.

He swallowed a bite and said, "I have a big family. Dad, stepmom, three sisters, two brothers, Nonna, my grandmother, aunts and uncles, cousins. Loud, obnoxious bunch."

It sounded nice. Although he'd left one person out. "Your mom?"

"She died when I was young."

I reached across the table and squeezed his hand. "I'm sorry. How young were you?"

"Really little. Maybe four?"

"You don't remember?" I asked.

Something flashed across Angel's face. Was it fear? Anger? Frustration? I couldn't tell. Before I could get more out of him, his cell phone rang.

"Excuse me," he said, setting his napkin beside his dish. "I have to take this."

He left the table and headed toward the restrooms. Bones angled himself so he could watch Angel without turning his back on me. I felt the weight of Bones's gaze as I took another bite. I swallowed.

Wondering what the heck his problem was, I leveled a stare at him and said, "What?"

"Trying to figure you out," he replied.

That made two of us. Okay, I'd bite. "What do you think so far?" I asked.

He steepled his hands on the table in front of him and openly analyzed me. "Small town girl. Parents were probably preachers or in law enforcement before they passed on. Your sister rebelled but you... you were the good girl, huh? I bet you got good grades; probably even went to college trying to be just like the folks."

He'd pretty much hit the nail on the head, which was a bit unsettling. But it didn't exactly take a detective to figure these truths out about me. Unfortunately, he wasn't finished.

"But something about all this doesn't add up. You were on track, and then you veered off and went to Africa. Why?" he asked.

"Why not?" I asked with a shrug, trying to go for relaxed while my insides churned. Bones couldn't know. He'd tell Angel and then everything would change. And although that would probably be for the better, I was having the time of my life and wasn't ready for it to end.

Bones started to say something else, but before he could get the words out, Angel returned. The worried expression he wore got both of our attention.

"We're running out of time," Angel said, signaling for the check.

Too thankful for the interruption to ask what he meant, I excused myself and hit the restroom.

CHAPTER TWENTY-TWO
Angel

THE DEAL WAS off. I heard the words, even understood their meaning, but they didn't make sense. How could the deal be off? Had I done something wrong? Overlooked some important negotiation tactic? I replayed the meeting in my mind, assuring myself I'd done everything the old man had told me to do. Still, I'd been sent to purchase the product—product he already had a buyer for—and I'd failed.

"We were able to secure a better offer," the voice on the phone told me.

A better offer? What sort of idiot would bid against my father?

The tracker on my Hummer had belonged to the Pelino family. They had to be behind this, which meant heads were going to roll. "You're making a big mistake." I replied.

"We are aware our decision might strain our relationship with your family, but we are first and foremost businessmen. I'm certain your father will understand our position."

They sure as hell didn't know my old man. "If you say so."

"We do look forward to the prospect of dealing with your family on future ventures. Please give my regards to your father."

The call disconnected. I stared at my phone, knowing what my next move should be. The old man would want to know immediately. But the minute I reached out to him, he'd expect my ass back on the road, headed home. We couldn't leave yet. There was only one more stop on the agenda, and it wouldn't take too long.

I'd call Father as soon as we were finished. He'd never even know I'd held out.

With time pressing against me, I returned to the table. Markie went to the restroom, which gave me time to fill Bones in on the call.

"You need to call the boss," Bones informed me when I was finished.

"I will. We have just one more thing... won't even take long. Then I'll call him and we'll head out."

"Angel, I got a bad feeling about this. You should call him now."

"I know I should, but I need this. Just a couple more hours, and then we'll get back to reality." The thought of heading back to Las Vegas filled my stomach with lead. I didn't want to go back.

"Then what?" Bones asked. He glanced in the direction of the restrooms. "What happens with her?"

"I don't know. The plan was to let her go, but to be honest, I don't think I can."

"Well you better figure it out, because we both know the old man will lose his shit when he finds out some stranger came sniffing around and you let her in. Especially right now, with the families at each other's throats." He shook his head and handed me his phone. "That picture on her phone. It's the first one that pops up when you google "African children"."

It did look similar, but then again, most of the pictures on his screen did. "Maybe she uploaded it?" I suggested. "Probably put it on social media or something. Who knows?"

"She's hiding something," Bones insisted. "I don't know what it is, but you know the boss will find out."

We all had our secrets, and I'd be a fool to believe Markie was the exception. All along I'd been waiting for that too-sweet filling and soggy crust. "I know. Please, Bones, one last stop, then I promise I'll fill the old man in and we'll head back."

My friend looked as convicted as I felt, but he gave me a barely perceptible nod as Markie returned.

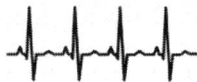

I parked the Hummer in the boat launch lot and herded Markie and Bones toward the restroom to change.

"What are we doing?" Bones asked as soon as we were alone.

"It's a cross between snorkeling and scuba diving. You only go about twenty feet down, so you don't need to take any classes first." I unzipped my bag and pulled out my trunks, stepping into a stall.

"Did you check out the instructors?" Bones asked.

"Yep, did my homework. It's a legitimate business." I'd also overheard a couple of distant relatives talking about the company at a Sunday dinner. "The family has used them before."

"You sure they're clean?" Bones asked, ever paranoid. "They could take us out to the middle of the ocean, pop us each in the back of the head, and we're sleepin' with the fishes. Literally."

I rolled my eyes. "That's actually figuratively. We'd literally be dead with the fishes, not sleeping."

"You know what I mean. Let's just hurry and get this over with so we can handle business."

There would be no hurrying and no getting anything over with. I intended to enjoy every last minute I got to spend with Markie. As if I needed more incentive, I stepped out of the restroom, and my breath was stolen by what I saw.

Growing up in Vegas, I'd been surrounded by beautiful women. What nature didn't perfect, doctors could, and the city fed almost as many plastic surgeons as it did casinos. Father had started taking me around town when I was seven. I'd danced with showgirls, flirted with bikini baristas, partied with pole dancers, and even dated strippers. My suits, made of the best Italian silk and tailored to fit me perfectly; my apartment, custom built with every luxury and overlooking the lights of the city; my car, designed to be the ultimate in safety and comfort… it was all shit compared to Markie. She wore a basic two-piece swimsuit—camouflage boy shorts and a black bikini top with matching camouflage lace—but it looked designed for her. Her suntanned skin complemented the print, and the innocent and conservative design managed to attract every atom in my body.

I gawked openly at her. She looked up and our eyes met. She chewed on her bottom lip, and her gaze held a note of uncertainty, making me want to reassure her. It loosened my lips and reminded me to breathe.

"Wow," I said, my voice sounding strange, matching the way I felt. "You look amazing."

"Thanks." She blushed and looked down, crossing her arms in front of her flat stomach. "You didn't specify which suit and I thought because we're at a boat launch that we'd probably be going for a ride and a chance for some sun."

Humble, rambling, gorgeous, I wondered if she had any idea what she was doing to my pulse. Certain she could hear my heart pounding, I fought the urge to scoop her in my arms and carry her off to a blanket on the sand. She would be my sun and I would soak up the rays of her presence. Stupid, crazy stanzas from long-dead poets churned in my mind, begging to be muttered. I swallowed them back before they burst through my mouth and made me sound like an idiot.

"Perfect suit," I replied, stepping past her on legs that felt strangely wobbly. "Bones, let's go see if they need help getting the boat in the water."

Bones followed, and I could feel his sideways glances. I wondered if he was looking at me, and seeing One Nut Brizio.

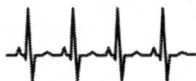

Two instructors, Tom and John, stood on the dock, waiting in front of their twenty-foot boat. A back compartment secured oxygen tanks and other equipment, and I knew as soon as Markie saw it, the jig would be up. And, it was. As we drew near the boat, she gasped behind me.

"We're going scuba diving?" she asked.

"Not quite. Scuba diving requires a class and a bunch more equipment. This is kind of a cross between snorkeling and scuba diving. It's safer and—"

"But we're going under the water to swim with the fish?" she asked.

It sounded immensely better than sleeping with the fishes, so I nodded. "Sure are."

She wrapped her arms around my neck and practically knocked me off my feet. I stumbled backward a few steps before catching my balance. Then I realized how much of her bare skin was touching mine. Before I could think too much about that, Markie released me and hugged Bones.

"We're going diving! Can you believe it? Have you ever been?"

Bones shrugged, cracking a smile. Even he couldn't resist Markie's contagious excitement. "Nope. Never been."

"Why aren't you as stoked as I am? This is amazing!" Then she turned her attention on the two men standing in front of the boat, offering them her hand. "Hello, I'm Markie."

They introduced themselves while Bones dropped a few names and a thinly veiled threat that if we didn't come back safe and sound, people would come looking for us. The confused instructors nodded and assured Bones they took dozens of divers out every week, all of whom returned unharmed. Then they handed us wet-suits, which we struggled into before climbing aboard. John pushed off the dock and we drifted for a few seconds before the engine purred to life. Bones and I sat in the center bench seat with Markie between us. She leaned her head against the back of the seat and closed her eyes. The engine revved and the boat picked up speed. A smile spread across her face, and her hair whipped back in the wind. She laughed.

"What's so funny?" I yelled over the sound of the motor.

"The salty air. It feels like a million angel kisses on my face. I love it!"

I couldn't help but smile as I watched her. She squeezed my hand but didn't open her eyes. The boat slowed and came to a stop beside a marker in the water. Tom killed the engine and John stood.

John gave us a quick lesson on the equipment, and then John, Bones, Markie, and I splashed into the water. We followed John down to a world of kelp and coral, surrounded by brightly colored fish, where neither my father nor the Pelinos mattered. Markie's eyes were bright and big in her mask as she reached out to touch a passing fish. Sea lions appeared. One nipped at the tip of Markie's flipper before swimming away. She pointed to it and gave me a dramatic thumbs up.

Even Bones had a good time. Head on a swivel, he looked determined to see everything. We watched fish and sea lions for a while and even managed to see a couple of rays before John motioned for us to head up. By the time I breached the surface, Bones was already climbing back into the boat. The sun was still high over the city, its reflection dancing across the waves.

I waited for Markie and John to pop up, but they didn't. Bones had removed his mask and was scanning the water from the boat. Worried something had happened, I dove back down to search for them. Finally, I spotted John holding Markie by the arm and slowly bringing her to the surface. Markie had both hands on her head. My heart lurched in my chest as they drew closer.

As soon as we surfaced I pulled the regulator out of my mouth and asked what happened.

Markie freed her mouth and said, "Headache."

John and I helped her into the back of the boat. Then she leaned over the side of the boat and got sick. Multiple times. I didn't know if I should look away and give her privacy or hold her hair. In the end, I patted her back.

When she was done, Markie apologized and slid down to the seat, hands still on her head. Her face was pale. Eerily pale.

"Nothing to be sorry about. What's going on? Are you okay?"

"Yeah. Just a migraine. I get them, sometimes. Will you please hand me my purse?" She pointed in the direction of her bag.

I passed it to her and she reached in and pulled out a prescription pill bottle. She popped a pill into her mouth and Tom handed her a bottle of water and Bones offered her a mint.

She accepted both before leaning against me and closing her eyes. "It's not a big deal. It will pass soon. I just need a minute. The change of pressure must have just been too much."

Bones and John shed their gear and wet suits, while I draped my arm over Markie's shoulders and pulled her closer. Tom started up the boat and took us back to shore. I could tell he was trying to be careful, but every time the boat hit a wave, Markie tensed.

Markie and I climbed into the backseat of the Hummer, and Bones got behind the wheel. We were almost to the hotel when my phone buzzed. Father was calling to find out about the deal.

With Markie leaning against me, and my decision to wait to call him weighing on my mind, I felt like I was navigating through a minefield. I needed to tread carefully. "I was just opening my phone to call you," I told the old man. "Deal's off. They got a better offer."

"A better offer?" Father swore. "The Pelinos?"

"He didn't say, but after what we found on my car..."

"I trust that you and Bones are on your way home?" Father

asked.

"Almost. We're stopping by the hotel to grab our stuff. We'll be on the road in ten, maybe fifteen minutes max."

"Adamo's a weasel. This was a bold move for him. He must be ready to show his cards. I don't know what they're up to, but I want you here when it goes down. Hurry up and get back." He disconnected the call.

I pocketed my phone and squeezed Markie a little closer, knowing our precious moments together were slipping away.

CHAPTER TWENTY-THREE
Angel

WE MADE IT back to the suite. Since Markie was already ready to go, she lay on the sofa with a pillow over her head while Bones and I packed our things. My phone rang again, this time with an unknown number. I closed the door to my room and turned on the television before answering.

"Hey, Angel. This is Bruno."

Bruno was the eldest son of Adamo, my father's sworn enemy and the boss of the Pelino family. We'd never exchanged phone numbers. In fact, I could have happily gone through life without ever hearing his voice. If Bruno was reaching out to me, shit was about to get serious.

"How'd you get my number?" I asked. I'd gone through a lot of work to make sure the only people who called me were those I wanted to hear from.

Bruno snickered. "We got a new tech guy. Might even be better than you."

It was a compliment, kind of. "What do you want?" I asked.

"You enjoying your little vacay with that pretty little blonde?" Bruno asked.

Of course he knew about Markie, because my day needed one more issue. "She's a nice girl, but just a friend. An innocent."

"Oh? Did she like my present?"

It took my brain a second to figure out what the hell he was talking about. The roses. They had to be from Bruno. The bastard had someone break into her room to leave her flowers. A warning. My blood ran cold at the thought.

"I left her alive and untouched, Angel. Remember that."

I had no reply, so I glanced at my phone. The built-in tracer was already busy tracking Bruno's location. I needed to keep him talking, but preferably not about Markie. Not unless I wanted to stroke out right there in the hotel room. "All right, Bruno, cut the bullshit and tell me why you're following me."

He chuckled again. "Following you? That's a little presumptuous, don't you think? San Diego's a beautiful city. Bountiful, too. Lots of establishments in need of representation."

"May your endeavors be ever prosperous," I replied.

"Heh. You're a respectful guy, Angel. I like you."

Another compliment. *Why? What's your game, Bruno?*

"You seem to know how to keep your mouth shut and stay in the shadows," Bruno said.

I shrugged. "I create useful things. No talking, no spotlight."

"So I hear. I also hear you and the old man aren't exactly close, am I right?"

Anyone who spent five minutes with me and the old man would realize we didn't exactly see eye-to-eye, but Bruno made it sound like he had eyes on the inside. My feathers effectively ruffled, I replied, "Everyone has daddy issues these days." It was no secret that Bruno and Adamo butted heads like mountain goats.

"Yeah, I like you, Angel. You're smart. Got your ear to the ground. Bet you already know there's a few people on the spot. I hear that if you keep your head down, you'll make it through this just fine."

There were hits being made and Bruno was going out of his way to warn me. *Why?*

"You should have my location by now. Don't worry, I left you a present, too. You're welcome." Bruno disconnected the call.

I glanced at my phone as the software I'd customized zeroed in on the exact location the call was made from. I sucked in a breath as the dot materialized. He'd made the call from right outside the hotel.

By the time I returned to the living room area, Markie was passed out on the couch. I went into Bones's room and gave him the rundown on my conversation with Bruno.

"Gift?" Bones asked. "What gift?"

I didn't know, but I had a hunch. "We need to scan the Hummer before we leave."

We left Markie asleep in the suite and carried the luggage to the parking garage. Easing toward the vehicle, I pulled out the device scanner and went to work. The scanner picked up a small, unknown device under the engine.

"Want me to get it?" Bones asked.

As my bodyguard, it was his duty. But we both knew I had a better chance of keeping the thing from exploding.

"No, man, I got this."

I handed him the scanner, got on my back, and slid under the front of the car. Sure enough, a bomb was attached to the undercarriage. It wasn't even a good bomb. In fact, I'd bet money the cheap piece of shit I stared up at had been sold by the wiseguys Bones and I had picked up from the airport. Since I'd seen the specs, I knew the bomb had sensors connected to the doors. I'd also seen how to disarm it. The Pelinos had to know I had this information. Did they think I was stupid? And why the hell would Bruno warn me?

"Sloppy piece of shit," I muttered, cursing the bomb, its makers, and the whole Pelino family for that matter.

"Can you get it?" Bones asked.

"Yeah. This is… this is bullshit." My tools were in the Hummer. Since I couldn't open any of the doors without exploding the vehicle, I whipped out the pocket knife I kept strapped around my ankle and cut the sensor wire. Then I severed the rest of the connections and pried the piece of shit from my engine. I climbed out from under the Hummer, gently handing the bomb to Bones.

Bones held it as far away from his body as possible. I climbed into the back of the Hummer and he handed it back to me. I disassembled the rest of it while Bones loaded up the luggage. Then we stashed the bomb in my bag.

Bones stayed with the vehicle while I went back for Markie. She was out cold, making me wonder what was in the drugs she'd taken. I half carried her back to the Hummer, belted her into the passenger's seat so I could keep an eye on her, and then we got the hell out of there. I don't think I breathed until the lights of San Diego faded from my rearview mirror.

Markie slept and Bones and I sat in silence, both of us keeping watch for a tail. I stole glances at Markie, wondering what to do about her. I tried to imagine her in my apartment, and with my family, but couldn't. The disassembled bomb in the back of the Hummer tugged at my thoughts, reminding me of how selfish I'd been to put her in harm's way to begin with. Scenarios of her opening a car door and triggering an explosion played in my mind. I forced myself to see every one of them, hoping they would change my mind. Hoping they would somehow give me the strength to push her away. Instead, I reached down and laced my fingers in hers. She stirred, but didn't wake.

I could always tell her. I could come clean about my family and let her decide her own future.

But knowledge about my family would only put her in greater danger. I needed to process, weigh my options, and figure out what the hell to do.

An hour from Las Vegas, Markie woke up.

"Hey, how you feeling?" I asked. Her skin had returned to its normal sun-tanned hue and her eyes were once again bright and lively.

She stretched. "Much better, thanks. My head still hurts, but it's manageable now."

Her stomach growled.

"Hungry?" I asked.

"Yeah, lunch..." She rubbed her stomach. "...didn't exactly stay down. I can just whip up something when I get home, though. Do you cook?"

Now she was speaking my language. "Do I cook? Damn, girl. I'm a chef."

"You went to culinary school?"

"Let's not get crazy. I didn't need to go to school for it. It's in my blood."

"So, your parents cook?" she asked.

A memory surfaced in the back of my mind. My mother picked me up and set me on the counter. The Temptations song "I Can't Get Next to You" blared through the house's sound system and Mom danced around the kitchen, tossing ingredients onto the counter for her widely-acclaimed marinara sauce. Garlic bread roasted in the oven while she dropped homemade ravioli into a pot of boiling water. She picked up a wire whisk and used it as a microphone, singing to me as I laughed. I held onto the moment, nurturing it, encouraging it to grow. Instead, it faded, leaving

161

behind a hollow ache.

I glanced in the rearview mirror. Bones slept, leaning against the window.

"My mother could have put every Italian restaurant in Vegas out of business, but she was content to stay home and cook for our family," I replied. "I have all her old recipes. Every time I use them, it's like she's not gone, you know?" I shook my head, wondering why I was confiding all of this to Markie. I'd never told anyone. Not even Bones. "I know that sounds stupid."

Markie patted my arm. "No it doesn't. I get it. It's like a pencil drawing you're always darkening to keep it from fading. But no matter how much you trace the lines, they keep losing their sharpness. You wake up one morning and can't quite remember her laugh, or the lines of her mouth when she's upset at you for breaking her favorite vase. Then even the memory of her sorrow is precious."

Her words evoked another flashback. It was late, and I was supposed to be in bed. Something was wrong, though. I crept down the darkened stairs, holding the railing to steady my steps. Mom sat on the couch with a newspaper in her hands, sobbing. I knelt on the stairs and clung to the railing, knowing I shouldn't interrupt her and wondering what could have affected her like this. The memory swirled around me, and suddenly I stood in front of an ornate wooden casket, holding my father's hand as family surrounded us. Father gave me a rose and pointed to the casket.

"Angel?" Markie asked, pulling me from my thoughts. "Are you okay?"

Her eyes were full of compassion, making me wonder how much of the memory showed on my face. My eyes burned. I didn't trust myself to speak, so I nodded.

She patted my arm again. Then she grabbed my free hand. Our fingers laced together. She gave my hand a gentle squeeze and smiled at me. Warmth rushed up my arm and soothed the pain the memory had brought. For the first time in my life, I felt like someone truly understood me. Only, how could she? There was so much about me she didn't know. And if she ever found out, she definitely wouldn't be smiling at me like that.

"Am I taking you to your sister's?" I asked, desperate to hide myself once again.

"Let me check." She released my hand and pulled her phone

out of her purse.

I missed the contact, and immediately regretted asking the question.

She sent off a text, and then a few moments later her phone buzzed.

"Ari's working. Any chance you can run me by the Tropicana so I can get the key to her apartment?" she asked.

"Yeah, of course," I replied.

"What does she do at the Tropicana?" Bones asked, leaning into the conversation. I wasn't sure when he'd woken up. Curious, I glanced into the rearview mirror, but he didn't look at me.

Markie turned in her seat. "She waits tables at the restaurant just inside the front door. Not exactly what she came to Vegas to do, but it's a job."

"She come to be a showgirl or something?" Bones asked.

"Not exactly. She wants to sing."

"Like everyone else in Vegas," Bones groaned.

"You don't understand, she has a phenomenal voice. And I'm not just saying that because she's my sister. She's really talented, Bones. Matt was supposed to set her up with some auditions, but…"

"But Matt's a *chooch*."

Markie arched an eyebrow.

"A loser," I clarified. Not quite what it meant, but close enough.

We stopped by the Tropicana, Markie got the keys from Ariana, and then we drove to their apartment. Bones and I helped Markie with her luggage, and Bones checked the apartment for intruders.

"You guys want something to eat?" Markie asked, heading for the kitchen. "I'm gonna make myself a grilled cheese."

We declined. I would have loved to hang out and let Markie make us sandwiches, but Father would be keeping track of our progress. I didn't want him to see the Hummer parked in front of her building for too long. While she was in the kitchen I scanned the apartment, finding it clean of any unexpected devices. Bones slipped out the door to give us some privacy.

Markie filled the sink with soapy water and started dumping dishes in while her sandwich was grilling.

She spun around and leaned against the counter, looking up at me. "This was the best weekend of my life. Thank you, Angel."

She tugged a rubber band off her wrist and put her hair up into a messy bun. Little wisps escaped the sides and fell back against her cheeks. She blew them out of her face and dumped a few more dishes into the sink.

My conscience kept tugging me toward the door, reminding me the right thing to do was to leave, delete her number, and forget her. Markie was a good girl who didn't need to be wrapped up in my family's mess. We'd danced, we'd kissed, and now it was time to end the fantasy and get back to reality. A stronger man would have done the right thing, but I wasn't that man. I was weak, and Markie was my strength. I breathed in deeply, and let the tropical scent of her invade my common sense. I couldn't walk away. Instead, I reached out and tucked the stray hairs behind her ears. My hand lingered against her face, and she looked at me, her eyes full of passion reflecting the desire I felt.

I leaned in and covered her mouth with mine. Warmth exploded on my lips and spread through my entire body. Her arms wrapped around me, and she pressed in, opening her lips to me. As I explored her mouth, my hands roamed, sliding down her back and to her waist. Markie broke away and rested her forehead on my collar bone.

"I can't do this, Angel," she said.

The finality in her voice made my chest ache. Confused, I put my finger under her chin and raised her face to look at me. Her bright blue eyes held sadness and regret. "Why?" I asked.

"There are things about me you don't know—things I don't want to tell you—and this isn't fair. I can't do this." Her chest expanded as she sucked in air. She took a step back, putting distance between us I couldn't seem to breach. "Please go."

But the way she looked at me, and the way she kissed me, surely she couldn't mean it. "What? Markie, please, let's just talk about this."

"I can't, Angel. Please leave."

I reached for her but she pulled away. "Markie, I know you feel something for me. Why are you pushing me away? Please don't do this. Talk to me."

"No. Go." She turned off the burner. "I need to think, and you're all in my head and I can't. Please just go away."

She wouldn't even look at me. My world crashed down around

me. My brain knew we had to call it quits, but my heart screamed that this was wrong.

"Please, Angel," she whispered.

It was such a dramatic difference. Just earlier today we'd been holding hands and laughing. Now *her* secrets were going to keep us apart? I hadn't seen that coming at all. Rejected, I trudged toward the door, dragging my feet and hoping she'd stop me, praying she'd come clean with whatever kept her from surrendering to her feelings for me. But she didn't. Not one peep.

Come on, Markie. Say something. Stop me.

I reached for the door handle. Still nothing. I turned, casting one last glance in her direction. Her back was still facing me. I swung open the door.

"I'm sorry, Angel." It was barely more than a whisper, yet it shattered me like a roar.

"Yeah. Me too." I fled from the apartment.

I climbed into the Hummer and Bones took one look at me and didn't say a word. I'd skipped dinner, I had a disassembled bomb in the back of my car I was dreading telling my father about, and our family was on the brink of war. The one person who made me feel like I was something more than a mob boss's son had rejected me. My chest hurt so damn bad I wanted to punch something. Vacation was definitely over, and I was back to business as usual.

♠ ♥ ♣ ♦

CHAPTER TWENTY-FOUR
Angel

FINALLY HOME, BONES and I carried our luggage out of the elevator and into the hallway. We rounded the corner to find two of Father's security guards positioned on either side of the door to my condo. As we approached, they nodded a hello and let us in. The old man lounged in my recliner, eyes glued to the cell phone in his hands. I set my luggage down, just inside the entryway, and walked over to greet him.

He kicked down the footrest and stood, pocketing his phone. "Angel, Bones. Good to see both of you back safe and sound. Come in, Son. Sit. How was the beach?" He gestured toward the sofa.

My father was the only man I knew who could walk into someone's home and make *them* feel like a guest. Seeing the power play for what it was, I handed the device scanner to Bones and perched on the edge of the sofa.

"Beautiful. The weather was perfect."

"Condo's clear," Bones said, handing me back the scanner. Then he picked up my luggage and headed for my room.

The old man leaned forward, his fatherly smile replaced with the intensity of an attentive businessman. "Good, now tell me everything."

I gave him the full, unabridged version of my weekend. Well, almost. I neglected to mention Markie, the security guard we'd hired to watch her, and the extra security we'd hired for the restaurant. When I got to the part about Bruno's phone call, veins started popping out on Father's forehead.

"Why am I only now finding out about this?" the old man asked.

"We were heading home anyway and I knew you'd want to meet."

His jaw tensed. He leaned forward and asked, "This bomb, you said you kept it?"

I gestured to Bones and he disappeared into my room, returning with the disassembled remains.

"Where did you say you found this?" Father asked, enunciating each word with tight control.

"Under my Hummer."

Father bolted out of his seat. "Someone made an attempt on your life, and you didn't contact me immediately?!" he shouted.

I inwardly winced, but managed to keep my back straight and my expression neutral. "It wasn't exactly an attempt. Bruno warned me. He even told me to keep my head down. He practically pointed it out for me."

"That cocky bastard! Angel, you still should have called. You know the protocol. What if this attack wasn't isolated? What if they targeted other members of the family as well?" His hands flew into the air. "Our people could be under assault as we speak, and you withheld information."

Unable to provide an answer that would appease him, I ducked and apologized.

Swearing under his breath, he walked to the window, whipped out his phone, and put it to his ear. Tense moments passed before he spoke into it. "Carlo, an attempt was made on Angel's life today. No, he's fine. Those bastards put a bomb under his car. I'm in the middle of something, but I'll call you after I'm done here. Contact everyone. Put more security on my family. You know the drill. Thanks." He disconnected the call, put his phone away, and then stared out the window for what seemed like forever.

A stupider man would have approached him, but my ass stayed glued to the sofa.

Finally, the old man's shoulders relaxed. He turned and walked back to his chair, sat, and asked, "Do you recognize the design?"

Emotion temporarily tabled, we were back to business.

"Yes. It was that cheap piece of shit those New Yorkers were trying to sell you."

"You're certain?"

I nodded. "Either they made it, or they sold their design and someone else did."

"Interesting." He laced his fingers in his lap. "Can you rebuild it?"

I glanced at the parts in Bones's hands. In my anger, I'd done a number on it. Putting it back together would take some time, but it wasn't impossible. "Yes."

Bones set the disassembled bomb on the coffee table and stood by the wall.

Father nodded. "Good. I knew those greedy bastards couldn't be trusted. I left them a breadcrumb trail that led straight to Adamo, and by God, if they didn't follow it. Adamo, that crazy son of a bitch, made his move quicker than I expected."

Give a sociopath a box of bombs... What the hell did you expect?

He rubbed at his face. "Still, Bruno warned you. Why? What's his game in all of this? Did Adamo pass down the order? Or is Bruno acting on his own?"

Father was worried about semantics, when all I could see was explosions. "The lives that could be lost to those bombs..." I shook my head, unable to wrap my mind around the potential for casualties.

"Necessary losses. They will be significant enough to unite the families and in the long run, save the city and all we have worked for. Balance sometimes requires sacrifice. You know that, Angel."

I definitely understood sacrifice. Friends, dates, trust, innocence... I'd given them all up for my family. But this was different. The bombs had the potential for massacre, destruction that would only be surpassed if the Pelino family gained control of the city. "There has to be another way. Maybe we can—"

My father threw me a look that chilled my blood. I closed my mouth.

"You said Bruno gave you two warnings. What was the other?"

"He told me they have a new tech guy."

"Interesting. Why is he showing their hand?" Father asked.

I shrugged. "Hell if I know. The whole conversation was strange." Maybe Bruno had grown a conscience and wanted to stop his old man? Maybe Bruno was just screwing with me?

Father keyed something into his phone and then returned his attention to me. "About your trip... Please continue."

My mind raced, searching for additional information I could give without mentioning Markie. "We headed home right after I disabled the bomb."

"That's it?" he asked.

"Yes," I lied.

Father lunged forward. I barely registered his movement before my cheek stung and my face whipped around. Stars danced before my eyes. Bones twitched, but kept his place. Father scowled at me, burning away the room's oxygen with his suffocating anger. His hand twitched, and I thought he would hit me again, but he didn't.

"Do you honestly think you take a shit without my knowing about it?" The old man bellowed.

I steadied myself on the sofa and reached for my cheek. My hand came away wet with blood.

Father grabbed a tissue from the box on the coffee table and cleaned his ring. I watched in open-mouthed awe. He'd never struck me. Oh, he'd whooped my ass good when I was caught skipping school in fourth grade and smoking cigarettes in sixth, but he'd never hit me out of anger.

He threw the used tissue in my lap and then flexed his hand a couple of times. He leveled a stare at me and said, "You come home to a place I bought for you, shower me with your half-truths, and question my methods? Who the hell do you think you are?" he asked.

"Father, I—"

"*Stai zitto!*"

Veins bulged out from his neck, adding to those throbbing out of his forehead. I did as he said and shut my mouth, lowering my gaze to the floor as I used the tissue to staunch the blood running down my cheek.

He paced in front of the recliner. "You think you're so smart, Angel. Think I don't know about the girl?" He pulled something out of his pocket and flung it down on the coffee table.

I stared at a five-by-seven photo of Markie standing beside me as we waited in line at the High Roller.

"Do you know who she is?" he asked.

"Yes." I rattled off the information I'd gleaned from Markie's driver's license.

"No, who she really is?"

I looked to Bones, but his face only reflected my own confusion.

Father laughed, and then shook his head. Veins were popping again. "Did either of you geniuses run a background check?"

"Yes sir," Bones replied, holding my father's gaze.

"Really?" Father asked. He pulled more photos from his pocket, flinging them down beside the first. Markie at the orphanage. Markie walking down the strip with Ariana. Markie leaning against the patio railing of our San Diego hotel. Markie looking very uncomfortable as she sat with a man in a suit in a booth at the Tropicana, his face hidden in the shadows.

"Interesting. Bones did a background check, but you—my son—clearly did not. Angel, you're thorough. You would know who that is." He pointed at the man in the picture. "And, you would have found this." He retrieved an envelope out of his inside pocket, pulled a stack of papers out, and tossed them on top of the photos.

I scooted forward and studied the transaction journal for Markie's checking account. Her balance showed a little over five grand. Usual withdrawals: restaurants, clothing, cab, grocery store. There were also monthly deposits in the amount of three thousand, twenty-one dollars and fifteen cents. It looked like an automatic payroll deposit, but Markie had never mentioned a job.

"What is this?" I asked, pointing to the acronym listed in the description column.

"And that's my question," Father replied. "Who does she work for?"

I shook my head. "She volunteers at the orphanage. She doesn't have a job."

The old man clicked his tongue. He paused in front of the coffee table and picked up the picture of Markie with the man in the suit. He looked from the picture to me. "So you don't know?"

His question hung in the air, forcing me to face my stupidity. Markie was employed somewhere; the proof was in my hands. Why hadn't she said anything?

"No, I don't know."

"Damn it, Angel, you're better than this. I can't believe after that last bitch, you'd blindly follow some broad. Will you ever learn?"

His words stung worse than his backhand. Mostly because I knew he was right. I also knew it didn't change how I felt about Markie. I was a fool.

Father shook his head, clearly disgusted with me. "What's her motivation?"

I thought back to each time I'd run into her, trying to find something that connected the experiences. Maybe I was just being optimistic, but I couldn't find anything.

"Follow the money to find the motivation." He pointed at the bank statement. "Do you know how much federal agents make?"

He thinks she's a Fed. The idea was so ridiculous, I had to stop myself from laughing aloud. I looked to Bones, but my friend's face was a mask.

Father shoved the photo into my face. "This man she's with... he goes by the name of James Frank. He's a known agent, and most likely her contact at the bureau. But there's more."

Father thumbed on his phone and showed me a picture of an unfamiliar man in his late fifties wearing a decent suit. He handed me the phone and said, "Scroll down."

The caption beneath the photo read, 'Jay Lawson, Boise County Chief Deputy Prosecutor.'

"What does the Boise D.A. have to do with Markie?" I asked, handing him back his phone.

"That's her uncle; her mother's brother. The man who had custody of your friend and her sister after their mother died. By the way, her mother died in the line of duty at the courthouse. Again, something you'd know if you weren't too pussy-whipped to do a goddamn background check. Always so desperate to see the good in people. Just like your mother," he spat, like it was some sort of curse.

He never talked about her. Not one word since the day we laid her in the ground. My ears perked up at the mention of her.

Father held out his hand. "Angel, don't. Now is not the time," he warned. His eyes were hard, and his frame shook with barely controlled rage.

My jaw snapped shut. I lowered the tissue to the coffee table, strangely mesmerized by the blood. Memories danced in the back of my mind. Clips and pieces. Laughter. Music. Mother sobbing, a newspaper clutched in her hands. The smell of bleach. Father leaning over the bathtub, washing blood from a mop. Then just like that, they were gone.

Father's expression shifted. Guilt and remorse flitted across his face for a brief moment before vanishing under hardened resolve. "This was sloppy, Angel. You disappoint me," he said. "Now, to clean up the mess ..." He scratched his cheek. He studied the photos for a few moments, and then looked from Bones to me.

If he ordered a hit—if he told us to make Markie disappear—I didn't know what I'd do. Would Bones take her out to save us both? Would I be able to stop him if he tried? Maybe we were destined for some Romeo and Juliet shit after all.

But Father surprised me. He didn't order Markie's hit. Instead, he steepled his hands and said, "The Feds have given us a valuable game piece, and we need to use it. I need you to stick close to her, Angel. Flip the script and romance *her*. Soon we can start feeding her information about the Pelino family, stuff we want leaked to the Feds. If we can use them to bring our enemies down... well, maybe you didn't screw up too badly."

He was justifying his decision to let me live. More importantly, he was letting Markie live. At least for now. There was only one problem.

"I don't think she's interested in a relationship with me," I said, Markie's rejection still weighing heavily on me.

Father leaned back on his heels. "Well, that's unfortunate. If I can't watch her, I'll need to get rid of her. I'd hate to do that, Angel. I don't need heat from the Feds right now, not with the Pelino family making their move."

It was a warning, and I heard it loud and clear. "I'll change her mind."

"Good. See that you do. And quickly. I want to meet her at dinner tomorrow."

He gave the coffee table one last glance, but left the photos and the bank journal where they were. I walked him to the door. His phone buzzed, and he paused in the door frame long enough to look at it. Then he swore and keyed in a response.

"Tech found Dante somewhere he's not supposed to be," Father said to me. "Turns out your brother is making the same stupid decisions you are. I need you and Bones to go handle this and set him straight. Tech will send you the details."

172

CHAPTER TWENTY-FIVE
Angel

"MARKIE... A FED?" Bones asked as he climbed into the Hummer's passenger seat. "Wow. Didn't see that one coming."

I nodded, still unable to believe it myself. "Yep."

"And not only does the Boss want her alive and unharmed, but he wants you to take her to Sunday dinner?"

My friend was clearly having as hard a time with this as I was. "Yep." One word answers were all I could seem to manage.

"How are you doing with all of this?" Bones asked.

"I don't know."

As an external processor, Bones liked to lay everything out, gauge everyone's reactions, and force it all to make sense. Although I knew what he was trying to do, I couldn't help him, because nothing made sense. Not one damn thing. I had approached Markie in the pizzeria. We had run into her the second time in Matt's apartment when Ariana almost died. After which, I had pursued her. How the hell could anyone set that up?

Besides, Markie wasn't like any woman I'd ever dated. Surely anyone setting me up would have surveyed the women I'd dated to get my type. Based on my history, Markie was the exact opposite of what my type would be. Would a federal agent have invited a homeless man to eat lunch with us? Would she volunteer at an orphanage?

And what about the way Markie looked at me? I swear it was like she saw past the money, past the cars and the clothes, past the family. Like she saw me. Not the bad-ass my father expected me to be, nor someone to always pay her way and solve her every problem. She looked at me like we were equals. No judgment, no expectations.

No reality. It was all a lie.

"You okay?" Bones asked.

I shook my head. Hell no I wasn't okay. "Let's just find my brother, all right?"

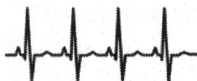

For Dante's sixteenth birthday, Father and Rachele had bought him a shiny red BMW. Tricked out with more horsepower than his now seventeen-year-old self knew what to do with, the Bimmer had a system like mine which kept him connected to Tech. As Father promised, Tech sent me Dante's location and the details of my little brother's most recent screwup.

Bones and I found the Bimmer parked on West Baltimore Avenue in front of a rundown two-story apartment building. I idled behind my brother's car and checked out the area. The few working streetlights didn't show me much. A chest-high chain-link fence surrounded the building, and a sign on the gate warned of security camera monitoring. Across the street lay a vacant field, cloaked in darkness. The dented old truck in front of Dante's Bimmer was missing a back tire.

I put the Hummer in park, killed the engine, and dialed Dante's cell. No answer. I hung up and called again. Still no answer. I hung up and tried a third time. Dante picked up sounding frustrated and out of breath.

"Yeah?" he asked.

"What, no hello? No 'how was your trip'? I'm hurt, little bro."

"Kinda busy right now. Can I call you back in a bit?"

"Nope. In fact, I'm going to need you to come outside. We have a few things to discuss."

Bones and I climbed out of the Hummer and leaned against it, watching the apartment building.

A mini-blind flickered in the window of the upstairs center unit. Dante swore. "You're here? Why?"

Some girl in the background asked what was going on.

174

"Is that a girl?" I gasped in mock outrage. "You got a broad up there with you? Is that why you're too busy to answer my calls?"

"Come on, Angel, stop screwing around. You know how it is."

By all accounts, Dante was the one screwing around. My frustrated little brother was flexing his independence and spending the night at his girlfriend's house. Too bad he hadn't realized his independence was a high-interest loan he couldn't afford and Father had sent me to repossess his ass.

"You want us to come up there and drag you down with your pants around your ankles?"

"Don't be a dick, Angel."

"Don't make me. Get your ass down here. Now." I glanced at my watch. "You have one minute."

I disconnected the call and waited. Within moments, feet hit the landing. Rusted metal stairs creaked under his weight as he pounded down the steps. Fifty-three seconds after I'd made the demand, a five-foot-seven disgruntled Italian stormed toward us. His feet were bare, and as he walked, he buttoned his rumpled shirt.

"D'Angelo. Bones." He nodded to each of us in turn, as little sparks of anger ignited in his eyes. Dante had our father's temper, but not the old man's power. If he didn't learn to rein it in, he'd end up pissing off the wrong person long before he became a made man.

Talking on the street was out of the question, even in times of peace between the families. I greeted my brother and ushered him into the front seat of the Hummer before settling myself back behind the wheel.

Bones climbed into the back. "Where's Pietro?" he asked Dante.

Pietro was my brother's full-time security guard. Also a senior in high school, Pietro was the son of one of Father's soldiers. The boy had rearranged his school schedule and life to align with Dante's so he could protect him. Yet he was gone.

"How am I supposed to know?" Dante asked.

I leveled my best I-will-make-you-eat-my-fist glare at him.

"Fine. I sent him to go get us weed. I wanted a little privacy with my girl and could use a little relax. No big deal."

I shook my head, chuckling. We were in the middle of a war and my little brother was without a guard so the two of them could get high. It was the very definition of a big deal. "So, you're alone in *this* neighborhood at night? I'll be sure to let Father know you don't think it's a big deal, though."

Dante swallowed, his Adam's apple bobbing up and down with the effort. "Okay, fine, it was stupid. But you know how it is with Bones always hanging around. Don't you ever want to get away from him for a while?"

I was lucky to have Bones watching my back. "No. That would be stupid. Especially right now."

Seeing he wasn't going to get any sympathy from me, Dante lowered his head. "Sorry. I promise not to do it again."

Rehearsed, meaningless words. I flicked them aside with a wave. "We both know you'll do it again, and you'll most likely die from it, at this rate. But your future suicide isn't my concern today. Father asked me to talk to you about the girl."

"What girl?" Dante asked. His gaze flickered toward the apartment before returning to me.

I chuckled. "My guess? The one you're trying to be alone with."

He sighed. "All right, fine, there's a girl. We're just having fun."

"Having so much fun you paid both her rent *and* her car payment last month?" I asked.

He shrugged.

"Father says you need to end it. Yesterday."

He paled. "What? Why?"

"Your buddy Rodge has been skimping on what he's been sending up to Father. The old man confronted him about it and Rodge rolled over on you. He says you shacked up with his best girl and now she's not showing up to work."

He glanced up at the apartment window. "Mia and I are together now. I don't want her hooking anymore."

If only it were that easy. "Everything comes with a price, bro, you know that." I leaned closer to him, lowering my voice. "You and me, we're privileged. We drive fast cars, we wear designer clothes, chicks throw themselves at us, we get whatever we want. But it all comes with a price. We have to play the game by his rules. He says end it, you damn well better end it."

"Yeah? Well, I'm sick of playing by his rules."

Bones cracked his neck and leaned forward, putting a hand on my brother's shoulder.

Dante rolled his eyes. "You can quit flexing, Bones. You wouldn't hurt me. Neither of you would."

Curious, I cocked my head. "Why don't you think I'd hurt you?" I asked.

"We're family. I'm a son."

Bones and I both got a good chuckle out of that.

"What?" Dante asked.

"You really think being family exempts you from being punished? Dante, look at my cheek. I'm family, too. Hell, I'm the eldest."

The anger in Dante's eyes was replaced by uncertainty as he studied my wound. "He hit you?" he asked.

"Yep. Ripped the skin off with his big-ass ring."

Dante's eyes widened.

Good. Time for a wakeup call, little bro. "Father will hurt you. Hell, *I* will hurt you, Dante. You're my brother and I love you, but if I call in and my capo orders me to whack you, I will. I would pull the piece out of my pocket and put two in your pig-headed brain. It would be quick and clean and you would be dead. Anyone in the family would do the same: Cousin Alberto, Uncle Carlo, even Pietro will put you on ice if the old man orders it." I glanced over my shoulder at Bones. "Bones is my best friend. You know we've been tight since grade school. He's always had my back and I know he loves me like a brother. If Father were to put out a hit on me, Bones would have to take it. If he didn't, Father would take me out anyway, and then send someone after Bones next. You get what I'm saying?"

"Yeah, but come on, Angel. You know what it's like to have a girl."

Oh, he had no idea. I leveled a hard stare at him. "Yeah. I've had a few girls. Like Leilana. Remember her?"

Dante's eyes widened. After Leilana's disappearance, my brother had drilled me for information. Wanting to shield him, I'd kept my mouth shut. Now he was old enough to know the truth.

"Hey Bones, you remember Leilana?" I glanced over my shoulder.

Bones shrugged. "Yeah, she was a babe. They ever find her body?"

"Never," I replied.

Bones frowned. "Tragic."

Dante stared back at the apartment building. I wondered if his girl was up there watching us now.

"You don't get a free pass because you're a son, Dante. Your blood got you the courtesy of this conversation. No more."

He looked like he was about to argue, but I cut him off.

"Besides, what's your plan? You're seventeen. You're still in high school. You gonna support this girl on your allowance? Bring her to family functions? Introduce her to your mom? How old is Mia, anyway?"

"Twenty-three."

Bones snorted.

I shook my head and tried to spell it out for him. "And what do you think a twenty-three-year-old prostitute wants with a seventeen-year-old kid?"

"It's not like that, Angel."

"It's exactly like that. Congratulations, you're a meal ticket."

He scowled at me. "You don't know that. You don't see how we are together."

But I could imagine, and I doubt their relationship ever left the bedroom. Mia knew what she was doing.

"I don't care if you're her goddamn soul mate. Doesn't matter. Father said end it. He's under a lot of pressure right now and he needs us out there making allies, not acting like entitled little bastards and pissing off earners. You hear me?"

His scowl deepened.

Frustrated, I let out a breath. Dante's fear of the consequences had to outweigh his libido, because truthfully, there was no way in hell I could kill my little brother. If Father gave the order, he'd have to kill us both.

I steeled my expression and stared at him, waiting.

He started fidgeting. Then finally his scowl broke and he looked down, defeated. "Yeah. I hear ya."

"Good. You won't get any more warnings, Dante. If I have to talk to you again, I'll blow up your car. I only hope Father lets me do it without you in it."

That got his attention. His fear stared back at me. I drank it in, refusing to look away. Both of our lives depended on it.

Congratulations, Angel. You've scared your little brother, you dick.

I released him and he turned to climb out of the Hummer.

"Wait." I grabbed his shoulder, remembering the bomb I'd found under my Hummer. If Dante wasn't being careful, I wouldn't need to blow up his car. "Be sure to use the scanner Father gave you. It won't protect you from me, but it should warn you about anything the Pelinos throw your way."

He nodded.

"Now go handle your business."

Head down, Dante lumbered back to the apartment building. Bones took his place and we sat for a moment, watching the area.

"I wouldn't take the hit," Bones said, breaking the silence.

Wondering what the hell he was talking about, I raised my eyebrows.

"If the boss put out a hit on you, I wouldn't take it." He climbed into the front seat and settled himself in. "I still got your back, Angel. No matter what."

The girl I was interested in was a federal agent, the families were warring, and I just threatened to kill my little brother if he didn't leave his girlfriend. My world thoroughly sucked, but at least I didn't have to worry about Bones's loyalty.

He held out his hand, waiting.

I tapped my fist to his, agreeing. "No matter what."

CHAPTER TWENTY-SIX
Markie

GUILT GNAWED AWAY at me Saturday night. Angel had done so many nice things for me and in return, I rejected him and sent him away. Feeling like the world's biggest hag, I woke up early Sunday morning, pulled a dust rag out of the cabinet, and took my self-loathing out on Ariana's apartment.

You did the right thing. It was bound to end. This is easier. Better.

So why did I still feel like crap? My chest ached. Instinctively, I reached for my phone and thumbed through until I found his number. I could call him and fix this. But it wouldn't fix anything. In the end, it would make it worse.

Be strong. You're better than this.

I pocketed my phone as someone knocked on the door. Just when I'd talked myself into not contacting him, Angel stood on the porch wearing jeans and a tight T-shirt that hugged his chest in all the right places.

Lord, have mercy!

My gaze traveled up to his uncertain smile. Then even higher to a nasty-looking gash on his cheek.

"What happened?" I asked, pulling him inside and checking out the wound. Bruising spread out from the cut, coloring his cheek in shades of blue.

His hand flew up to cover it, but I stopped him. "Stupidity."

"Stupidity?" I asked.

"Clumsiness?"

Definitely a question. I arched an eyebrow at him, but he didn't expand. Bones stood quietly behind him, not even looking at me. Frustrated, I sighed and pointed him toward the sofa. "Sit. I'll go get something to clean it." I hurried to the bathroom without waiting to see if he complied. When I returned, Angel was sitting and Bones was walking around the room with something in his hands.

"What are you doing?" I asked, pointing at the gadget.

"Checking for bugs," Bones replied.

Bugs? I paused on my way to doctor up Angel. "Why would my sister's apartment be bugged?"

Bones pocketed the device and headed toward the door. "It's clean. I'll be outside if you need me." Then he left, closing the door behind him.

I sat beside Angel. "What's with him?"

Angel shrugged, without looking at me. He stared at the wall in front of him, lips drawn in a frown, eyes hooded with hurt. My chest tightened at the sight, but I couldn't change my stance on us. With nothing more to say, I treated the wound on his face.

"There you go. All clean and medicated," I said.

I expected him to tell me why he was there or leave, but he just stared at the wall like it was the most interesting thing he'd ever seen. I wanted to talk to him, but didn't trust myself not to complicate things further.

"Why are you here?" I asked finally.

Then he looked at me. His dark eyes seemed to drink me in like a man dying of thirst. I couldn't take it.

"Angel, you should go," I whispered.

"Why?" he asked.

The biggest reason lingered on the tip of my tongue, but I was too much of a coward to voice it. I was scared it would change everything between us, and terrified it would change nothing at all. I didn't have the strength to fight what I felt for him, and needed him to leave so I didn't have to.

"Why do you keep trying to push me away?" he asked. "It doesn't make sense. Your whole objective should be to get close to me, but you keep pulling away. Why?"

I blinked. *My objective?*

Angel pulled something out of his jacket pocket and flung it onto the coffee table. Then he stood and started pacing.

It was a photo. I picked it up and saw my face staring back at me. I was sitting with someone... someone Angel shouldn't know about. The invasion of my privacy made the hair on the back of my neck stand up. "How did you get this? Have you been following me around?"

Angel stopped pacing and faced me. The expression on his face was cold and unreadable. "That's all you have to say about it?" he asked.

"Angel, this is none of your business. You had no right to—"

"No right? Do you understand the position you've put me in? The position you've put my family in? I trusted you. You made me want... something. Something real. And the whole time you were lying to me?"

Lying? Had I lied? No. I just hadn't told him everything, which was perfectly acceptable for the beginning of a relationship. Nobody just walked in and dumped all their drama on the other person. So why did his accusation make me feel so bad? Maybe I had lied. But there was a reason for it. Surely he'd understand.

"Was any of it real?" Angel asked.

His hurt and anger washed over me, and I opened myself to it, knowing I'd caused it. I'd been stupid to listen to Ariana. Stupid to think I could dabble in a relationship and not give myself fully. Stupid to believe no one would get hurt. I'd wounded us both, and for what? A couple of dances? A few great kisses? A selfish moment of bliss? Was it worth the pain I now saw in Angel's eyes?

His expression hardened at my silence.

I stood, wanting to go to him, but stopped myself from stepping forward. This was my chance to release him for good. I bit my lip and locked down my emotions, knowing it was better this way.

"My father knows about you," Angel said, his voice softer, quieter.

Okay.

"He's ordered me to bring you to dinner with the family tonight."

I opened my mouth to tell him what a horrible idea that was, but he was suddenly in my personal space, his hand brushing against my cheek.

"I know it wasn't all a lie, Markie. Helping Max, working with the kids at the orphanage, the dancing, the way you kissed me... no way that was all a lie. You showed me the real you, and I want it. I want you."

His breath was warm against my lips. I wanted to close my eyes and lean into him, but that would be sending the wrong signal. We couldn't be together. There was no future in it.

Forcing myself to stay strong, I whispered, "I'm not going to dinner with your family."

Angel sighed. "It's not optional. If you don't come, very bad things will happen to you."

That woke me up from my stupor. I pushed away from Angel and asked, "Are you threatening me?"

He watched me without saying a word.

He *had* threatened me. Wow. I couldn't believe it. It felt like a slap across the face, waking me up to see how wrong I'd been about him. I'd felt guilty about the pain I'd caused him, and he had the nerve to threaten me? I didn't care how hurt he was or how rich and powerful his family was, he couldn't go around threatening people when he didn't get his way. And to think I'd almost fallen for the guy!

"You need to leave, Angel."

He looked from me to the door, and then back to me. He wasn't going to leave. Ariana was asleep in her room, but even if I woke her, there was no way the two of us could force him out. Especially not with Bones right outside the door. If I couldn't get Angel out of the apartment peacefully, we'd probably end up on some Lifetime special, warning girls about dating charming, well-dressed guys.

"Please, Angel, just go," I begged.

His expression softened. He was once again the Angel I'd danced with on the beach. The Angel who'd shaken Max's hand and put him up in a hotel. He nodded and stepped past me, heading for the door. Hand on the doorknob, he froze.

"Markie, you don't understand. This isn't me. It's my family, and they don't threaten. I'm trying to give you a warning here. If you don't come to dinner with me, they will come for you." His eyes found mine. They were so full of raw emotion, they made my breath hitch. "And I... I care about you and I will try to stop them. It will end badly for both of us. Not only us, but those closest to us." His gaze flickered back to Ariana's room. "I'm sorry, but we have no choice. I'll be here at four-thirty to pick you up. If you care at all about me—about Ari—you'll be here." Then he walked out.

Seconds later, Ariana emerged from her bedroom wearing only her bra and panties with her phone and her clothes in her hands.

"Ohmigod, Markie, Bones has been blowin' up my phone. You're going to dinner with the Mariani family tonight. You have to."

I was about done with people telling me what I had to do, but I couldn't speak. My sister's safety was at stake.

She stopped walking long enough to lean against the wall and pull her jeans on. "I don't think you understand the severity of the situation. You've been invited by the family boss. Nobody says no to him. Nobody."

"Yeah, I'm getting that. What are you doing?"

The look she gave me openly questioned my intellect. "Getting dressed." She slid a shirt over her head. She stomped her barefoot way over to me and showed me her phone. "This is Angel's ex-girlfriend."

I glanced at the photo. Dark hair, long dark lashes, a smile that held both challenge and promise, thin, very beautiful. "So?" I asked.

"She's missing. She's been missing for a long time. Well over a year now."

"Are you saying Angel made her disappear?" I asked, mortified.

"No. Listen. Angel *is* the guy you think he is, but his dad... his dad is a scary son of a bitch. People who tell him no disappear and nobody finds them. Bones says this isn't just about you. Angel will be in deep shit if you don't show. You need to do what the boss says."

"You've been talking to Bones a lot," I said, mulling her words over in my head.

She blushed. "Yeah. He's a nice guy. Fine, too. But don't change the subject. Tell me what's going on with you and Angel. You said you had a great time at the beach, then you freaked out and rejected him last night. Now you really think he's trying to manipulate you into going to a family dinner with him? That doesn't sound like the Angel you've been telling me about."

I sighed. It didn't sound like the Angel I knew, either. "I can't go, Ari. I don't have anything to wear."

A smile tugged at my sister's lips. "Easily solved with a little shopping trip. What the hell do you think I'm getting dressed for?"

♠ ♥ ♣ ♦

CHAPTER TWENTY-SEVEN
Markie

ARIANA DRESSED ME in a pale pink dress that hugged my upper body and fell in layers past my knees. Then she put my hair up in some sort of complicated braid with feathers weaved throughout it and pronounced me beautiful.

"This isn't too fancy for a forced dinner with the fam, is it?" I asked, eyeing my reflection in the mirror. "I kinda look like I'm heading to prom."

"That's right, get all that snarky crap out now, because you need to be sweet and charming when you meet Angel's father."

"When am I not sweet and charming?" I asked.

"When you're in the presence of snobby rich people who think they're better than everyone else. Maybe this isn't such a good idea, after all. We should probably ditch the dinner and go into hiding."

Ariana's idea had serious appeal, but before I could give it too much thought, Angel and Bones were knocking on the front door. Ariana hugged me and reminded me to be careful before practically shoving me out her door.

"You look nice," Angel said. "Thank you for doing this."

"I don't have much choice, do I?" I asked, walking past him toward the Hummer.

The drive was quiet and tense. After what seemed like an eternity on the road, we pulled past two security gates into the driveway of what could only be referred to as a mansion. Tough-looking big guys in suits lined the driveway, looking threatening. That's when I realized I was in way over my head.

Angel got out of the car. I started to open my door, but Bones grabbed my shoulder, holding me in place.

"Angel has a really nice family. Don't trust any of them, you hear me?" he asked.

Okay, that's contradictory.

"You hear me?" he repeated.

I nodded.

"Answer their questions, but don't volunteer any information. We're gonna do our best to keep you alive, but you need to help us out. Okay?"

To keep me alive?

That sounded ominous, and a little over the top. I nodded again.

Angel opened my door and offered me his hand. Because I was wearing three-inch heels and was in danger of rolling an ankle and breaking my neck, I took it. He led us into the house, where he introduced me to Nonna, his grandmother. She clicked her tongue and muttered something under breath while eyeing Angel's cheek.

"It's fine, Nonna, doesn't even hurt," Angel assured her. "Markie cleaned it out and doctored it up for me."

She didn't ask how he'd gotten it, which was strange. But before I could think too much about it, Nonna took me under her arm and led me into the kitchen where she introduced me to the rest of the ladies. They all hugged me, some kissed my cheeks and went back to their work. Nobody asked how I'd met Angel or how long we'd been together, or any of the other questions families usually asked. Before I knew it, I was finished in the kitchen and Angel was whisking me toward the back door.

Young squeals of laughter came from the hallway, followed by a great whooshing noise, and suddenly two little kids were attached to Angel's legs like two overzealous Chihuahuas.

Rachele, Angel's stepmother, looked over the kitchen bar, saying, "Luci, you're wearing a dress! Stop that right now, young lady."

The dark-haired little girl released Angel's leg, crossed her arms over her dress, and stuck her bottom lip out. "I'm just telling Angel hi, Mom."

Angel picked her up. "Well, hello there, beautiful. I'd like to introduce you to my friend, Markie. Markie, meet my youngest siblings, Luciana and Georgio."

"Luci," the girl corrected holding out her hand to me. "Pleasure to meet you, Ms. Markie."

Black curls, big dark eyes, olive skin, pouty lips, Luciana was adorable. "The pleasure is all mine," I said, squeezing her little hand.

Georgio stood, smoothing down the front of his dark slacks. He placed himself at my feet and said, "My friends call me Georgie."

I squatted down so I was eye level with him and offered him my hand. "Good to meet you, Georgie."

He flipped my hand over and kissed the back of it. It was so sweet it almost made me forget I was forced to be in that mansion meeting those people. "Aren't you the little charmer?" I asked.

"I am a gentleman," Georgio said by way of explanation. "If you'll excuse me, I have to go help my father now."

"Yes, of course." I inclined my head, biting my lip so I wouldn't laugh.

The gentleman gave me a slight bow before making his departure.

"He's so weird," Luciana groaned.

"That wasn't weird. It was sweet," I said, returning my attention to Luciana. "And you are very beautiful. I love your dress. Teal complements your skin tone very well."

"Thank you." She reached out and touched the feathers braided into my hair. "These are pretty."

This was an exchange I could handle. It felt natural and I wasn't worried that anyone would make me disappear like Angel's ex-girlfriend. "Why thank you."

"Markie needs to meet Father, Luci," Angel interrupted, gesturing toward the back door.

"Great, I'll come with you." Luciana slid her little hand into mine.

The women in the kitchen seemed surprised by this, but I wasn't. Children usually felt comfortable around me. It wasn't uncommon for random kids to walk up and ask me my name. I'd read somewhere that children were better about following their instincts, and this was why. They instinctively knew I wouldn't do anything to hurt them. And I wouldn't. Even if their dad was a horrible person.

Luciana's hand in mine seemed like an endorsement of sorts. Feeling safer and better than I had since I'd entered the mansion, I let her lead me out the back door to a group of men standing in front of a barbecue grill.

A big man who looked like an older, bigger version of Angel was waving a pair of tongs around as he spoke. He saw me and paused, midsentence, dropping his gaze to the girl holding my hand. He tensed.

"Hi Daddy," Luciana said.

"Luci, tell me who you've got there."

Luciana smiled up at me. "This is Markie, Angel's friend."

"Thank you for the introduction, Luci. Now, doesn't your mother need help in the kitchen?" he asked.

"Yes, Daddy." Luciana's shoulders slumped. Then she made me promise to sit by her at dinner before scurrying off.

I watched her go, and when I turned back around, all of the men who'd been surrounding us had moved away. Angel and Bones were off to the side, hanging back.

Angel's father watched me, making me feel like prey locked in the gaze of a very big predator. For someone so eager to get me there, he sure didn't seem happy to see me. "Hello, Markie." He offered me his hand. "You can call me Dom."

I swallowed back my fear and shook his hand. Goose bumps sprouted across my flesh. "Hello, Dom. Nice to meet you," I lied.

He gave me a crooked smile, telling me he'd seen through the lie. "Beautiful young ladies are always welcome around here. Come now, let me introduce you to everyone else."

He led me around the group, filling my head with names and stories about each person while making my skin crawl from the tension between us. I could feel Angel and Bones watching us, waiting.

'I'm trying to give you a warning.' Angel said in the back of my mind. *'If you don't come to dinner with me, they will come for you. And I care about you and I will try to stop them. It will end badly for both of us, and those closest to us.'*

He'd been afraid of this man—of his own father—and now I understood why.

'Angel has a really nice family. Don't trust any of them, you hear me?' Bones had said.

Now I got it. I understood exactly what I was dealing with

189

here. Dom was a terrifying man, and for some reason he wanted *me* here. Why? The more I tried to figure it out, the more my head hurt.

After the introductions were made, Angel took my hand and put it in the crook of his arm, rescuing me. I'd never been so happy to feel someone's arm before. "Are you okay?" he whispered as we walked toward the house.

"Yeah. I just need a minute. Where's the bathroom?"

He pointed toward a door and told me he'd wait for me in the kitchen.

The new shoes were already killing my feet, making me want to strangle Ariana for talking me into them. I kicked them off the second the bathroom door closed and gave my feet some time to breathe while I dug through my purse, searching for my pills. They weren't there. I'd checked for them before we'd left the house, so they had to have fallen out in the Hummer or on the way into the house.

Hoping it was the former and not the latter—because boy wouldn't that be embarrassing?—I tiptoed out of the bathroom and out the front door. I could feel the guards watching me, but I didn't pay them any mind and retraced our steps to Angel's vehicle. The pill bottle hadn't rolled under the vehicle, so I cupped my eyes and tried to peer in through the darkened glass.

The second my hands made contact with the vehicle, its alarm blared.

Suddenly my body was airborne, and then I was half-sprawled across the hood of the Hummer with my hands in the air. Two guys were yelling, and someone was patting me down. I tried to search for Angel or Bones, but every time I moved the guards would slam me harder into the vehicle. My head hurt and tears stung the back of my eyes.

The Hummer's alarm beeped off, and Angel and Bones stood on either side of me, helping me up. The relief of seeing them freed my tears. I tried to blink them away, feeling like an idiot.

"I'm sorry," I told them. "I didn't think it would be locked here, with the security gate and all. I… I got a headache, but my pills aren't in my purse. I thought they might have fallen out in your car."

Everyone had poured out of the house to witness the spectacle. I'd never been so embarrassed in my life.

"It's okay," Angel reassured me. "I'll find your pills."

He opened the passenger's door and started looking. He emerged empty-handed, and I started to panic. What if he didn't find them? Would the guards think I was lying? Did they think I was trying to steal his ride? And how the heck did they think I could stash a weapon in this dress? I'm all for being vigilant, but the slamming up against the vehicle and the pat-down had gone a little too far.

Why would they do that to me?

"Found them," Angel announced, shutting the back door and holding up my pill bottle. When he handed them to me, I couldn't help but notice that his hands were shaking, too. He pulled me into an embrace and squeezed me tight.

"I'm sorry," I whispered.

"No big deal. Just a misunderstanding." He patted my back.

The crowd disbursed leaving only me, Angel, Bones, and the guards behind. Angel continued to hold me. After a while, he released me and tilted my chin up to look at him.

"I'm sorry. My family… There's been kidnapping attempts and money makes people crazy. Paranoid. If you want to leave, I understand. In fact, that's probably a good idea. Come on, I'll take you home."

He grabbed my hand and started walking toward the passenger's door. I looked from him to the house. Angel had dealt with this his entire life. He'd been raised among these people and yet he'd turned out to be a well-adjusted, caring human being. If he could do it his whole life, then I could sure as heck last a dinner. Especially if it made things easier on him.

Resigned, I took a deep breath and closed my eyes, willing my nerves to calm and my hands to stop shaking. My head still pounded away, but that would get better after I took a pill. I'd be much more relaxed then, too.

"No. Every family has issues. I can handle this, Angel," I said.

"You sure?" he asked. "You don't have to."

I shrugged. "Yeah, but you do. It's just dinner. It won't kill me."

The look on his and Bones's face told me they were worried that it might.

♠ ♥ ♣ ♦

CHAPTER TWENTY-EIGHT
Angel

THEY SAY SITUATIONS are only awkward if you let them be, but after my entire family had watched Father's guards detain Markie for trying to get her headache medicine out of my vehicle, awkwardness was inevitable. Thankfully none of my siblings had seen the spectacle, so they had no problem talking to Markie. In fact, the twins clung to her like a couple of blue-hairs at a hot slot machine, talking her ear off about their birthday last weekend.

"She's good with them," Nonna observed after dinner while I helped her carry desserts to the table.

I followed Nonna's gaze to find Markie sitting at a small poolside table playing Go Fish with the twins. Sonia and Sofia, clearly believing they were too old for silly card games, sat beside Markie, talking to her. After Markie played a card, she turned and ran her fingers through Sonia's dark curls, saying something that made my sister smile.

"She volunteers with orphans," I explained. "Kids seem to understand she's a kid-person and they flock to her."

Nonna inclined her head. "Children are more intuitive than adults give them credit for. They know a good person when they see one. Are they right? Is she a good person?"

Markie laughed at something Georgio said, and my little brother grinned.

I nodded, and then wondered if Feds were usually good people. "I think she's the best person I've ever met."

By the time I tore my gaze away from Markie and my siblings, Nonna was walking away.

Moments later, my cousin, Renzo, took her place. "Looks like someone's big-ass ring took a chunk out of your cheek," he said, sidling up to me as he eyed my wound. "Did the golden child finally manage to piss off his daddy?"

If Renzo thought he could goad me into responding, he had another think coming. I shrugged off his question, my gaze never faltering from Markie. She laughed at something Cousin Alberto said.

Out of the corner of my eye I watched Renzo as he leered at her, his hand rubbing the stubble on his chin. "Pretty face, hot body. She looked pretty good sprawled across the hood of your ride. Looks like she'd be fun for a tumble or two. Think you can set that up for me?"

If he knew how much I wanted to strangle him, he'd never let up, so I shrugged off his question like I didn't care. "Sorry, but she's smarter than the pole dancers you usually hook up with. You'll need an IQ above eighty-four, and since you can't seem to tell the difference between your ass and a truckload of checker terminals... it's probably not gonna work out."

His jaw tensed. He forced a smile. I wanted him to move along, but he leaned closer. "I hear they're opening the books up soon. You ready to become a real man, golden child?" he asked.

No.

As a Mariani, my fate was pretty much sealed from birth. But I wasn't made yet, so there was still a smidgen of hope something could change. The minute the family opened the books and made me, that hope would be extinguished. There was no going back once a man was made. I'd be in the family business until death. Father would elevate me to capo, and build an army beneath me.

"Didn't think so," Renzo said. He chuckled as he walked away.

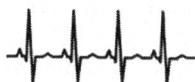

⎍⌁⎍⌁⎍⌁⎍

After dessert was cleaned up, Father ordered the kids to head inside so the adults could talk. With the children gone, Markie sat beside me playing with her coffee cup while Uncle Mario questioned me about a new 3D tablet he'd seen commercials for.

Markie seemed so lost and uncomfortable, and none of the women tried to engage her. It was past time for us to leave, and I started looking for a tactful way to excuse us from the rest of the evening. Uncle Mario wouldn't shut up about the tablet, though.

A hand fell on my shoulder. "Angel, honey," Nonna said, "would you mind taking me home? I think I forgot to take my blood pressure medicine this afternoon and I need to check." She sighed. "Growing old is the pits. The memory goes, and it's all downhill from there."

Whether Nonna really had forgotten her medicine or saw the situation and decided to intervene, I will never know. She might have been just an old woman trying to get into heaven, but she became a saint in my book.

My father started to object and I saw my window of opportunity shrinking. I jumped out of my seat before it could disappear. "Of course, Nonna." I turned to offer Markie my hand.

She was already standing, a relieved smile spreading across her face. "Thank you all for dinner. It was really nice of you to invite me."

Everyone stood. We said a hasty good-bye before heading out the door. Bones was out front, talking with a few of Father's guards. He joined us on the way. We helped Nonna into the passenger's seat and climbed into the Hummer. Then, I took my first deep breath of the night and pulled out of the driveway.

"Well, that was interesting," Nonna said, settling herself in her seat. "Markie, dear, I apologize for my family. They're wary of strangers. That's the problem with having money, you know? There's always someone trying to take it away."

"They say some people are so poor, all they have is money," Markie replied. Then she must have realized how judgmental that sounded, because she was quick to add, "I mean... I'm not saying that about your family. It's just something I heard once, and I thought it was profound."

Nonna laughed so hard she buried her face in her hands. When she came up for air, she turned to smile at Markie.

"I can see why my grandson likes you. You're about as politic as a sidewalk preacher."

Markie arched eyebrow. "Thanks, I think?"

"Oh, it's a compliment, girl. We have enough politicians and thieves around. We could use someone brave enough to speak their mind. I just hope you live long enough to do that." Nonna tugged on her sleeve. "Oh, shoot, would you look at that? A hole in my favorite dress, and what am I going to do about it? My eyes have gotten so bad I can't even thread a needle anymore."

I stopped for a light and glanced over. Sure enough, a large hole ran down the inside seam.

"Looks like it's time to go shopping, Nonna."

Her eyes squinted at me. "That's exactly what's wrong with your generation, Angel. Every time something gets damaged, you throw it out. Whatever happened to fixing things?"

"Nonna, it's just a dress," I insisted, wondering what the big deal was. "Clothes aren't supposed to last forever."

"But I like this dress. It's comfortable and a good fit."

"I could sew it for you?" Markie offered.

Nonna turned to look at her. "You can sew?"

Markie nodded. "The women in Africa taught me how. It's how we entertained ourselves after the children went to sleep and the orphanage was cleaned."

Something about Nonna's sugary-sweet smile told me we'd all been played. No matter how sweet Nonna acted, she was still my father's mother, a fact it was dangerous to forget.

"Well, isn't that nice?" Nonna asked, Cheshire grin still firmly in place. "I'd love for you to come in and sew up my sleeve for me. Thank you for offering."

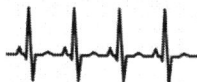

Nonna lived in an upscale retirement community not far from my father's house. The facility sign boasted of everything a retired person could want: a beauty salon, a library, a movie theater, and an activities director who knew how to keep the clientele busy without blowing up their pacemakers. I'd always assumed Nonna loved the place, but as we parked in front of her door, her grumbles did not sound complimentary.

"What's that?" I asked, leaning closer.

She sighed, watching a group of women clustered in front of the clubhouse. "Look at them, gossiping about who's got more money and who's sleeping with whom. Like it even matters at our age. Not a one of them has anything useful to do with their time.

I'm so sick of this place and its pretentious old crones."

"I thought you liked it here?" I opened my door and hurried around to help her out.

"No, I like being with my family. This place... it's the pasture your father has put me out to in order to keep me out of the way. It looks nice and welcoming on the outside, but here I'm just another old nag waiting to die."

"Nonna, don't talk like that," I said, helping her out of the Hummer and toward her door.

Bones and Markie followed us but hung back, giving us privacy to continue our chat.

"Why not? It's true. I am a grandmother, Angel. I should be fattening up my grandchildren with homemade treats and reading them stories *every* day. Not just coming over for Sunday dinners." Her tone sounded genuinely hurt and offended.

"I'm sure the family would love to have you over more often," I insisted.

Hand on my arm, she leaned closer and whispered, "Rachele doesn't want me there any more than she wanted you there. Neither of us has ever fit in. Not since your mother died." Nonna made the sign of the cross. "*Dio l'abbia in gloria.*"

"God rest her soul," I repeated in English, mimicking the gesture.

"Yes, well, nothing to be done about that now, is there?" We reached Nonna's door and she looked back and waved Markie forward. "Come along now, young lady, and we'll let the men get on home."

Nonna unlocked her door and I opened it for her.

"We can come in and wait to take Markie home," I said.

"No, you most certainly may not." She looked at Markie and her face softened into a warm and welcoming smile. "I'd like to chat with your friend one-on-one. Come along, dear."

Without batting an eye, Markie marched past me and followed Nonna into the house. Then she turned and said, "I can take the bus home, Angel. Thanks anyway, though."

The women said good-bye and the door closed. Bones and I were left standing on the sidewalk, wondering what had happened.

"The boss is gonna shit a brick," Bones muttered.

"I think that's an understatement," I said. "But what do we do? Bust down Nonna's door, or sit out here like a couple of schmucks?"

Bones shook his head. "I don't know, man."

We ended up getting back into the Hummer, driving to a nearby convenience store, and grabbing a roll of antacid to help my sudden indigestion. Then we returned to the parking spot in front of Nonna's door and waited.

It had been over a half hour since I'd dropped off Markie when my phone rang. Grimacing at the display, I answered.

"Where are you?" Father asked.

When the old man wanted to know where someone was, he didn't call them up and ask. Instead, he accessed Tech's software and saw for himself. He knew damn well where I was, which is why he'd made the call.

"Nonna wanted to have a chat with Markie, so we're waiting outside."

Father sucked in a breath. "You left an FBI agent alone with your grandmother? What the hell are you thinking? Get her out of there."

Right. Bust down her door and drag Markie out. Why didn't I think of that?

"Nonna said—"

"She's an old woman, Angel. If you can't figure out a way to get that broad out of there, I will. And it will be in a body bag. *Capisce?*"

"Yes, Father."

"Good. Do it now."

The call disconnected. I took a deep breath, and then Bones and I climbed out of the Hummer and approached Nonna's door. She answered before we knocked.

Nonna gave me a knowing smile and a wink. "Oh, good, you're right on time. I promised Markie you'd be back in time to give her a ride."

Markie eyed me. "I told you I could take the bus."

"Angel's a gentleman. Enjoy it, dear. It will probably end after you spread your legs for him."

Markie turned beet red.

I barely resisted the urge to pound my head against the door. "Did you ladies have a nice time?" I asked between gritted teeth.

"Oh, yes. Markie stitched up my sleeve and painted my finger-nails as we chatted. They look lovely, don't you think?" Nonna held up her hands for my approval.

I tried to smile. "Yes. She did a great job."

Father wants to kill her now, but yes, your fingernails are beautiful. I hope it was worth it.

"Angel, don't worry," Nonna said, pulling me forward to kiss my cheek. "Everything will work out. I will make sure it does. Your Nonna always takes care of you."

Then she shooed us out of her apartment so she could get some rest.

CHAPTER TWENTY-NINE
Angel

HAND-IN-HAND, I WALKED Markie to her apartment door while Bones leaned against the Hummer, hand on the gun in his pocket as he watched us.

"Tonight was… interesting," Markie said.

Interesting wasn't the word I'd use, but I nodded anyway. "How's your head?"

"Better. Nonna gave me some tea that helped quite a bit. Even sent some home with me." She patted her purse.

"Good. You gonna tell me what you guys talked about?" I asked.

She dimpled and shook her head. She'd been incredibly tight-lipped about the whole experience, making me very curious. Seeing that she still wasn't going to open up, I left it alone.

"Sorry about… well, everything," I said.

"Thanks for uh… saving me from those guards," she replied.

We stood in silence for a while before I asked, "Are we good?"

"Yeah."

But she was still holding back. "You gonna tell me about the guy in that picture?"

She nodded. "I will. Just give me some time, okay?"

I had no other choice, so I nodded. "Yeah, okay. I'll give you as much time as you need."

They were empty words since I didn't know how much time Father would give me and couldn't promise anything. If Markie came clean as an agent and asked for my help, I would do my best to make us both disappear. Maybe together—with Bones's help—we could outrun the old man. Most likely, we'd all end up dead, but I'd try anyway.

Thoughts of the future made me appreciate the moment we were in. Markie looked beautiful beneath the street lights. The time we had together was precious, and I didn't want to waste a second of it.

"Can I kiss you?" I asked.

She shook her head no. Disheartened but determined to honor her wishes, I started to turn away. She grabbed my arm and pulled me into her. Her lips met mine and all our problems disappeared for a few breathless moments. All too soon she pulled away, said good-bye, and slipped into her apartment.

"The old man's got something on you now," Bones said once we were back in the Hummer. "He's gonna use her. You know that, right?"

I nodded. "What should I do about it?" I asked.

Bones rubbed his chin and stared out the front window. "He thinks he's found your kryptonite. Make him question himself."

"Okay, how?"

More rubbing of his chin. "If it was me, I'd call Terrance."

You could find anything in Vegas if you knew the right guy. When it came to girls, Terrance was definitely the right guy. "You want me to call for a hooker?" I asked, completely confused.

Bones chuckled, nodding. "Hell, yeah. You don't have to do anything with her, just pay her to say you did. Word'll get around to the old man and he'll wonder why you're paying for it. Why you're not gettin' it from Markie. He'll question how committed you are to this broad. If nothing else, it'll screw with his head."

And that, right there, was worth the cost. Convinced, I dialed Terrance and asked him to send me a companion for the evening. He asked if I had any preferences.

"A local. Someone born and raised in Vegas," I told him.

"I've got just the girl. She'll be there within the hour," Terrance said.

He always had just the girl. That's why he was the man.

Bones and I headed upstairs. We'd just changed into sweats and gotten comfortable when a knock sounded on the door. Bones answered, and a tall, thin, redheaded knockout sauntered into the room. She was in her early twenties and wore a black business jacket, skirt, and pumps, all working double time to accentuate her curves. Her hair was up, and a single strand of pearls hugged her neck. More pearls dangled from her ears. Her makeup was heavy, but tasteful. Had anyone seen her walking into my condo, they would have assumed we had a business meeting. Except it was after eleven p.m.

"Damn," Bones said, openly ogling her.

She gave him a coy smile before dismissing him and sashaying over to stand in front of me. "You must be Angel." She looked me over, from head to toe, and licked her lips like I was a T-bone steak and she was one of the tigers from the safari park. I stayed perfectly still, certain that if I made any sudden movements, she'd pounce.

"What's your name?" I asked.

"You can call me Ginger. What can I do for you, sugar?"

I was holding the answer behind my back. I brought the deck of cards forward, offering them to her with a sheepish smile.

She grabbed the deck from me and her eyebrows rose in question. "Okay. Do you want me to wear these or something?"

Now that had potential. It evoked all sorts of images I had to ignore. "No. I want you to play cards with me."

"Ah. Strip poker. Got it." Her hips swung as she strolled to the dining table and sat down, tugging the cards from their case.

Bones chuckled.

"Not exactly." I sat in the chair across from her, pulled out my wallet, and started stacking hundred-dollar bills on the table. She played it cool—pretending not to watch me—but I definitely had her attention. "We need to see how good you are at bluffing."

"Bluffing, huh?" Her smile turned predatory. "All right. I'm game."

Of course she was game; she was a local. Locals knew better than to ask questions, and they pursued easy money like bulls charging a Matador's flag. Ginger stretched her fingers, and then dealt the cards.

Bones stood off to the side, fiddling with his phone and looking completely disinterested in the game. But I knew differently. My friend caught every detail.

Not only was Ginger a great bluffer, she was also quite the card shark. By the fifth game, I was confident she could do the job.

With a scratch of his neck, Bones told me he'd got what he needed as well.

I set down my cards and palmed the stack of hundreds.

Ginger sat up.

"The job's a simple bluff," I said. "You arrived, we had wild, passionate sex, I compensated you well, we made plans to do it again, and then you left."

She was staring at me, but watching the cash fold over in my hands. "And who do I tell this story to?"

"Anyone who asks. You in?"

"Yes." No questions. No hesitation.

"Good." I handed her the money. "Because if they buy it, next time I'll double this."

She struggled to keep a straight face and tucked the bills into her bra. When she stood, Bones stepped in front of her, blocking her path.

"Ginger. Or Elaine Jones. You share an apartment with your friend, Samantha King, and your three-year-old son, Brock, on Esmeralda Avenue. Brock attends the Montessori academy a few blocks from your house."

She stared at him, unblinking.

"Angel's given you a generous opportunity, and you've agreed to do as he asks. You get greedy and screw him over, and you will not be able to hide. *Capisce?*

Bones used Italian when he wanted to remind people who he was. Who we were. Ginger... Elaine... swallowed hard and nodded. "I understand."

"Good." He smiled and stepped out of her way.

She fled. In her position, I would have done the same thing. Bones had packed more malice into that thinly veiled threat than if he'd written a step-by-step manual for what he planned to do to her. I hoped Ginger was smart enough to realize Bones never bluffed.

Needing to dispel the intensity of the situation, I shoulder-checked my friend. "Wow. You're getting better at this," I told him.

He flipped me off.

"No, no, I mean it. I gotta hit the john. You straight scared the piss out of me."

He told me exactly what I could do with my pisser.

Feeling hopeful about the curve ball we'd just thrown my father, I laughed and headed to bed.

CHAPTER THIRTY
Angel

"ANGEL. ANGEL, WAKE up!"

The urgency in Bones's voice snatched me from my dreams and shoved me upright, reaching for my gun.

"Whoa, no need for that," Bones said, his leg pushing against the nightstand drawer to block my access.

Confused, I sat up, shielding my eyes from the light. "What's going on?"

Bones pulled a T-shirt over his head. "Ari called. Markie's in the hospital."

"What?" My mind raced. Father had threatened her life, but she'd left Nonna's. Why would he go after her now? "Wait, the hospital? She's alive?"

Bones nodded, his expression unreadable.

The old man never left anyone alive. Especially not anyone who could pick him out in a lineup. If he'd gone after her, she would have disappeared. I let out a breath and asked about the next likely suspects. "The Pelinos?"

Again, Bones shook his head. "No, it's not like that."

"Not like what?" I asked, reaching for my phone. "And why didn't anyone call me?"

"Ari tried. You didn't answer."

I thumbed on my cell phone and confirmed Bones's words with a blinking notification that I had six missed calls and two voice mails. The last one came in at four thirty-four a.m., seven minutes ago. My phone was silenced. I felt disconnected and angry. Someone had hurt Markie and Bones was acting strange. "What the hell's going on?" I demanded.

"Um… I don't know how to say this." Bones collapsed into the chair in the corner of the room, socks in hand, a blank expression across his face.

"Just tell me, dammit!"

"Ari wasn't making much sense. She was talking about a tumor."

I had to have misheard. "A tumor?" I asked.

"Yeah, a brain tumor. Markie has cancer."

Cancer?

The word slammed into me like a wrecking ball, throwing me off balance. It wasn't true; it couldn't be. "What? She doesn't have cancer! Are you sure she said tumor?"

Bones shook his head, looking as shocked as I felt. "Yeah. It doesn't make sense, but what else sounds like tumor?"

I shook my head. "I don't know. There's got to be some mistake. We were just with her. We'd know if she had cancer. Her hair would be falling out or something."

Bones nodded. "Yeah. You're right." But he didn't look too convinced. In fact, he looked like a damn zombie, staring straight ahead as he put his socks on.

And why was I still in bed? I jumped up and headed for my dresser. "We'll get to the hospital and straighten this all out," I said, trying to reassure us both.

But the knots forming in my stomach told me something was very wrong.

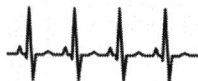

"Angel, you need to slow down," Bones said.

We were halfway to the hospital and I looked down to see the speedometer clocking me at eighty-three in a fifty-five. Surprised, I eased off the gas pedal.

Bones had his hand on the dashboard, as if he could manually slow our speed. "Do you want me to contact Tech and get us the lights?"

I shook my head. Until I knew exactly what was going on, I

sure as hell didn't want to draw my father's attention to the matter. No doubt Tech was already monitoring our early morning drive.

Maybe it was made to look like a brain tumor?

I dismissed the ridiculous thought as soon as it popped into my head. Certain poisons could cause reactions that would point to a heart attack or a stroke, but I'd never heard of anything that could mimic the symptoms of a brain tumor.

The admittance clerk buzzed me and Bones back, and a nurse greeted us and led us to a small examination room where we found Ariana. Still in her pajamas and bare feet, she leaned against the bed, hands clasped in front of her. Bones marched in and hugged her. I squeezed past the two of them, desperate to get to Markie.

Markie lay under a pile of white hospital blankets. Her eyes were closed, and cords connected her to an IV and a couple of ominous-looking machines. Her face looked worrisomely pale.

"How is she?" I asked, turning back toward Ariana.

Ariana pulled away from Bones and glanced at her sister.

"Awake," Markie interrupted. Her eyelids flickered, and then she raised a hand to shield them. "Can you hit the lights, please?"

Bones flicked the switch and she lowered her arm.

I looked from the machines to Markie, searching for clues. A tumor? It sounded too unbelievable to say aloud.

"Are you just going to stare at me all day?" she asked.

Dreading the answer, I summoned my courage and asked, "What happened?"

"Minor complications." She gave me a weak smile.

"Like …?" I asked.

"Swelling and pain. The doctors got the swelling down and the pain is… tolerable. I'm still a little nauseous, but nothing some saltines couldn't cure. You don't have any, do you?"

She seemed so calm and collected as she skirted the real issue. Whatever that was. Surely someone with a brain tumor would be freaking out.

I squeezed her hand and shook my head. "We'll ask for some."

"Thanks." Another weak smile, this one barely hinting at her dimples.

I couldn't take it anymore. "Stop bullshitting me, Markie. What's really going on?"

"Let's give these two some privacy," Bones said. He put his hand on the small of Ariana's back and led her from the room.

"We'll be right outside if you need us."

The door closed. One of the machines beeped, and the cuff around Markie's arm tightened. Her blood pressure levels showed up on the monitor. Silence stretched between us. I opened my mouth to break it, but she beat me to the punch.

"His name is John," she whispered.

I gave her a blank look.

"The man in the photo. His name is John. He's my end-of-life counselor."

My blood turned to ice and the hair on the back of my neck stood up.

Not an agent. An end-of-life counselor.

Markie wasn't working for the government. She was getting counseling for the end of her life.

My legs came out from under me and I collapsed into the chair beside her bed, elbows on my knees, head in my hands. The world spun out of control, and I couldn't make it stop.

"Your end-of-life counselor," I acknowledged once I finally found my voice.

"Yes. I have a brain tumor. It's terminal."

"This was your secret," I breathed. Now that she'd shared it, I wanted her to take it back. I'd rather her be a federal agent. That, I could have dealt with. This... well, there are some options for cancer. I leaned back and stared at the ceiling. "What about surgery or chemo? Isn't there something they can do?"

"Expensive, risky, and painful, with no guarantees."

"How much time do you have?" I don't even know where the question came from. It just spilled right out of my mouth.

"They don't know. They keep changing it."

My mind struggled to wrap around what she was telling me. "So, it's like there's a bomb in your head. Nobody seems to know when it will go off, and the odds are against them defusing it?"

"Exactly." She chuckled. "Where were you when I was looking for a way to explain this to Ari?"

I didn't laugh with her. I couldn't. I couldn't say anything.

"You're right, Angel. And everyone I've told expects me to sit around and wait for my life to go boom. They want me to play it safe to stretch out my days."

"Even Ari?" I asked, finding that hard to believe.

"She's the exception. She thinks I'm nuts, but she gets me. She understands why I'm trying to live every single minute I've got left."

"But surgery or chemo wouldn't—"

"No," she interrupted. "I'm not going to wait around on some list for the surgery, and I can't shoot hoops with Myles and the other kids when chemo is sapping my strength."

She sounded resigned, but not upset. Markie had come to terms with her tumor, but I had not. I would not. I reached for her hand. Her skin felt warm and soft beneath my touch, and I rubbed my thumb over it.

"You are such a selfless, giving, beautiful person," I whispered. "It doesn't seem right that you should have to go through this."

She cracked a smile. "Trust me, Angel, I've committed my share of crimes."

"Sure."

"No, seriously. After my mom died, I kind of lost my mind a little."

"That's probably to be expected," I interjected, not wanting to hear her degrade herself.

"No, let me finish. I want you to know everything. My mom was amazing. After Dad died, she was all I had. All Ari and I had. Strict as could be, but in a loving way. She worked as a courtroom stenographer and was hit by a stray bullet when this criminal, Tristan Bougher, tried to bust his cousin out of jail in the middle of a trial. He took everything from me and Ari. There were a dozen witnesses, but Bougher got off on a technicality. Since Ari and I were both minors, our uncle got us hefty settlements from the state. But nobody could give us back our mom."

That explained the government paycheck. My father had to have known the truth. With eyes and ears everywhere, nothing could hide from him. Which meant he knew exactly who the end-of-life counselor was and had intentionally lied.

Why?

"Mom—" Markie's voice cracked.

I patted her arm. She was finally spilling her guts. I desperately wanted to know it all, but the information seemed to be costing her too much. "Rest. You don't have to do this right now. We can talk about it later."

"No we can't, Angel. You've been so great. You deserve to

know the truth about me."

There was a warning in her voice, eluding to darker secrets. "Wait," I said. I stood, pulled the device finder from my jacket pocket, and scanned the room. "All clear."

She took a deep breath and started again. "All those witnesses, and Bougher got off on a technicality. Can you believe that? I was already in the Running Start program, earning college credits in high school, but I changed my classes when it happened. I wanted to become a cop, like my dad, so when I arrested him there'd be no technicalities. Everything would be text book and the law would bury him under the jail, bars nailed shut so he couldn't take away anyone else's mom."

A cop. She'd gone to school to become a cop. Of course she had, because that's how my life worked. Yet she'd left for Africa shortly after she'd gotten her degree. Why? "What happened next?"

"This." She gestured toward the machines. "I was enrolled in police academy when they found the tumor. Game over. Dad died, Mom died, I would die, and Tristan Bougher would be free to wreck lives. It was such a slap in the face. My parents were good people and they were killed. Ari and I were good people and our lives were wrecked. Then cancer? Really? I was so angry. It was unfair, and I wanted to make it fair." Tears welled in her eyes. "That's when I lost my mind. It was like I became obsessed. I stalked Bougher. I saw him selling drugs to kids, I watched as he hit his girlfriend. He was a bad person, Angel."

Tears leaked down Markie's face.

"Shh. You don't have to justify yourself to me. I'm not gonna judge you."

"You should. Tristan *was* a bad person, but I became worse. I started hanging out at clubs, meeting people. I bought a gun." Her eyes glazed over as she stared at something only she could see. "I didn't even know where the guy had gotten it. What it had been used for. I bought it anyway. I didn't care. The law had failed my family and I wanted Bougher dead." She fell silent.

Markie, my beautiful ray of sunshine, had been driven to want to kill someone. I smoothed her hair out of her face and wiped tears from her cheeks. She smiled up at me and I realized despite what she'd been willing to do, I wasn't looking into the face of a killer. Markie was innocent. Relieved, I let out a breath. I knew the weight of taking a life, and it wasn't a burden I wanted Markie to bear. "But you didn't do it," I said.

"No. My uncle somehow knew what I was planning. He found the gun and freaked out on me, insisting that Bougher was protected. If I would have done anything to him, people would have come for my uncle and Ari. He said I'd talked to the wrong people and he needed to make me disappear. Then he shipped me off to Africa."

Everything suddenly made sense. Father knew who she was. Hell, he probably had connections to whoever was protecting Bougher. Markie's uncle, the district attorney, had to be connected somehow, too. I wondered who Father knew in Idaho, and how deep the roots ran.

Still, something bothered me. If Markie was in danger, her uncle should have sent Ariana away as well. "What's your sister's role in all of this?" I asked.

"She doesn't know anything. My uncle said we needed to keep her in the dark to keep her safe. Please don't tell her."

"I won't. I promise."

"I didn't want you to know." She sighed. "I've changed so much since it all happened. Sometimes it doesn't even seem real. In Africa… the people I met… the conditions I saw… talk about a perspective shift. I'm not angry anymore. I've forgiven Bougher. I'm over… everything. I've accepted the fact I'm dying and I want to enjoy the time I have left."

"And you want to make the world a better place before you go." Now I understood her. Everything I'd heard her say and had seen her do made sense. "You've gone through fire, but it didn't burn you. You came out beautiful and perfect. Like gold, refined by flames."

Markie watched me, her eyes leaking more tears.

"I'm glad you told me, but your past doesn't matter. I want to be involved in your future. No matter what that requires or how long it lasts. Late night hospital visits, I'm there. Days with orphanage brats, you already know. You don't have to carry this alone anymore. We're in this together now. I love you."

She blinked back tears while a giant smile dimpled her cheeks. She grabbed hold of my shoulders and pulled me forward until our lips connected. Markie kissed me until my breath was gone.

"Thank you, Angel. I love you, too," she whispered against my cheek.

A knock on the door interrupted our moment.

♠ ♥ ♣ ♦

CHAPTER THIRTY-ONE
Angel

THE DOOR CRACKED open and Bones poked his head into the hospital room. "Doc's here," he said.

I waved him in. Bones opened the door and he and Ariana entered, followed by a silver-haired, bespectacled man wearing scrubs and carrying an electronic tablet. The man introduced himself to me as Doctor Johnson, studying the machines as his fingers flew over the buttons on his tablet.

He paused long enough to glance at Markie. "How's your pain?" he asked.

She gave him a thumbs up. "Much better."

He pointed toward a pain management printout on the wall. "From one to ten?"

"A two, maybe?"

"Good. It looks like we got the swelling down, too. How's the nausea?" He turned and put his stethoscope on, leaning in to listen to Markie's heart.

"Crackers would help. Can I have some?"

"I don't see why not. I'll have the nurse bring some in."

"Thanks. Do you know when I'll be able to go home?"

He eyed her, pulled the stethoscope down to rest around his neck, and then looked at the machines again. "There's no real reason for us to keep you here. Pain management seems to be all we can do for you at this point. Have you spoken to Hospice yet?"

It's a good thing I was sitting, because the word would have taken my legs out from under me. Hospice meant the end.

"Hospice?" Ariana asked, gripping the end of the bed for support. "Are you— Is she—"

Bones rubbed her back.

"You think she's already to that point?" Ariana finally spit out.

"No," Markie hurried to say. "I can hold off for a while longer."

Doctor Johnson lowered his electronic tablet and leveled a stare at her. "Calling in Hospice doesn't hurry along the end. They can help control the pain, though."

"It's usually not this bad."

He lowered his shoulders and looked to me, like I could help him. I couldn't even wrap my brain around her tumor, so I didn't know what he expected from me. I shrugged.

"It's going to get worse." Doctor Johnson glanced down at his tablet, and then back to Markie. "Don't wait too long. Okay?"

She nodded. "I won't."

"All right. I'll have the nurse get you some crackers. They'll be serving breakfast soon. If you can manage to keep that down for a couple of hours, I'll release you."

She beamed him a smile. "Thank you."

He nodded and hurried out the door.

I stared after him, feeling like an outsider, watching someone else's life crumble. Then I remembered this was my life—my Markie—and I stood and ran after him. He was about to enter the next room, but I called out and he paused.

I caught up and asked, "What options does she have?"

He eyed me over his spectacles. "I'm sorry, but that falls under doctor-patient confidentiality."

"I'm not asking you to read me her file. I just… there has to be something we can do. Some sort of procedure or chemo? Can't anything save her?"

"Without breaking confidence with Ms. Davis, I can tell you there are few doctors who will operate on someone whose diagnosis is as advanced as hers. Her tumor's location is ideal, making her a perfect candidate for a new laser procedure several surgical oncologists have had great success with. The procedures are expensive and risky, and the waiting lists are long."

Hope sparked inside of me. "But they do exist?"

He nodded. "Now, if you'll excuse me, I have another patient to tend to." Without waiting for me to reply, he stepped into the room.

I leaned against the wall and let his words sink in. *Expensive. Risky. Waiting list. Will she do it? Will I be able to find her something in time?*

I couldn't. In my own right, *I* was a nobody. My entire life I'd hidden in the shadows of anonymity, cloaking myself from my family's influence. If I wanted Markie to get help, I'd have to go through someone well-known and powerful enough to pull strings and hoist her to the top of the waiting list. My father. I closed my eyes and rubbed the bridge of my nose, dreading the conversation. He'd lied about her and threatened her. Now I had to beg him to save her.

"You okay?" Bones asked, leaning beside me.

I closed my eyes and shook my head, unable to reply.

"Right. Well, let me know if there's anything I can do."

I nodded. "Thanks, man. I'm gonna need the old man's help for this one, though."

Bones didn't miss a beat. "When are we going?" he asked.

"Soon as they release Markie," I replied, thankful Bones was by my side. Thankful he'd be with me when I begged my father to save the woman I loved.

Confirming my thoughts, Bones patted my shoulder as he followed me back into Markie's hospital room. "I got your back, bro. No matter what."

CHAPTER THIRTY-TWO
Angel

MARKIE KEPT DOWN crackers and breakfast, so she was released from the hospital a little after nine a.m. We dropped Ariana off at their apartment so she could shower and get ready to work her scheduled lunch shift. Still dressed in the pajamas she'd gone to the hospital in, Markie slipped inside to change. She emerged minutes later, wearing jeans, a sweatshirt, and sneakers. Her coloring seemed better, but she still winced when she stepped into the sunlight.

"How are you feeling? Really?" I asked as soon as she climbed back into the Hummer.

She leaned back and closed her eyes. She'd dozed quite a bit while we were waiting for her release, but there were still dark circles around her eyes. "It hurts. Not sharp pains like last night, though. Just an annoying dull thud. Like my pulse is pounding against my brain."

I reached for her hand and intertwined our fingers. "You should have told the doctor."

"Why? So they could drug me up and keep me longer? I don't want that." A smile tugged at her lips but didn't reach her dimples. I stopped for a light, and she opened her eyes and looked at me. "I don't want to be stuck in some hospital."

A lump formed in my throat. I squeezed her hand, silently promising she would get more time. That I would get more time with her. I turned on my bluetooth and made a call to my father.

He was home and surprisingly available for a quick meeting as long as I came immediately. I disconnected the call and squeezed Markie's hand again.

"I know you're tired, and this didn't exactly go well last time, but do you mind if we swing by my parents' house for a couple of minutes?" I asked. "It won't take long, I promise. Then I can take you back to my place and you can pass out for as long as you want."

"You sure it's a good idea to take her with us?" Bones asked from the backseat.

Hell no, it wasn't a good idea, but I didn't exactly have a wealth of options. The second her doctor suggested Hospice, I knew we were fighting against the clock. I couldn't leave her alone in her state, but I needed to speak to the old man immediately.

Markie squeezed my hand. "I know you have things you need to do, and I don't want you rearranging your schedule for me. Of course we can swing by your parents' house."

I was still trying to figure out how to approach my father when we pulled into the driveway and I helped Markie out of the Hummer. We stepped into the house and were attacked by the twins. Their loud, happy laughter bounced off the walls, crashing into us. Markie winced, but kneeled and opened her arms to them. They bounded against her, no doubt wreaking havoc on her head, but she smiled anyway.

"Daddy said Angel was coming, but he didn't say you'd be here," Luciana announced.

"Careful. Markie's got a bad headache, so I need you to be quiet and not so rough, okay?" I plucked Luciana out of Markie's arms and gave her a bear hug. "And what are you two doing home on a Monday? Did you get kicked out of school again, you little hooligans?"

"We've never been kicked out of school," Georgio laughed, grabbing hold of my legs. "No school today, so Mom's taking us to the park."

"Hey! I was going to tell them." Luciana elbowed Georgio, glaring at him. Then she smiled up at Markie and added, "She has to run out our energy so we don't drive her crazy."

Markie's smile lit up her eyes, returning life to her face. "I'll bet."

"Would you like to come with us?" Georgio asked.

Markie looked to me.

"Sorry, guys, but we're not going to be here long. I need to meet with Father for a minute. Do you know where he is?"

"In his office," Rachele said, coming around the corner, cell phone in hand. She looked frazzled and worn. "Angel, Markie, good to see you both. I forgot there was no school today and the nanny's not here yet. I'm trying to get this proposal approved. Can you keep an eye on the twins for a few minutes while I make some calls?"

Rachele was on the board of directors for one of Father's companies. As near as I could tell, her position required her to bully, coerce, and stroke egos to get the board to do whatever Father wanted.

"I'm actually here to meet with Father," I replied.

"I'd be more than happy to watch them while you two are busy," Markie said.

"Oh good, you can help us!" Georgio exclaimed, tugging at Markie's shirt. "We're making a giant Lego castle in the playroom."

"Then we're going to set up our dragons and knights and have a battle," Luciana added.

"Markie should be resting," I replied, giving my stepmother a pointed look and hoping she registered the seriousness in my tone.

Markie reached up and grabbed my hand, using it to pull herself up. "It's Legos, Angel. Not like I'm going to be running a marathon or something." Then she turned back to the twins and added, "Sure, I'd love to help build."

"Great, thanks. You're wonderful." Rachele paused long enough to key something into her phone before heading toward the kitchen.

Still hesitant, I squatted until I was eye level with the twins. "Okay, but you guys gotta promise me you'll take good care of Markie, okay? Don't let her overdo it. You promise?"

They nodded enthusiastically, like little bobbleheads hopped up on sugar.

"Angel, it's fine," Markie whispered, her hand on my arm. "Go do what you need to do. The twins and I will have a blast."

"You sure you'll be okay?"

"Are you kidding? I have the two most adorable babysitters in the world." She gave me a peck on the lips, much to the disgust of the twins, and then let the two of them tow her up the stairs.

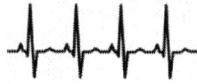

My father's office was located to the right of the entryway. As we approached, Cousin Alberto emerged from the room, leaving the door ajar. He said a quick hello and headed for the front of the house. Bones and I entered the old man's office in silence, our footfalls echoing against the dark walnut hardwood floors. Father sat in a high-backed chair, his gaze fixed on the dual computer screens in front of him. We stopped beside his desk and waited for him to address us. Without taking his eyes off the screens, he gestured for us to sit.

He didn't greet us. We waited in tense silence as he pounded away on his keyboard. Then he finally graced me with a cold stare that made my hackles rise.

"I hear that Ms. Davis spent some time in the hospital this morning," he said.

"She has a brain tumor, but I'm sure you knew that as well."

He inclined his head and spread his hands across the desk.

"Why did you lie?" I asked.

"I'm surprised you care so much, after your visitor last night."

So the old man had found out about the prostitute. Good to know. Had Markie not ended up in the hospital this morning, the plan Bones and I were working on might have actually been a success. He still hadn't answered my question, so I stared at him, waiting.

Finally, said, "Because I was trying to avoid this conversation. The one where you come and ask me to solve your problem."

My problem. That's what Markie was to him.

"But it's not that easy," Father continued. "This girl you're messed up with… she has some big enemies. Tried to kill a made man."

"That's not exactly the truth."

He shrugged. "They say the first casualty of war is the truth, and she's not exactly my problem."

He knew it wasn't true, but he had every intention of using it anyway. Markie was valuable to him now, because she was a card he could play against me. Her cancer just increased his power.

Now he had me by the balls.

"What do I need to do?" I asked.

Bones shifted. He was trying to warn me, but I was fully aware of what I was getting into.

"You know what I want, Angel."

I swallowed back the lump in my throat. "I have done everything you've ever asked me to. I contribute to this family just as much as anyone else. My inventions have opened the doors for us to—"

"Your inventions? Angel, you are my heir apparent. You shouldn't be hiding in some lab, building shit. You should be elevated to Capo by now, learning the business and serving at my right hand."

My throat was dry. I swallowed again, envisioning myself sitting behind my father's desk, my hands dripping with blood. I didn't want that life. Didn't want it, but I had no choice. I'd never had a choice. But at least now I'd be exchanging my future for something that mattered. For someone who mattered.

"And if I promise to do this?" I asked.

Father stood. "Well, then I will—"

His desk phone rang, interrupting. He scowled at the readout and then pressed a button. Tech's face popped out into a 3D image at the base.

"This better be good. I'm in a meeting."

Tech's 3D image spun around the room. After seeing Bones and I were the ones in attendance, he turned back toward my father. "Yes, sorry sir, this can't wait. Dante's car has disappeared from radar."

My father's eyes widened. "What do you mean, disappeared?"

"There's been an explosion, sir."

Father sat down hard. "And Dante?"

My phone rang. Dante's number. I answered and put it to my ear.

"You bastard!" my little brother shouted. "How could you? I told you I would tell her and I did. You couldn't give me one more day?" A sob ripped through him. "She's dead, Angel. She's dead and I will never forgive you for this!"

Shocked and confused, it took me a minute to put two and two together. Tech said Dante's car—the same car I'd threatened to blow up—had exploded.

His girl. Oh no.

"Dante, you've got to believe me. That wasn't me."

"Dante? You have Dante on the line?" Father asked, his tone desperate.

I nodded.

"Go to hell, Angel!" my brother shouted.

He really believed I blew up his car. Of course he believed it. I'd promised him I would, and I'd bluffed my ass off to make sure I sounded convincing.

"No, Dante, listen. Bones and I have been at the hospital since early. I'm in Father's office right now."

"Give me the phone," the old man ordered.

I handed it to him and slumped down in my chair. My little brother thought I'd tried to kill him. He thought I was that type of guy.

"Dante?" My father let out a breath. "Oh, thank God. There's an ambulance on the way. They're going to take you to Summerlin, and Angel and I will meet you there. You go and get checked out." Father listened for a moment, looking down at his desk. "Yes, well there's nothing we can do for her now. But you get in that ambulance. I'll see you soon."

He disconnected and handed me back my phone.

The door crashed open and Rachele came bursting through it, her face a mask of terror. "Dante?" she asked.

"He's okay," Father assured her. "I just spoke to him. He's fine. He's heading to the hospital to get checked out, just in case."

She let out a relieved sob, and he engulfed her in his arms. "Shh. He's fine."

"Who did this?" she asked. "Who would want to hurt my baby?"

"I'm not sure, but I promise you I *will* get to the bottom of this."

"What about the girls?" she asked. "What if someone tries to attack them?"

Father pressed a button on his phone. When Uncle Carlo answered, Father directed him to get security to Sonia and Sofia's school.

"I'm going to the hospital with you," Rachele announced.

"What about the twins?" Father asked.

"The nanny will be here soon."

"No. No nannies. Nobody outside of family. Got it?"

Rachele nodded. Her entire body was trembling.

Father slipped his suit coat on and continued talking to Rachele. "Good. Call Mom and have her come sit with the twins. Then you can join us at the hospital. Make sure you take at least two guards, though. I don't know what these bastards have planned, and we can't let them catch us with our pants down. You understand?"

Her gaze was vacant, but she nodded.

Bones and I left so my parents could finish their conversation in privacy while we went upstairs to find Markie. She and the twins had thousands of Legos dumped on the floor and were busily laying out the ground floor of what would soon be a giant building. When Markie saw my face, she stood and asked what was wrong. I gestured for her to follow me out of the room.

Once we were out of earshot from the twins, I whispered, "It's my brother, Dante. He's been in an accident."

"Oh no. Is he okay?"

"Yeah, but Father and I need to get to the hospital. Are you okay to stay with Rachele and the kids for a while? I'll try to get back here as soon as I can. I'm sorry to leave you here like this, but I've gotta—"

"Yes, of course. Go, Angel. I'm fine."

I leaned in and kissed her, relieved. "Thank you. I'll be back as soon as I can."

She gave me a reassuring smile. "I'll be here."

♠ ♥ ♣ ♦

CHAPTER THIRTY-THREE
Markie

MY PERIPHERAL VISION was blurry. I probably should have told the doctor that, but there was nothing he could do for it, so why tell him? So I could stay in that stupid hospital bed longer? No thank you. Then I would have missed out on building a lovely castle with the twins. Their laughter was all the medicine I needed. I reached forward to stack another Lego. It slipped out of my hand and rolled out of my line of sight.

Well, dangit.

"You okay, Markie?" Georgie asked.

"Yep. I'm good. Just trying to figure out which block to place next."

He eyed me. I was a horrible liar. I couldn't even fool a seven-year-old.

Angel appeared in the doorway, which was thankfully in my line of sight, looking worried. I followed him into the hallway where he told me the bad news about his brother. He needed to leave. I'd stay behind with the twins. I watched him go, and then returned to our castle building.

"This section needs to be pink, because it's the princess's room," Luciana announced, placing a rose-colored wall. "This next area will be blue for the prince. They're going to get married." She glanced up at me. "Are you and Angel going to get married?"

You'd think I'd be used to the bizarre out-of-left-field questions kids ask, but every once in a while a child still caught me off guard. This was one of those times.

"No," I replied, hoping she wouldn't pry.

In true child-like fashion, she did. "Why not? Don't you like Angel?"

"I like Angel very much."

"Then you two should get married. I'll be your flower girl and Georgie can be the ring bearer."

Tears stung my eyes. There'd be no wedding, no flower girl, no ring bearer. Not to Angel nor anyone else. It had never bothered me before, but at that moment, it seemed like the most tragic truth of life.

Must be the pain meds.

I took a deep breath and blinked away useless tears. "You'd make a beautiful flower girl, Luci. And Georgie would make a handsome ring bearer."

"But you're not going to marry Angel?" Georgio asked, sounding confused.

"No, I'm not."

"Well, will you marry me, then?"

Okay, that was sweet. And I had no idea what to say.

Luciana had no such trouble. She sighed and rolled her eyes dramatically. "She can't marry you. She's *way* older than you."

That wasn't so sweet. Before I could tell her as much, it sounded like fireworks went off outside. All three of us jumped at the noise.

"What's that?" Georgio asked, rushing to the window.

Shouts followed the fireworks. Then there were more explosions. Only this time I knew they weren't fireworks. My training kicked in.

"Georgie, get away from the window!" I shouted. "Come here."

Doors slammed open downstairs. Men shouted. Shots were fired. A woman screamed.

Luciana's eyes grew round. "It's the bad guys," she whispered.

That seemed to ignite something in Georgio. "This way. Hurry!" He motioned us toward the closet.

Luciana grabbed my hand and tugged me toward the closet.

More gunshots rang out. Feet slammed against the stairs. I looked behind us, expecting someone to bust through the door and find us. There was another tug on my hand. Luciana shoved me through a small door in the closet. She followed me, and then closed it up. Darkness engulfed us. I could hear the twins breathing heavily. Or maybe that was me? I couldn't tell.

"Now we wait," Georgio whispered. "Dad will find us here."

"It's just like hide and seek. You don't have to be scared," Luciana added, her voice wavering.

I turned on my phone to give us a little light. We were in some sort of hidden passageway in the wall. It went on past Georgio. I angled my phone, but couldn't tell how far it continued.

The twins were visibly scared, but also eerily calm. They'd acted so quickly.

"Does this happen often?" I whispered.

Heavy footfalls on the other side of the wall kept them from answering. Luciana was trembling, so I pulled her in for a hug. All three of us held our breath and listened.

"They're not in here," a muffled voice said.

"Well, they've gotta be here somewhere. Check the rest of the rooms." Names and directions were called out as the footsteps retreated.

My cell phone rang.

It pealed through the darkness, startling me. I jumped, and then fumbled to silence it. Angel's face appeared, and then vanished when I hit the button to send him to voice mail.

"You hear that?" someone asked.

"Sounded like a phone."

"Where?"

More footfalls. They were searching for us.

Georgio grabbed my phone from my hand. He took out the battery and set both phone and battery on the floor. "They can use it to track us," he whispered. "We have to go."

He was like a seven-year-old James Bond. His father had prepared him for an attack. Why? Who would break in to a well-guarded mansion, in the middle of the day, and assault a mom and a couple of kids? A memory tickled the back of my mind. Something Angel had said …

There's been kidnapping attempts and… and money makes people crazy. Paranoid.

Maybe his family wasn't so paranoid after all.

The three of us held hands so we wouldn't get disconnected in the dark, and tip-toed through the dark with Georgio in the lead.

"This way," he whispered.

There was a faint click, and then light flooded the space, intensifying my headache. As my eyes adjusted the two of them grabbed my hands and tugged me into a bush. Staying low, we crawled for several minutes, pausing every time a twig snapped, and stopped at the fence.

Loud banging came from the house. Whoever was in there was tearing the place apart. I glanced back before following the twins through a hidden gate. Once we were on the other side, Luciana looked up at me with big trusting eyes and asked, "Which way?"

Sirens blared in the distance. The cavalry was coming to save us. "We wait here for the cops," I said.

Georgio shook his head. "No cops. This is not a drill."

What? "You have drills like this?" I asked.

The look he gave me made me feel like the stupidest person on the planet.

"Right. Of course you do. Who doesn't?" Building a Lego castle was normal for a seven-year-old. This was not.

"No cops," Georgio repeated.

Gunshots coming from the back of the house told me we needed to move. I grabbed both their hands, gritted my teeth against the pain in my head, and ran. We continued on for blocks, until Luciana started to lag behind. I didn't know if we were being followed and didn't want to take the chance. I picked her up and kept going.

When Georgio and I ran out of steam, I lowered Luciana to her feet and we slowed our pace to a walk. By then, I was lost and couldn't even tell which direction we'd come from. Part of that was probably from having no peripheral vision. We continued on for hours, mostly traveling down side roads and alleys. My pain medicine wore off and I felt completely disoriented.

"We should get a map," I suggested, pointing toward a convenience store. Of course, I had no idea what I'd purchase a map with since my purse was still in Angel's vehicle.

"No. There's cameras," Georgio said.

"And?"

He sighed, clearly disgusted with my lack of knowledge. "And the bad guys can take over the cameras and see us."

Certain he was messing with me, or quoting something he'd heard on television, I started to laugh. But Georgio was serious.

"No they can't," I replied.

Stone-faced, he said, "My dad does."

And that was pretty much the most terrifying thing I'd ever heard a kid say. I tried to dismiss it as something someone had told him to scare him, but every time I walked toward the convenience store Luciana started crying. No crocodile tears, either. She was legitimately panic-stricken about it. My vision was getting worse and my brain felt like mush, but I stayed away from anyplace with security cameras.

My legs went numb from walking, and I knew the kids had to be suffering as well. The temperature dropped with the sun but we trudged on, searching for a landmark we recognized.

It was well past dark when we finally caught a break. I recognized a bus stop and followed it to a coffee shop I'd frequented. We were only a few blocks from someone I could trust.

Feeling hopeful, I urged the kids on.

CHAPTER THIRTY-FOUR
Angel

BONES AND I followed two of Father's black SUVs to the hospital. As I maneuvered through traffic, I felt my friend's gaze burning a hole in the side of my face.

"What?" I asked when I couldn't take it any longer.

No answer.

Markie was dying, someone had just tried to blow up Dante, and I had almost made a deal with the devil. I had no time for his games. "You might as well just spit it out," I said, not bothering to mask the anger and frustration I felt.

And spit it out he did. "You can't do this, Angel. It will kill you."

"Thanks for your concern, but I'm not *that* weak," I growled.

He chuckled. "Weak. Right. That's *exactly* what I mean."

He wasn't helping my mood. "Well then, what the hell do you mean?"

"Your old man snaps his fingers, and half the city comes to heel like dogs waiting for table scraps. We're the weak ones, Angel, not you."

Sure he was screwing with me, I scowled. His expression was serious, though.

"Then there's you," Bones continued. "Every day you resist him. Every day you fight."

I started to object. Resisting and fighting my father would be stupid, and I sure as hell wasn't stupid.

"Oh you play the game," Bones said, holding up a hand to stop me. "But it's different. He hasn't found your currency... your motivation for playing. Most of these fools, you show them the money or the girls, and they're all in. None of that shit matters to you. Never has. It still won't. You make this deal, and you'll have to commit. You'll have to stop resisting, and the shit he'll make you do will eat you alive. More than it already does. And for what? A chance to save Markie? What if she doesn't make it?"

I understood everything he was saying, but it didn't matter. "I can't just sit here and watch her die, Bones."

He nodded. There were no easy answers, and we were both smart enough to acknowledge when all our options sucked. We rode the rest of the way in silence, following Father's motorcade into the hospital parking garage.

Dante was in an examination room. He had a gash across his forearm, but was otherwise fine. He watched me with eyes full of suspicion, which both hurt and frustrated me. I'd already said my piece on the matter, so I didn't bother trying to defend myself again. Father would set him straight eventually. Or not. In fact, the more I thought about it, the more I wondered if the old man had set up the whole thing. In one genius move, he'd have gotten rid of Dante's girl, made Dante believe I was a badass, and given the families incentive to unite against the Pelinos since they'd attacked my brother before he was a made man.

Well played, old man.

No. I had to believe Father wouldn't have risked hurting Dante. At least, I had to hope he wouldn't.

"We'll get those bastards," Father said, patting Dante on the shoulder. We were still waiting in his room for the staff to release him. "The family is preparing. We'll strike back hard and fast. I promise you they'll regret this."

The last time the Vegas families were at war, I was just a child. Father had ordered the women and children to hit the mattresses, so to speak, while he and his crew struck the reigning boss. Too young to know what was going on, I remember hiding in a cabin in the woods. Before Father left us there, he promoted me to "man of the house," making me promise to watch over the family by any means necessary, showing me the handgun he stored in my nightstand.

"Two in the head, make sure they're dead," he said. Then he

ruffled my hair and left.

I was holed up in that cabin with Nonna, a pregnant Rachele, Aunt Mona, and Dante for what seemed like an eternity, praying my father would live to come back for us. Each sleepless night, I pressed my face against the window and watched for his return, my hand resting on the nightstand in case the bad guys came to hurt my family. Now my father was the boss being attacked.

"By now, the whole city knows the Pelinos failed. They will need a successful strike—or a really good score—to save face. We can't let them have that chance. They struck out at my second son, so I will hit their first."

"Bruno," I breathed, a sense of dread washing over me. Bruno seemed like the least dangerous of his family. But as the eldest son, his death *would* hit the family the hardest.

Father nodded.

"What do you need me to do?" I asked.

"Get in touch with your team, and find that bastard. I need a location and a plan for how to take him out."

"Yes sir." I pulled out my phone and sent a mass text to the guys on my team.

As I hit send, an alarm went off on my father's phone. He looked down at it and his brow furrowed.

"What is it?" I stood.

"Something's haywire with the house alarm." He dialed a number and then put the phone up to his ear. "Tech, why the hell is my house alarm showing as offline? What do you mean it's been disabled? I got that system because *you* assured me it couldn't be disabled. How could someone hack into our system? Has Rachele been contacted?"

I stared at my father straining to hear Tech's response.

"What? What about the guards? How could you lose all contact with my house?" Scarlet crept up Father's face, ending in a vein that throbbed against his forehead.

Lost contact with the house?

It felt like the floor fell out from under me. I grabbed the arm of a nearby chair to steady myself. If the Pelinos were making their move…

No. They wouldn't attack a house full of women and children. That's against the rules. The families would wipe them out. They'd have to be crazy!

Reassuring myself, I dialed Markie's number. It rang once, and then went to voice mail.

"You get her?" Father asked.

"No sir."

Guards surrounding us, Father and I rushed from the hospital waiting room into the garage. Thin slits in the concrete let in traces of the midday sun and kept the place from being pitch black, but the garage was dark. It hadn't been like that when we'd parked. Immediately, the hair on the back of my neck stood up. Glass crunched under my feet and I glanced up, squinting until my eyes adjusted. The lights had been busted out.

Bones closed in on my right, his presence reassuring me I wasn't alone. On my left, Father kept his hands firmly in his jacket pockets, stepping over the glass without breaking stride. In the dim light, I could barely make out the vicious grin spreading across his face.

A chill went up my spine. I squinted into the dark, searching for whatever had the old man smiling. Figures emerged from the shadows in front of us, and chaos erupted. Gunfire shattered the silence. I tried to duck, but someone grabbed me from behind, yanking me backwards. The hard steel of a pistol jabbed into my ribs.

No.

It wasn't the first time I'd had a gun pointed at me—not by a long shot, thanks to Father's drills—but this time was different. It made me desperate and angry at the distraction keeping me from Markie and the twins. I spun and threw a punch at my attacker, hearing the satisfying crunch of impact before his gun went off. Fire burned through my side as I hit the ground, drawing my weapon. Father's guards fell in, swinging at each other. Dark-suited men jumped, kicked, and swung to the thunder of bullets bouncing off the cement walls. The fray looked like an out-of-control mosh pit. Ears ringing, I searched for Bones. His fist slammed into the face of my attacker. The attacker flew backwards and slapped against the cement floor. Bones followed and kicked him.

I raised my weapon, but couldn't get a clean shot.

"You're surrounded Mariani. Give up and step down, and we'll let the kid live. All your kids."

The familiar voice came from the shadows in front of us. I

peeked around a car and squinted into the dark. Bruno's voice came from the center of several dark shadows.

"You want me to trust a bunch of cowardly bastards who attacked a house full of women and children?" My father asked.

"We thought you were home."

"Is that what you plan to tell the other families? That you blew up my son's car and expected me to hide in my house?"

Bruno laughed. "You think the other families will step in? Ha! The borgatas are sick of being tied down to your rules, old man. The wolves want to be unleashed. They would have pulled you down years ago, but they're just a bunch of bitches... not enough balls between them to attack. Well, my father's just crazy enough to do whatever needs to be done."

Father twitched. A little red beam raced across the shadows, ending in the center of Bruno's forehead. Before I could register what I was seeing, a shot rang out. The Pelino heir apparent crumpled to the ground. His stunned guards took a few seconds too long to react, and the little red light traveled down the line.

Bam. Bam. Bam

Bodies fell in its wake. I aimed and fired off a shot. A bullet whizzed past my head and I ducked back behind the car.

"You cocky son of a bitch; this is my city!" Father roared. He ducked down, slammed another magazine into his Glock, and the little red beam resumed its deadly dance. I thought the old man was crazy when he'd tasked me with adding a laser sight to his Glock, but in that darkened garage he was a genius. In fact, if we made it out of the garage, I fully intended to get myself a gun just like it.

For now, my Desert Eagle would have to do. I peeked back around the car and took a few blind shots. The fighting behind us began to die down, and more of my father's guards joined us in the frontal attack. The Pelino men started to retreat. One guard slung Bruno's body over his shoulder before the entire group turned and ran, weaving through cars and dodging our bullets as they disappeared deeper into the darkness.

My father had lost several guards. The remainder of the force piled into one SUV, leaving the second in the garage. Bones and I followed in the Hummer. I drove while Bones fumbled with the first aid kit.

"You're gonna need to take off your jacket so I can get a look at your side," he said, tugging bandages out of the kit.

I stopped at a light and struggled out of the ruined coat, stinging the hell out of my side with every twist of my stomach. The bottom right quarter of my T-shirt was soaked with blood. Bones tugged it upward and swore.

"How bad is it?" I asked. The light turned green, so I focused back on the road.

"You got a chunk of meat missing; needs stitches."

I chuckled. "Yeah, we should probably call the Pelinos and ask them to chill the hell out so I can get back to the hospital. That gash on your cheek could probably use a stitch or two as well."

Bones pulled down his mirror and snorted. "I've cut myself worse shaving."

"Yeah? They probably have classes to teach you how to do that..."

"All right, wiseass, let me get that bleeding stopped."

Bones rolled up the bottom of my shirt and taped it to my chest. Then he doctored my side while I drove. "Not bad for your first gunfight," he said, admiring the wound.

I nodded. "Bruno's dead." My father's bullet had splattered Bruno's brains all over his men. No surviving that.

"He was stupid to goad the old man... and standing out in the open like that? Why? Almost like he wanted to die."

I considered Bones's words as my adrenaline rush faded, sapping my strength and leaving behind a bone-deep weariness. Bruno was free of our fathers' war now. He wouldn't have to take any more lives or watch the people around him suffer. Maybe Bruno had wanted to end it all. If I didn't have Markie, Bones, and my younger siblings to think of, I might have been tempted to do the same.

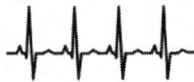

The street in front of my father's house was lined with cop cars and ambulances. Father's SUV parked behind a police cruiser and Bones and I pulled up behind them. What was left of the old man's guards surrounded us as we made our way past the cruisers and into the mayhem.

The mansion looked like a war zone. Bodies were strewn from

the broken security gate to the front door that hung from its top hinges. Authorities clearly hadn't been there long, because they were still checking for pulses and bagging and tagging the dead. A fallen man moaned and writhed on the ground. The guards around us tensed, but an EMT hurried over to deal with the wounded. I scanned the faces of the fallen as we passed; some I recognized, and some I didn't. I knew I should feel sorrow for those who'd given their lives to protect my family, but all I felt was outrage. How many men had we lost? How many had the Pelinos sacrificed? How many more would it take?

Where are Markie and the twins?

My father saw my blood-soaked shirt and hurried over to check out my wound.

"I'm fine," I said, waving him off. "It grazed me. We'll deal with it later."

"You should let me have a look at that," one of the EMTs said.

"Not now," I replied, walking past him.

Renzo and his team met us in the driveway. "Sir, I'm glad to see you're okay."

"Where's my family?" Father asked.

Renzo's gray T-shirt was darkened with sweat in several areas and he held a semi-automatic in his hands. "Rachele's inside. They're loading her onto a stretcher. She's been shot in the leg. We can't find the twins anywhere, sir."

"Did he get them? Did that bastard get my children?"

Renzo shifted his weight and continued, "We don't think so. Rachele said—"

"Dom!" Rachele's high-pitched voice strained.

Renzo snapped his mouth shut, bowed his head, and stepped to the side, revealing the gurney that rolled my stepmother out of the house and toward us. One EMT navigated the route while a second held a mass of white cloth to Rachele's leg, applying pressure as they walked.

Rachele broke into tears and stretched out her hands.

Father rushed to her side. The gurney stopped and Rachele leaned against him, sobbing harder. The old man's jaw clenched as he stroked her hair. "I'm sorry you had to go through this. They'll pay for what they did."

"She's lost a lot of blood, and we need to get her to the hospital," the EMT pushing the gurney said.

233

Father nodded, and the gurney started rolling forward again. He stayed beside Rachele, and she clung to him.

"I'm coming with you," he told Rachele.

"No. Please… our babies. Those bastards didn't find them."

"What about Markie?" I asked.

"She's with them. I hope she knows what she's doing. She better keep them safe."

I let out a breath I didn't realize I'd been holding. "She'll protect them." I was certain of it.

Father continued to stroke Rachele's hair. "Shh. Relax, we'll find them, but I'm not leaving you again. I can do what I need to do from the hospital."

Rachele ignored him, focusing on me. "Find them," she commanded.

It was the closest I'd ever felt to my stepmother, because, for once, our goals aligned. "I will. I promise."

She leaned back and closed her eyes, releasing my father's arm as the EMTs loaded her into the ambulance.

Father pulled me aside. "Get that wound looked at, and then get to Tech's office. I'll message him on the way. I want you both staring at that goddamn screen until you find the twins."

I nodded.

"Good. I don't know who to trust right now, Angel, but I know I can trust you. You do whatever you need to do, you hear me?"

"Yes sir."

"Excuse me, sir, but we need to go," an EMT said, leaning out of the back of the ambulance.

"Right." Father got the attention of another EMT who was checking the vitals of a fallen guard. "See to my boy's side," he demanded, pointing at me.

As the EMT walked my direction, Father climbed back into the ambulance. They closed the doors and he and Rachele rolled away.

CHAPTER THIRTY-FIVE
Angel

I FIRST MET Tech over Skype when I was eight years old and trying to network my father's computer to the new security system. Tech walked me through a compatibility issue, and then showed me how to program the outside lights so we could turn them on remotely. He was the smartest person I'd ever talked to. Over the years, we worked on several more projects together, and I gained an awestruck respect for him. Although I'd never met him in person, Tech was my idol. In seventh grade, I faked poor eyesight so I could get glasses like his. The glasses had long since gone in the trash, but my hero-worship for Tech was still going strong.

Excited to finally meet him, I leaned against the retinal scanner and waited.

"You sure about this?" Bones asked.

The scanner beeped and the door unlocked with a click.

I nodded, turning the handle. "Yeah. I need you on the street. If I find them, I want you to be the first one there. I can't trust anyone else. Text me when you get to Ari's. Maybe the two of you can figure out where Markie would hide. Drive around. You search your way, I'll search mine, and maybe one of us will get lucky."

I could tell my friend wanted to argue, but I didn't have time for it. I pulled open the heavy iron door and walked into every geek's wet dream. Over one hundred square security camera feeds were projected onto the white wall to my left. I froze and took it all in, hearing the door close and lock behind me. Tech's messy blond mop peeked over the top of a high-backed desk chair, positioned in front of the wall. Keyboard keys clicked, and then the images on the wall rotated.

Wondering if he realized I was there, I cleared my throat and stepped forward.

"Take a seat." Tech directed me to the empty chair beside him. "I'm dividing the screen in half, and you have a keyboard and a mouse to control the feeds on your side. If you have any... wait a second. What do we have here?"

My gaze shifted to the feed he was studying. Blonde woman, two small children. Thinking he'd found them, I ignored the chair and rushed to his side. He zoomed in until we got a clear view of the faces. Not Markie, and not the twins. His only reaction was to switch to a different feed.

"You shouldn't have any questions. DOS commands, it's self-explanatory." Then Tech seemed to realize I was standing right beside him. He leaned away and looked up at me over dark-framed glasses. "Angel."

"Tech." I nodded.

His gaze shifted to the limited space between us. Right. I was too close. Who knew when he'd last had someone in his office? I slipped away, eased into my own seat, and looked around. Tech's workspace was immaculate. He had a yellow smiley-faced stress ball in front of his keyboard, but that was the only decorative element. Everything else was functional. Coffeepot, phones, computers, screens.

"So this is the Tech cave, huh?" Obviously. It was a stupid question, but I was strangely nervous.

He turned and gave me a smirk. "Yep. This is where I watch the world." He was somewhere in his midforties, wearing a black-and-white checkered button-up shirt, and black joggers tucked into classic red Chuck Taylors like some wannabe hipster.

"I'm sending you a feed. It should populate right in the center."

A second later, the back of my father's house filled the middle of the screen. Markie and the kids slipped from a hidden door and into the bushes. I tracked their movement to the fence and then lost them. Moments later, Pelino's goons filled the backyard.

"This one's from the end of the block," Tech said.

Another feed populated. Markie and the twins were still running. Luciana was lagging behind. Markie slowed long enough to scoop up my little sister. Cradling Luciana in her arms, Markie said something to Georgio. He nodded and broke into a sprint. Still carrying Luciana, Markie followed. Once again, Pelino's goons were right behind them. They pointed in the direction Markie and the twins had headed.

"Those are the only two confirmed sightings we have of the twins. The Pelino family is still scouring the city for them." He clicked a few more keys and several of my feeds were highlighted. I watched as grown men hunted for Markie and my siblings.

"I also have the facial recognition software scanning, so it may highlight a feed from time to time. Let me know if you see something," Tech said, resetting the feeds.

I watched the wall for a while. My phone buzzed. Hoping for correspondence from Markie, I checked it to find a text from Bones. He'd picked Ariana up from work and the two went to her apartment. There was no sign of, or word from, Markie. He and Ariana were going to go look for her, but they planned to circle back by the apartment periodically just in case she showed up there. I thanked him, and then turned my attention back to the screens.

I'd always known Tech had access to most of the city, but I didn't grasp the extent of his reach until I shuffled through the feeds, populating my half of the wall. It was like watching all of Las Vegas at once. I saw the fountain Markie and Ariana had sat on, and the High Roller we'd rode on. Someone jumped from the tower of the Stratosphere.

Markie, where are you? I wondered while scanning faces of strangers. *Maybe they checked into a hotel?* Only they couldn't have, because her purse was in the Hummer. We'd found her phone in pieces in the hidden passageway of my father's house. No credit cards, no phone. It was getting dark. I rotated the feeds again. Hours passed in a blur of energy drinks, snacks, and staggered bathroom breaks. Still no sign of them. It was as if they'd vanished from the street.

The sun was beginning to rise by the time my phone rang again.

"Hello?" I couldn't answer it fast enough.

"Rachele's out of surgery and in recovery," Father replied. "Any word on the twins?"

"We're still looking. The good news is so are the Pelinos."

He took a deep breath. "Those bastards still haven't given up, huh? Sounds like they need something to do. I've got just the thing."

He disconnected, and I returned my attention to the screens, wondering what the old man was up to. Tech's phone rang. He answered it and changed feeds as he listened. The right side of his screen populated with what looked like GPS readouts. He pulled addresses from the screens and sent them to the GPS readouts. I watched in awe as he worked, amazed by the speed in which he had six of my father's SUVs en route.

I continued to watch for Markie and the twins until activity on one of my feeds drew my attention. An SUV pulled into an alley behind the strip. The doors opened, spilling out men with semi-automatics. They gunned down a group of Pelino's men who'd been searching the area.

"Team one was successful," Tech confirmed into his phone.

Only seconds later another SUV pulled up in front of a hotel. But this time, the Pelino soldiers seemed to expect the attack. They pulled their guns and opened fire before the SUV full of my father's soldiers had even rolled to a stop. The feed disappeared.

"Team two, successful," Tech said.

Successful? I searched for the feed, but it was gone.

"Team three, successful," Tech said.

Team three? Where the hell is team three?

Tech's police scanner pealed in the background, reporting the shootings. All of my feeds were rotated, removing the Pelino goons from my view. I tried to bring them back, but those feeds disappeared, too. He had to be blocking my access.

"Team four, five, and six—all successful."

I glanced at his screens, searching for the battles, but saw nothing.

He looked at me and asked, "Have you found them?"

I startled. "No. Still looking." I went back to my feeds, wondering what the hell was going on. Tech had been loyal to my family for as long as I could remember. He was the best at what he did, yet someone had hacked into his system to break into my father's house. Had someone hacked him again to get the jump on the attacks?

No, not that fast. Impossible. And he told Father the attacks were successful. Why?

Tension crept up my shoulders, stiffening my back. I kept one eye on Tech and the other on the feeds.

"Angel, I know you saw that," Tech said, watching me.

"Saw what?" I feigned. "Did you find them?"

His forehead scrunched up in response. "You know what I'm talking about."

He was on to me. "You tipped them off, didn't you?" I asked.

Tech pulled out a pistol and trained it on me.

Hell of a confirmation. He was a traitor. It explained so much and made me feel so stupid. How had I not seen it before? I raised my hands in the air. My gun was in the pocket of my jacket, hanging in the closet. The only weapon on me was a knife strapped around my ankle, and there was no way I could get to it before he got a shot off.

"I want out, Angel."

"Out?" I asked.

He nodded. "Yeah. Out of everything."

"Okay. I can understand that."

"I knew you'd get it. That's why I had Bruno approach you. This is the chance for both of us. We can get out."

I couldn't get out. I had to find Markie and the twins. Then I needed a doctor who could fix her. Even if I could get out, I'd never trust the Pelinos to make it happen. Besides, there was one more little matter... "You want me to turn on my father?"

"Some father," Tech spat. "Manipulative bastard. He doesn't care about you. He doesn't care about any of us. He deserves whatever he gets."

I loved my old man, but I couldn't exactly argue. "What about the rest of my family? The people you're helping are hunting down the twins, Tech. They're just little kids."

"I've kept their location hidden."

Red spots dotted my vision. Tech—my friend and mentor—had known where Markie and the twins were and he'd kept it from me, knowing I was going out of my mind with worry. "Where are they? I swear to God, if you've hurt them ..."

He raised his hands. "Calm down, Angel, I haven't done a damn thing with them. That girl of yours has led them to safety. She's smart."

She led them to safety.

I wanted to feel relieved, but was having a hard time trusting him. "You expect me to believe you? After you turned on my family?"

"I didn't turn on your family, they turned on me." Gun still in his hand, Tech stood. "Fifteen years, and do you know how many vacations I've gotten?"

I stared at him, shocked. *This is about vacations?*

"Zero! You know why? Because I'm not a person to him, Angel. I'm an asset. You're an asset. We're all assets... pieces of this game he plays. I thought you, of all people, would understand that."

"I do understand. I just... he's my father."

Tech shook his head. "And so he can be an asshole and still deserves your loyalty? Because of blood?"

He was pointing a gun at me, so I didn't answer.

"Disappointing, Angel." He steadied the gun. "You should have come with me."

There was a finality to his tone that left me no time to think. I lunged forward, ducking low. A shot rang out. My shoulders connected with Tech's stomach, knocking him back. He fell over his chair, taking me with him. We bounced, and then slid to the cement floor. I grappled for the gun on the way down. Impact relaxed his grasp and the gun slid away. Rather than go for it, I pressed my arm against his neck until he blacked out. Then I stood, retrieved his gun, and called my father.

"Tech's dirty," I said, glaring at my former friend and mentor.

"Is he dead?" Father asked.

"No."

"Why not?"

"Because I need to go find the twins and I don't have time for this shit. You want him dead? Send someone else to do it," I growled.

It was brazen and stupid to speak to my father in such a way, but I was pissed.

"Did he tell you where the twins are?" Father sounded hopeful, ignoring my outburst.

"No, and he's out of commission right now. I have an idea, though." I grabbed my jacket from the closet.

"Take Bones," Father ordered. "Do not go alone."

We disconnected, and I called Bones as I exited through the secure doors.

CHAPTER THIRTY-SIX
Angel

TECH'S OFFICE WAS well-hidden beneath a self-storage building toward the north end of Las Vegas. I sneaked out of the warehouse and crept into the shadows of nearby buildings to hide and wait for Bones. Before long, a hunter-green Honda Civic with darkened windows pulled into the neighborhood. It slowed and idled at the corner. I kept Tech's Glock in my left pocket and pulled out my Desert Eagle. I switched off the safety and watched the car. The driver's side window rolled down. Bones stuck his head out and looked up and down the road. Relieved, I flipped the safety back on and hurried out to greet my friend.

"Whose ride is this?" I asked, sliding into the small backseat.

"My mom's. We had just stopped by her house when you called and you sounded like you could use a vehicle nobody knows about."

I patted him on the shoulder. "Good thinking."

Ariana turned around, her mouth pressed into a thin line and her eyes red and swollen. "Good. Now that that's settled, can one of you please tell me where the hell my sister is?"

"Ari—" Bones reached for her.

She deflected his hand. "Don't you touch me. You guys promised to take care of Markie and now she's missing. I swear to God if one of you doesn't tell me what's going on right now, I'm calling the cops."

"I think she's at the orphanage," I blurted out.

"That doesn't make sense. Why isn't she answering her phone, then?" Ariana asked.

Bones put the car into gear and flipped a u-turn, heading toward the orphanage.

I sighed, wondering how much I could tell Ariana without dragging her into this mess, too. In all actuality, she was already in it. No need to make things worse, though. "It's just a hunch.

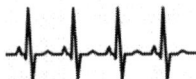

The orphanage door was locked, so the three of us took turns banging on it until we pissed someone off enough to open it. A woman I didn't recognize cracked the door and told us Markie hadn't been there in days. I'd been so certain, and now I had no clue where to look. I ran a hand through my hair and pulled out my phone to let the old man know I'd failed. Maybe the Pelinos had nabbed Markie and the kids and Tech had lied.

"Angel. Pst, Angel."

Bones and I both had our hands on the guns in our pockets as we spread out and searched for the source of the whispers. Bones nodded toward the bush on the side of the building and we crept over to find Myles crouched down behind it.

"What are you doing out here?" I asked, releasing my hold on my gun.

"Waiting for your slow ass. I thought you'd never get here, but Markie made me promise to wait for you."

My heart skipped a beat. Before I could say anything, Ariana lunged forward. "You know where Markie is?" she asked.

"Yeah, I know where she is, but who the hell are you?"

That helped me find my voice. "Myles, this is Ariana, Markie's sister. Can you take us to Markie?"

"Fool, what do you think I'm waiting here for?" he asked. Then he turned and motioned for us to follow him down the side of the building. We crept past the open field to a small storage shed. A broken lock dangled from the hook beside the door. Myles knocked out a little tune, and then opened the door.

Luciana and Georgio stared up at me with dirty, tear-streaked faces. Recognition widened their eyes and they both lunged at me. Overjoyed to see them, I kneeled down and gathered the little monsters into my arms, squeezing them tightly. Then I let go so I could examine them. Their clothes were torn and filthy, and several small cuts and scrapes covered the exposed area of their arms, but they were alive.

"Where's Markie?" I asked.

The two stepped aside so I could see behind them. Markie was lying on the ground, her skin worrisomely pale.

"Shh, she's asleep," Georgio whispered. "She still has a head-ache."

I could tell by looking at her that she was more than sleeping. My feet felt glued to the floor as I watched her chest, hoping it would rise and fall with a breath.

She should have heard us. She should have woken up. Why is she so pale?

"Markie?" Ariana asked. She rushed past us and fell to her knees beside her unconscious sister. "Wake up. It's time to go home."

Markie didn't even stir.

Ariana gave Markie's shoulders a firm shake.

No response.

"Get up." Ariana's voice cracked. "This isn't funny, okay?"

"Is she messin' with you?" Myles asked.

Ariana shook her head. "No. I think something's wrong. She's not... she's not responding."

I couldn't move. All I could do was stand there and watch as my world shattered. I'd found her, but I was too late.

"Is she breathing?" Bones asked, stepping forward to check.

Tension and fear mounted. The twins started crying and asking what was going on.

My mind raced back in time. I saw my father kneeling on the floor holding my mother. He rocked back and forth, stroking her hair. "No. Don't leave me. I'll change, I promise. Just don't go." An empty pill bottle rolled out of my mother's hand and across the floor.

"Breathing. She has a pulse," Bones announced, pulling me from my stupor. "She's not dead, Ari. We need to get her to a hospital."

Ariana pulled out her phone. "I'm calling for an ambulance."

I reached out and grabbed her phone, stopping the call. "No. It'll come across the police scanner and..." I glanced at the twins.

"Just no."

Ariana looked like she was going to argue, but she didn't. I gently lifted Markie, cradling her in my arms as I carried her to the car. We sent Myles back to the orphanage, and then Bones, Ariana, Luciana, Georgio, Markie, and I all piled into Bones's mom's tiny Honda and headed for the hospital.

"Angel, you need to call your father," Bones said.

With my arms still wrapped around Markie, I somehow managed to phone the old man and tell him we were taking the twins to the hospital.

"Will she ever wake up?" Luciana asked, her big, innocent eyes heavy with tears.

I tried to be strong for my little sister, and for Markie, but I lost it. Tears rolled down my face. I choked up. "I don't know."

We made it to the emergency room where a nurse had me lay Markie on a stretcher. I was vaguely aware of my family surrounding us and taking the twins. Nurses wheeled Markie through the double doors and out of my sight. Not knowing what else to do, I stood there feeling hollow, wondering if I'd ever see her again.

Bones and Ariana joined me. I don't know how long we waited there, staring at those damn double doors. People came and went in a blur. After a while, I felt a tug on my shoulder. Nonna wrapped me in a hug, but I couldn't bring myself to return the gesture. She grabbed my hand and pulled me down the hall and into a small private waiting room. Bones and Ariana followed, but Nonna had them wait outside the room.

Father stood at our entrance. He looked haggard and haunted, and I doubted he'd gotten any more sleep than I had. "Thank you for finding the twins," he said, embracing me.

I nodded. "It was Markie. She kept them safe."

Father ducked, his expression unreadable. "I'm grateful, and sorry to hear about—"

"Are you?" I asked.

He stared at me.

"This is what you want, right? Her in that hospital bed so you can control me. So you can get me to promise to be just like you. Well here I am, Dad. Fix her, and I'll sign whatever you force me to."

His face contorted, but I didn't care. I held my ground.

Nonna slipped between us. "It's been a rough couple of days, and emotions are heavy right now. We all need to take a step back and think about what we're saying," she said, patting my chest.

I knew exactly what I was saying. My gaze didn't leave my father's face.

Seemingly oblivious to the war going on between me and the old man, Nonna plunged ahead. "Angel, I've taken the liberty of looking into a doctor for Markie. Dr. Westfall is a highly recommended neurosurgeon who owes me a favor. It will be risky and expensive, but that young lady rescued my grandchildren. She won't have to wait for treatment."

Father's scowl shifted to Nonna. "You forget yourself, *Mamma.*"

She gave him a tight smile. "Yes, I have forgotten myself. For far too long, but not anymore. You lied to me, Dom."

Father sighed. "Mamma, this is not the time."

"When will be the time? When all my grandchildren are dead? No. This needs to be discussed now."

"Mamma—" There was both warning and frustration in the old man's voice, but she paid him no mind.

"My father was a horrible man, Angel. We had to flee our home and come to this country because of the crimes he committed. When I was barely out of school, he married me to a worse man, your *Nonno.*"

"Mamma, do not speak ill of the dead."

She gave him a blank look before insisting, "I would speak well of them, but there is nothing good to say. You, of all people, should know that, Dom. After what he did to your family. Do you remember your Nonno, Angel?"

Memories of my grandfather were hazy. He had a predominant Italian nose and always wore a scowl. "Barely."

She nodded. "He died when you were young. Your *Bisnonno* was dead long before you were born. Same with my only brother, Bartolo, and my eldest son, Michael."

Father sat and put his head in his hands. Michael was another name our family wasn't allowed to mention.

"Your Nonno was ruthless and mean, everything my father had trained him to be," Nonna sneered. "Your great-uncle Bartolo had already given his life for the family, so my father *made* my husband a Mariani." She put a lot of emphasis on the word made. "He trained your Nonno to be abusive and cruel. Mariani men," she spat. "My poor, sweet Michael, *Pace all'anima sua.*" She made the sign of the cross.

"God rest his soul," Father repeated, and we both mimicked the gesture.

Before I could ask what had happened to Uncle Michael, Nonna cupped my face in her hands. "When Michael died, your father made me a promise. He swore to me that no more Mariani men would be forced into the lifestyle. He said you would have a choice."

Father bolted out of his seat. "I did give him a choice!"

"You used his girlfriend's life to blackmail him. That's hardly a choice." Nonna eyed him. "And after what happened to Annetta, I'd think that you, of all people—"

My ears perked up at mention of my mom.

"Annetta killed herself!" Father shouted. "I screwed up and she found me cleaning up that hit and—" He looked at me and then looked away.

Nonna shook her head, clicking her tongue. "Oh, Dom, I thought for sure you'd see through it. Annetta loved you. She loved Angel. Yes, she was upset, but suicide? You knew her better than that."

His brow furrowed. "But the coroner said—"

"Your father was very good at what he did. He never got caught cleaning up *his* hits." Nonna inclined her head, a secretive glint in her eye. "He did manage to make some powerful enemies, though, and that's what got him in the end. Why you didn't have to grow up with that beast, Angel."

My father gaped at her. "Mamma, you didn't?"

"That wretched man beat on me for years and I put up with it. But then he got Michael killed and took away your happiness. He went too far."

Father leaned against the wall, looking very much like he was about to pass out. "You killed him?" he whispered.

Nonna steepled her hands and smiled at him. "Kill him? Oh no, I've never had the stomach for violence. But after what he did to you and Angel, I didn't exactly cry at his funeral."

I gaped at both of them. This was too much to take in. For my father as well. He lowered his head and rubbed the back of his neck. Then he looked up at the ceiling. I couldn't imagine the magnitude of what he was feeling. Several emotions flickered across his face, but none of them stayed.

Nonna stood and went to him, grabbing his hand. "It's this life... this path my father chose, then my husband chose. You were pushed into it, and now that's what you want to do to Angel." She shook her head. "This lifestyle... stuffed full of everything money can buy, but it's hollow. Today you almost lost everything: your wife, your children, your life. Half of your borgata has turned against you. And you want Angel to follow in your footsteps?"

My father's gaze landed on me. His expression softened and he looked back to Nonna. "He's a Mariani, Mamma."

"And you promised to give him a choice. Angel isn't like you. He needs a normal job where he can die of natural causes when he's old and ready. I want to see grandchildren who live long enough to grow into men and women, marry, and give me great-grandchildren to spoil." She held his hand, pleading, tears welling up in her eyes. "Don't make me bury them."

Father rubbed his face. He looked at the ceiling again and then shuffled his feet. I wondered what was going through his mind. Was he really considering it? Would he really let me walk away from the business and live like a crumb with a legitimate job?

The look Father gave me made me break out in a sweat. "Is that what you want?" he asked.

I bowed my head, unable to answer.

"You'd abandon the family? You'd leave us in the middle of this war? I lost Tech today, Angel. I need you."

"Why should he have to give up his hopes and dreams to fulfill yours?" Nonna asked. "You are the parent. You sacrifice for him, not the other way around." She stood inches from him. "You owe it to Annetta—to his dead mother—to give him his own life. A life he would choose."

Father tensed. I'd never seen him hit a woman before, but for a second I feared for Nonna. She didn't seem afraid, though. She reached out and cupped his face, pulling him closer to her. "Give me Angel. Let us go and make a life away from this valley of greed and death. Let the remainder of my days be full of laughter and life."

Father's shoulders drooped. "He is my son," he whispered.

Nonna smiled. Tears filled her eyes. Her gaze shifted to me, and then back to my father. "Then let him live his own life, Dom."

Her final blow rocked him. He took a step back and looked at me. "Angel, if this is what you want, you may go."

Then my father stormed out of the room.

CHAPTER THIRTY-SEVEN
Angel

THE NEUROSURGEON SAID Markie's surgery was a success, but when the anesthesia wore off she didn't wake up. She didn't wake up the next day either, or the day after that. Hooked to machines and with a fat white bandage wrapped around her head, she slept peacefully while I worried.

Father waged his war while I stayed by Markie's bedside, holding her hand and thinking about the decision I had to make. The old man was willing to let me go, but could I really leave my family?

"What's the alternative?" Nonna asked on day three when she stopped by the room to check on Markie. "Will you lock yourself in that basement and replace Tech? Will you become an enforcer? How long until he expects you to step into the position he's been preparing for you? And what about her?" Nonna nodded to Markie. "Will she marry a killer?"

I stroked Markie's arm, silently promising to become whatever she wanted me to be if she'd just wake up.

Nonna didn't relent. She captured my face in her hands and asked, "What have you always wanted to do? To be? I know you have dreams and aspirations. You will be free to follow them now. Dream big, Angel."

She was wrong, though. My dreams for a future had shattered more than eleven years ago, over my first cappuccino. I hadn't allowed myself another one since. After she left, I considered her advice, and fantasized about my future. What would I be? With no idea, I used my tablet to search possible career paths.

I spent the next couple of days researching while I waited for Markie to wake up. Father checked in a few times, lines of stress and frustration tugging at his features. I felt guilty for abandoning him when he clearly needed me, but each time I looked at him I wondered what it must have been like when my mom found him cleaning up after that hit. What it would be like if Markie found out about some of the things I'd done. My father never said anything about our talk with Nonna. He never asked me for my decision or pushed me to stay. I knew he'd honor my decision when I made it.

By the fifth night, I'd almost convinced myself that Markie wasn't coming back. I replayed our adventures in my mind, wishing I could do things differently. If I could have gone back in time, I would have jumped from the Stratosphere tower with her. I would have held out for one more dance in that Mexican restaurant and I would have held her on the beach until the sun came up. I would have spent more time with her at the orphanage. I would have fed and sheltered every bum in Las Vegas just to see her smile again. When she asked me to write my regrets in the sand, I would have gladly accepted her driftwood pencil. I was ready to let the ocean wash away my past so I could start a new life with her by my side.

But she didn't wake up.

On day six, I felt Markie stir. I was half asleep at the time—knee-deep in self-pity, mourning the sound of her laughter—and convinced myself I was feeling things. I watched her sleep for a while, and then wrote it off as some sort of involuntary twitch or muscle spasm. Desperate for the contact, I squeezed her hand.

She squeezed mine back.

My heart leapt into my throat. "Markie?" I asked.

Ariana and Bones were sitting on the guest bed/couch. They both jumped up and rushed to the bed.

"What? What's going on?" Ariana asked. "Is she awake?"

"I think she just squeezed my hand," I explained.

Ariana grabbed Markie's other hand. We stood on either side of the bed, waiting for her to do something. Anything. Nothing happened.

"Maybe it was a muscle spasm or something?" Bones suggested.

Hope made me feel high, and I wasn't ready to come down yet. "No. She squeezed my hand, I promise. Markie? Can you hear me? Please wake up."

It was the same plea I'd been making for the past week, but this time her eyes opened.

Ariana gasped. "You're awake! Quick, someone get the doctor!"

Bones rushed off and Ariana and I stayed with Markie. I stared into her beautiful blue eyes, thankful to finally see them again.

She looked at us and then glanced around the room. "Are the twins okay?" Her voice sounded weak, but it was the most beautiful music I'd ever heard.

Ariana burst into tears and hugged her. Markie patted Ariana's head, still looking at me.

"Yeah, they're fine." I choked up. Trying to get my emotions under control, I kissed her fingers one by one.

"What's wrong? Are you guys okay?" Markie asked, her eyes wide.

I nodded. "We're fine, and now so are you." The truth of it was overwhelming. My legs felt weak, but I wasn't about to leave her side. Even to sit down.

"What are you talking about?" Markie asked.

Ariana stood back up, wiping the tears from her eyes. "Y-you were in a coma, so I s-signed the release for the doctor to operate. They removed your t-tumor."

"What?" Markie asked. She pulled her hand away from me and rubbed at the bandage on her head. "It's gone? But how? There were waiting lists and—"

"Nonna did it." I still wasn't sure how she'd made it happen, but over the past week my sweet little Nonna had proven she was a powerful and influential force to be reckoned with.

Markie's eyes flooded with tears. She blinked, and they slid down her cheeks. "Seriously? It's gone? For good?"

Bones returned with Markie's doctor in tow.

"It's really gone," the doctor confirmed, smiling. "You have been officially cancer-free for six days now. It's about time you woke up so we could share the news with you. Now tell me, sleepyhead, how do you feel?"

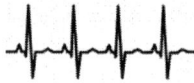

Markie was released from the hospital two days later. We stopped by Ariana's apartment long enough to pack their meager belongings, threw everything they couldn't live without into the back of the Hummer, stopped by the retirement community to pick up Nonna, and headed to my place. I made us all dinner, and then we sat around the table and Nonna and I broke the news to everyone.

Bones eyed me. "You and Nonna? You're leaving the city?" he asked. "But what about—" He glanced around the room. "What about your job?"

"I've been released from my contract."

"How the hell did you manage that?" he asked.

Nonna gave him a wide smile.

Bones's jaw dropped.

"What? Why would you want to leave the city?" Ariana asked.

We all gaped at her. Her gaze shifted from the scar on Bones's cheek to my side. My stitches had been removed the day before.

"Right. Stupid question. Sorry."

"Where will you go?" Markie asked.

I winced, stung by the casual way she'd excluded herself.

"And what the hell will you do?" Bones asked, anger creeping into his tone.

Nonna held up her hands. "Let Angel talk. I'm sure he'll answer everyone's questions."

Bones snapped his mouth shut, but his eyes told me he was hurt and irritated.

I gripped the arms of my chair and plunged ahead. "I'm not sure. It's not my decision to make alone." My throat dried up. I sipped water and waited, hoping for the right words. They had to be perfect. I needed Bones and Markie, and if they refused to come with me... I wasn't sure I could go.

Nonna stood. The sound of her chair scraping against the hardwood floor drew everyone's attention. She smiled and walked over to me, putting her hands on my shoulders.

"What Angel is trying to say, is that we'd like to extend an invitation for the three of you to join us. We can make the decision of where to go together. Angel and I will cover the costs of the move. We don't all have to live together, just close. Perhaps the same neighborhood." She patted my back and bent to kiss the top of my head before returning to her seat.

"And the boss would release me from my contract, too?" Bones asked.

"Yes." I nodded.

His expression fell. "This is all I've ever known, Angel. I don't know what else I'd do."

"I will need someone to protect my interests," I replied. "Someone I can trust to run security and make sure my family's drama doesn't follow us. I know this is a lot to take in and a huge decision to make. Please think about it. Let me know."

He gave me a curt nod. Not a nod of acceptance, but a nod telling me he understood and would think about it. Good enough for now. I finished my glass of wine, hoping it would give me the courage to get through what I had to do next.

Posing the question to Markie would be more complicated. I needed to speak to her alone, so I stood and offered her my hand. I led her through the living room, out to the balcony I'd never stood on. There, several stories above the strip, I kissed her and took a giant leap of faith.

"Markie, listen, my family is involved in a lot of crap. I've had to do stuff for the family that I'm not proud of, stuff I never wanted to do. But I don't want to be that guy. I want a life and maybe a family someday, and I don't want to have to worry about my kids being kidnapped or my wife being shot. It's... it's too much. I need to get away from all of this." I gestured out to the city.

She nodded, watching me.

I let out a breath, wishing I'd had another glass of wine, and grabbed her other hand. "Come with me?" I pleaded.

Her breath caught.

Already committed, I couldn't stop. "You got a peek into what it's like to be part of my family. It's jacked up. I've seen some scary shit... stuff I wouldn't wish on anyone. But sitting by your hospital bed, waiting for you to wake up, not knowing if you even would... I've never been so terrified in my life."

She looked down.

I gave her hands a gentle squeeze, forcing her attention back to me. Tears filled her eyes. I didn't know if they were tears of sadness or joy, but I kept going.

"I know we haven't known each other for long, but I have never been as happy as I am when I'm with you. I want that. I want your smile, your laughter, your courage, the way you treat people… it's so beautiful and I want it all. I want you. Please say you'll come with me?"

Tears rolled down her face. She pulled away and wiped her cheeks.

When she looked back at me, the hope and love written all over her face made my knees weak. I leaned against the wall and recaptured her hands in mine.

"I gave up on this life, Angel," she whispered. "The doctors said I was going to die and I'd accepted their diagnosis. I let all my hopes and dreams for a future go. And then you show up and sweep me off my feet like I'm living in some sort of fairy tale. Your grandmother found me a doctor and saved my life, and now this…" More tears slid down her cheeks. "It's all so overwhelming. And so wonderful." She dimpled up at me. "Of course I'll come with you. Can we live by the ocean?"

Vegas was the only home I'd ever known, and the thought of leaving it both terrified and thrilled me. Father was winning his war against the Pelinos, but he'd be cleaning up for months. He needed me, but I couldn't let myself get sucked back into his world.

I kissed Markie and pulled her close. "As soon as the doctors give us the okay, we can go anywhere you want."

Once we left, there'd be no coming back. I'd no longer be living under my father's rule, but I'd also lose access to his endless resources. Markie and I would have to make it on our own. I squeezed her close and kissed the top of her head, excited about the possibilities.

This was my life, and I'd finally get the chance to live it.

Thank you so much for reading **Making Angel**. I hope you've enjoyed the journey and will watch for the next book in the series, **Breaking Bones**, coming in 2016. Please help support my work by writing a review on Amazon. Reviews only require twenty words and help me tremendously. I appreciate your support!

Also be sure to visit my website and sign up to be included on news about future releases:
http://www.amandawashington.net

Find me on Facebook, too!
https://www.facebook.com/AmandaWashington.Author

Other books by Amanda Washington

Rescuing Liberty: Perseverance Book 1
Liberty's Hope: Perseverance Book 2
Fallen: Chronicles of the Broken 1
Cut: Chronicles of the Broken 2
Forsaken: Chronicles of the Broken 3

Made in the USA
Charleston, SC
28 October 2015